THE FUTURE UNFOLDS IN NEVER-BEFORE-PUBLISHED STORIES FROM

PHILIP JOSE FARMER—A hilarious spoof on sex and the science fiction writer that starts off with a whimper, but ends with a bang...

R. A. LAFFERTY—A world called Paleder, where life is flawless and uninspiring—with one deadly exception...

KATHERINE MACLEAN—A cartoonist's not-so-funny view of "reality" — and what his psychiatrist tries to do about it...

RICHARD A. LUPOFF—A spine-tingling tribute to Lovecraft, bringing back *The Dunwich Horror* in all its hideous glory...

MILDRED DOWNEY BROXON—A mother's love for her dying child sends her knocking for help on a neighbor's door — a galaxy away...

ELIZABETH A. LYNN — A paradise planet of peace and tranquillity where a chess match ends in violent death...

Plus **EIGHT MORE** daringly original, never-before-published stories by the top science fiction writers of today — and tomorrow!

CHRYSALIS
VOLUME 2
EDITED BY ROY TORGESON

ZEBRA BOOKS
KENSINGTON PUBLISHING CORP.

ZEBRA BOOKS

are published by

KENSINGTON PUBLISHING CORP.
21 East 40th Street
New York, N.Y. 10016

Copyright © 1978 by Roy Torgeson

Don't Look At Me copyright © 1978 by Elizabeth A. Lynn
Quiz Ship Loose copyright © 1978 by R.A. Lafferty
Where is Next Door? copyright © 1978 by Mildred Downey Broxon
The Bulldog Nutcracker copyright © 1978 by Robert Thurston
One More Song Before I Go copyright © 1978 by Craig Gardner
Just in the Niche of Time copyright © 1978 by Thomas F. Monteleone
Dragon Story copyright © 1978 by Alan Ryan
The Devil's Hop Yard copyright © 1978 by Richard A. Lupoff
EMMA copyright © 1978 by Evelyn Lief
Canary Bird copyright © 1978 by Katherine MacLean
Caught in the Crossfire copyright © 1978 by David Drake
Eclipse of the Son copyright © 1978 by Jayne Tannehill
The Last Rise of Nick Adams copyright © 1978 by Philip Jose Farmer
The Works of His Hand, Made Manifest copyright © 1978 by Karen G. Jollie

All rights reserved. No part of this book may be reproduced in any form or by any means without the prior written consent of the Publisher, excepting brief quotes used in reviews.

First Printing: August, 1978

Printed in the United States of America

**for
Andy
Cayley &
Eli
   my three sons**

CONTENTS

INTRODUCTION by Theodore Sturgeon	9
Elizabeth A. Lynn DON'T LOOK AT ME	11
R. A. Lafferty QUIZ SHIP LOOSE	25
Mildred Downey Broxon WHERE IS NEXT DOOR?	57
Robert Thurston THE BULLDOG NUTCRACKER	79
Craig Gardner ONE MORE SONG BEFORE I GO	91
Thomas F. Monteleone JUST IN THE NICHE OF TIME	107
Alan Ryan DRAGON STORY	141
Richard A. Lupoff THE DEVIL'S HOP YARD	149
Evelyn Lief EMMA	173
Katherine MacLean CANARY BIRD	183
David Drake CAUGHT IN THE CROSSFIRE	199
Jayne Tannehill ECLIPSE OF THE SON	221
Philip Jose Farmer THE LAST RISE OF NICK ADAMS	239
Karen G. Jollie THE WORKS OF HIS HAND, MADE MANIFEST	255
AFTERWORD by Roy Torgeson	283

INTRODUCTION

A complaint I have been making for some years now is that the taxonomists are taking over more drastically, even, than the tax collectors. I tell the story of my son who, at age ten, when I pointed out to him a paragraph in a magazine I thought might interest him, took it from me, held it in the right position, got his nose aimed right, and then asked, "What is it about?" Thus do the taxonomists, the labelers, the putters of things in coded cubbyholes, taint our defenseless innocents. I have railed loudly against the increasing specialization in all things everywhere, but especially in literature, because of the insidious and growing conviction that if you can put a precise name to a political trend, a musical innovation, an architectural style, or anything else, you thereupon understand it. Taxonomy is useful to supply handles with which to grasp and hold an idea or theory or trend, but it is not the same thing as examination and analysis. Editors reject books out of hand because they seem to be another "road" book or a "costume" book or a "shrink" book, without really reading them; taxonomy and faddism substitute for intelligent examination, and what might be a real experience for you and me goes spinning off into limbo, breaking an author's heart along the way. (I am thinking, at the moment, of Jerry Sohl's magnificent *The Spun Sugar Hole*. Ever read it? Of course not.) Anyway, I usually end this diatribe by mourning the loss of the general fiction magazines and books: *Collier's*, *Liberty*, the *Saturday Evening Post*, *Red-* and *Golden-*and *Yellow-* and *Bluebook* magazines, and the long-forgotten, much beloved *Argosy*, a pulp that came out every *week*. You could sidle up to any of these and say simply, "Hey. Tell me a story," and it would whisk you away to dusty cowtowns or Philippine insurrections or high-handed flappers defying Prohibition or beast-ridden rainforests.... But no more. Now you demand, "What is it about?" before you crack it open.

Then along comes Torgeson. Yes, the Chrysalis series looks and often tastes like science fiction (whatever that is; it still awaits a tight definition) but the intuitive Mr. Torgeson will not be rammed into anyone's cubby. Right here, right now, is a second package of stories whose chief merit is not that they wear the uniform of anyone's regimentation, but that they tell good stories—that, first of all. Let the taxonomists take it from there, and may their neat heads ache. Here at last is a book you may trustingly sidle up to and say, "Hey. Tell me a story." And the book will say, "Why sure. Sit right down. Once upon a time there was this dragon..." And off you go. So enjoy.

—Theodore Sturgeon
Los Angeles, 1978

A Master's in English and philosophy from Chicago and a brown belt in aikido tailor themselves well on Elizabeth A. Lynn, a spring-steel and velvet lady who lives in San Francisco, and the sale of her new novel *A Different Light* (which I have read in manuscript, and like enormously) makes her one of the twenty or so writers on this planet who make a living exclusively on science fiction. She is a joy to be with; she's one of those rare up-front human beings who will take you as they find you, and expect to be taken as nothing else but what they are. She is articulate and delightfully quick-witted, and she lives by things like loyalty and conviction and honesty. Folks like this don't grow in bunches like grapes, more's the pity.

"Don't Look At Me" will give you a glimpse of her feeling for strength and tenderness and compassion. It will be many a long moon before you'll forget little Mischa and the exquisite Elsen, and jovial Atawak, and the quiet dreadful things that happen to them.

—Theodore Sturgeon
Los Angeles, 1978

DON'T LOOK AT ME
by Elizabeth A. Lynn

The magician's hands say: *Look at this!*
His feet and legs crossed yogi-fashion in the seat of the armchair in the lounge, Mischa Dramov is playing with the cards. He cuts, shuffles, makes the picked card disappear, plucks it out of the air again. A crowd gathers to watch the impromptu performance. He speaks no patter; he mimes. They murmur applause.

"Misdirection," he says to them. "Illusion."

("Mama, why is he so small? I'm bigger than he is!"—"He's a dwarf, that's why."—"Is he sick?"—"No. It's a thing you're born with, honey, like the color of your hair.")

ALL PASSENGERS DISEMBARKING ON ZOLL REPORT WITH HAND LUGGAGE TO THE LOUNGE.

The metallic voice repeats the command twice, in six languages. The magician stacks his cards and folds his hands atop them. All but one of the spectators drift away: to the bar, to their staterooms, or closer to the giant observation window across the huge lounge through which they can watch the stars. She stays. She had been sitting way in the back during the show the night before. It helps to have a face to play to; hers had stood out, pale skin and tight pale curls singular in a mass of dark faces, dark hair. He had played to her. She says: "That was fascinating."

"Thank you."

"I loved the show last night."

"Most of it was improvised. Our big pieces of equipment are crated."

"When your partner did the trick with the linking rings I tried to watch her hands but I couldn't. She's dazzling, with that height, and the silver skin and hair!"

"That's the effect we work for," he answers, pleased. Proud.

"Is it a wig?" she asks.

"Chaka's hair? No, it's real."

She nods. It's the first gesture he has seen from her. She sits with straight back, very controlled, hands still, not moving, except for her eyes. Her eyes are light turquoise, and very wide. *Cosmetic lenses?* he wonders.

She says, "My name is Elsen Zakar."

He inclines—a bow. "Mischa Dramov."

"Where are you from?"

"From Earth—Terra."

"Are you? Maybe I will go there one day. What is it like?"

"I never think about the places I have left," says the magician, "only about the place I am going."

"Where are you going?"

"To Zoll."

"So am I," she says softly.

To vacation, he thinks, *to lie in the sun, to be entertained, to watch the show. Ah, well. Mischa, she is making polite conversation with you, the funny little magician, that's all.* "I'm told it's one of the most beautiful planets in the Living Worlds," he says politely.

"It's a paradise."

"You've been there before?"

"I was born there. It's warm, gently warm, all over. If you like cold, there's cold at the poles, and snow in the mountains. You can float a glider off a snow-covered peak and ride the currents down into the valley.... I've done that. The oceans, too, are warm. But now," she says, "I live on Gilbert's World."

He cannot remember what it is he knows about Gilbert's World. It is famous for something. As Zoll is famous for its beauty and because it is a world of telepaths. Mischa thinks, *I have never met a telepath before.* Automatically he begins to shuffle the cards. Misdirection. Illusion. "We will be working at a hotel in Rigga—the Embassy Hotel."

"I'm staying in Rigga. At the Embassy Hotel."

ALL PASSENGERS DISEMBARKING ON ZOLL SHOULD BE ASSEMBLED WITH HAND LUGGAGE IN THE LOUNGE.

Space between the chairs begins to fill. The ship will be landing soon on Zoll's larger moon. People press towards the window. Mischa says, "You don't want to watch the landing?"

"I've seen it before. Many times. You?"

"I can't. My eyes are on a level with most people's waists. Chaka rubbernecks for both of us."

"Yes. I can see her there." She is watching the

crowd. Five people float out of it to hang, legs decorously crossed, above everybody's head, even Chaka's. Large brown ghosts in sport clothes. One of them is holding a tennis racket. She waves to them. The one with the tennis racket waves back.

("Mama, look, they're flying!"—"No, they're teleports from Gilbert's World. It's a thing they can do, like you can read music, and Uncle Harry can dance.")

Mischa watches her, half-expecting her to float up and join them. But no, her feet remain firm against the metal floor of the ship. "You have family on Zoll?" he asks.

"My father is Elk Zekar, the chess player. You've heard of him?"

"No."

"I visit him every year."

Then why is she staying at the Embassy Hotel? he wonders, *if she has family to stay with?* and then feels a fool. He fumbles with the cards. Drops one.

"What is it?" she asks.

"I'm sorry. I've never met a telepath before."

"You haven't now. I am not a telepath. And you won't on Zoll. The Zollians never go to the Embassy Hotel, or anywhere else the tourists go, and the tourists may only go to certain places on Zoll. Non-telepaths are too coarse, too insensitive and raw for Zollian telepaths to be near."

"But you—"

"I stay at the hotel when I come to Zoll, or I would destroy my father's peace, his harmony. Peace and harmony are very important to good chess, you know. I visit him for a few hours. That is all of me he can stand—and I of him." Her mouth twists.

"I understand."

"Do you?" She looks at him. He almost puts his hands up to hide his eyes. "Yes, you do." Her voice softens. "You know what it feels like to be a freak, to be gawked at and then shoved out of sight, to be teased and scolded for something you can't hide and can't change."

"Yes."

"You don't want to meet a telepath, magician, take my word for it." She leaves him.

Chaka strides up and sinks into the vacated chair. "What's her name?"

"Elsen Zekar," he says.

"Those people in the air are blocking my view," Chaka says, bemused. She stretches her long legs out into the aisle, and kicks someone in the ankle. "Sorry." She curls her legs with a grimace—"Fooey! Everything on this ship is so damn small!"

Mischa Dramov, who stands four feet three inches tall with shoes on, and for whom everything everywhere is so damn tall, smiles.

Yoshio Atawak is the owner of the Embassy Hotel. He is a mammoth of a man.

"Come in, come in! Sit down! They call me the Ambassador. Want some lunch?" Two platters piled with food take up the entire top of his six-foot desk. "No? Not even a snack?" He leans forward—the chair groans—to offer Chaka a can of what could be salted nuts or sautéed bacon bits or tempuraed grasshoppers. "No? How about some beer? *Beer!*" he roars. His secretary staggers in with a pitcher of dark foamy beer and three huge steins. "Glad to have you with us. *Contracts!* Your shows will be a welcome change from the usual entertainment— bad bands and worse dancers and rotten comics. You thought this was a classy joint, right? Nobody intelligent comes to Zoll. If I didn't own the hotel I wouldn't be here either. *Sign here.* The Zollians are a pack of standoffish wet fish, and the tourists are rich bums. Rich and drunken bums."

Chaka asks, "What do they come here to do?"

"Swim, sun, climb moutains, ski, sail, play tennis, fly gliders, and talk to each other about it. They won't appreciate you. But I will."

"What do you do?" asks Mischa, liking him.

"Eat. And play chess with Vadek. You have heard of Vadek Amrill. He is chess champion of the Living Worlds, here to play a match. He is staying at the hotel, and every morning I play chess with him, over breakfast. I am *his* breakfast. You must meet him; he is intelligent, he'll like you."

As they cross the lobby, Mischa sees a familiar face. Hair like pale wire. Turquoise eyes.

A woman with a surfboard nearly knocks him down. "Watchwhereyuhgoing!" she snarls. "Creep!"

He ignores her—he maneuvers across the room. "Elsen."

Turquoise eyes like beams of coherent light. She looks at him. *She looks at him.* "Mischa," she says. "Hello."

"May I take you to lunch?"

Chaka says, "Mischa, we're doing a show tonight!"

A short lunch?"

"Well—I'm due this afternoon at my father's house. Lunch—I would like lunch. Maybe I'll wait till tomorrow to see my father. He won't care. I would like to see your first show on Zoll."

"Mischa!"

Lunch. Dinner. They meet and touch in a dark

room. "How old are you?"

"How old are you?"

"Are you happy, Elsen?"

"Happy..." Her hands are small in the darkness.

"May I stay with you tonight?"

"Yes," she says, "stay. Stay."

In the morning she says, "I cannot see my father today, I am too content."

"I am glad."

"I will go tomorrow, I must."

"I will stay with you until you leave the hotel."

"You will not!" She turns on him. "No one sees me then. Anger is ugly."

"You hate him so much?"

"Wouldn't you hate someone who never saw what you were, only what you were not, and despised you for what you couldn't be or do, and claimed nevertheless to love you?"

"People cannot always see the thing they love clearly."

"Zollians know nothing of love. They suppress and fear it, like all emotion. Love, hate, pain, joy, you never let go, you are never free to feel—" She is crying. "Leave me, Mischa. Please go."

"No," he says, touching her back.

She trembles in the bed, and then turns to him again.

He meets Vadek Amrill in the hotel lobby. He is small, for a non-dwarf. On sight, Mischa likes him. He is thin and tense and powerful.

"I liked your show last night," he says.

"Thank you."

"Have breakfast with me?"

"I don't play chess," says Mischa.

"I cannot palm cards."

They sit and talk about nothing. Vadek sets up a practice game. Almost under the table, the magician's hands play with his cards, turn them, stroke them, ace of spades, ace of clubs, ace of diamonds, ace of hearts, jack of diamonds, *look at this, look at this!*

Vadek Amrill says, "You do not have to do that with me, you know."

Startled, Mischa stops.

A commotion at the lobby door heralds the emergence of Yoshio Atawak from his office. "Good morning, Vadek! Ready to beat me?"

"Certainly." Vadek clears the board of his practice game and together they set the pieces up. They make an odd trio; the huge hotelier, the thin chess champion, (eyes of dark grey, like stone) and the beardless dwarf. "But you shouldn't be so certain of your loss, Ambassador. You're improving."

"*Beer!* Vadek, you flatter me ridiculously. You played better chess when you were nine than I do now. *And sandwiches!*" They bring an extra chair to hold the platter of food.

Vadek says to Mischa, "It's too bad you don't play chess."

Mischa picks up a black pawn and makes it disappear. "Check." Vadek laughs. Mischa brings the pawn back. "I can't sit for hours with my legs dangling."

"If you played chess you could."

Yoshio Atawak says, "Only if you are a monomaniac. Vadek, you'd sell your soul to the devil for the chance to beat him at chess. When is your match with Elk Zekar?"

"Yoshio, I thought you knew everything."

"I do not. Almost everything. Is it tonight?"

"No—a few days."

"His daughter is staying in the hotel, you know. Elsen Zekar." Yoshio is looking at Mischa. Under the table Mischa's hands are moving: look at this, look at *this!*

Vadek says, "Is she?" He examines the chess board, unconcerned. But after a moment he says, gently, "Mischa, stop that."

Mischa stops.

Yoshio Atawak looks at them both, and then shrugs.

Mischa asks, "What is Elk Zekar like?"

"I like him," Vadek says. "I like the way he plays chess."

Atawak says, "I admire you. I would not agree to contest a telepath at tying shoelaces."

"Can you still tie your own shoes?" says Vadek. He moves a pawn.

"Of course. No matter that it takes me an hour to bend down." Atawak moves a pawn. Vadek moves a bishop. "Now why the hell did you do that?"

Mischa asks, "Will you win this time, too?"

"I think so."

"Are you still happy, Elsen?"

"Happy ... Yes."

"Don't go tomorrow. Stay another day in the hotel with me. One more day."

"Another day ... But then I must go."

"Why, if it makes you so unhappy? Why must you see him at all?"

She will not answer him.

Yoshio Atawak sticks his head into the closet dressing room. It is all that he can get inside the door. "Message for you from Vadek," he says. "He will not be at the show tonight, because he is playing that chess game, but he sends his regards."

Mischa nods. He has become used to the champion's presence during the shows, just as he has become used to Elsen's warmth in the dark night.... "I wish him well."

"I saw him off. He seemed confident. Chess games take hours sometimes. I don't think he ate enough dinner, either—"

"By whose standards, Yoshio?"

"Oh, not you too, Mischa!"

Mischa escapes to the stage. He misses Vadek—but Elsen is there, pale skin, pale hair, eyes like gems. She is going to see her father in the morning, he has not been able to talk her out of it. *What is a telepath in a bad mood like?* he wonders. *Do Zollians let themselves have bad moods? Will her father be in a bad mood if Vadek beats him at chess?*

Almost, he wishes that Vadek would lose.

He looks for Elsen after, but she is gone, and he guesses that she is hiding from him. ("Anger is ugly, Mischa. Go away, don't look at me!")

"Mischa, Mischa." Chaka's voice. Reluctantly he comes awake in a bed that is too big for him. Chaka is leaning above him. "Mischa, please wake up. Vadek's in jail!"

"Jail?" A nightmare—he is not awake.

"Wake up! They say he murdered that Zekar person."

Mischa comes awake. "Atawak."

"He isn't here, he's at the jail. He called from there. It's morning. He asks us to come there, Mischa. Vadek asked for you."

"For me?"

They meet Yoshio Atawak at the jail. His face is blotchy. His secretary is with him. "I spoke with Dov Dolk, the prosecutor. It seems that Vadek went in to play the match with Zekar—and walked out of the room a few moments later, dazed, with a bloody letter opener in his hand. Zekar was dead on the floor. They let me see Vadek a moment, only a moment. He asked for you. Then he kept saying my name over and over, as if it were a rock he could hold on to." The secretary holds out a sandwich. Atawak takes it and stares at it in loathing. "I don't want it. Take it away."

"But you haven't eaten!"

"Take it *away*!"

The room in the jail is bare, white, dreadful, and Vadek sits in its center and shivers, as if cold. "I can't remember," he says. Panic nibbles the edges of his voice. "I went to the study—the pieces were all set up; it's a beautiful set, blue and white on a crystal board—Zekar came round the desk to meet me. He was smiling. I *think* he was smiling. I felt warmth, and then a wave of fear, anger, hatred and rage, like an electric shock. It was horrible. I don't know what happened then. I was holding the letter opener and Zekar was bleeding on the floor." He shakes. "They took away my chess set, the little peg one. It was in my pocket. I wish I had it."

The prosecutor deigns to speak with them, her distaste for non-telepaths plain in her thinned lips, her shuttered eyes. "We have ascertained that there were no other visitors to Elk Zekar's house. Vadek Amrill was alone with Elk Zekar. The story he tells, the hatred he says he felt, were his own. Zollians do not hate, we are disciplined."

"Vadek—Vadek's not like that," Mischa says. Dov

Dolk looks down at him and does not answer. "What will you do to him?"

"We have doctors for such people. We will fix him."

"Change him?"

"For the better, I assure you. It does not hurt."

Vadek says, "What do they say, Mischa?" Mischa tells him. Atawak is roaring protest in the halls. "Change me? What am I, an animal? A freak? What will they turn me into? They cannot make me a telepath. What will they take from my mind?"

"Don't, Vadek."

"Will they take my *chess*?"

Mischa walks out into the hall. Atawak is raging; Dov Dolk is icy cold. Mischa holds his cards, shuffles, palms. Misdirection. Illusion. Atawak is purple and his voice is shaking the walls. *In another minute they will throw us out.* Dov Dolk is holding her head in pain.

"Yoshio. Yoshio!"

"What!"

"Shut up." Yoshio shuts up. Mischa says to the prosecutor, "Please listen to me. For just a little while."

They have drugged her and blindfolded her. "Elsen?" he says.

"*You* told them."

"Yes."

"Why did you tell them?"

"For Vadek—and all of us."

"How did you know? I handed *him* the letter opener."

"You used my techniques. Misdirection. Illusion. You gave the Zollians Vadek, knowing their dislike and contempt for non-telepaths would blind them.

But I know Vadek. The hatred was not his, it was yours, funnelled through your dying father's mind. Your fear, your anger, your rage. It dazed Vadek as you knew it would."

"It did. Why didn't it blind you, too?"

"I looked at you, and remembered where you live, where you chose to live. On Gilbert's World. A planet of teleports."

"You looked at me. Mime, magician, freak, why did you look, why did you speak? It was easy; it was so easy. You gave me the courage to do it, Mischa. I loved you a little. Trapped—you trapped me. Tell me, will Chaka be your lover, freak? Will Vadek? Will anyone again? Who would want you, with your little boy's body, but a freak and a fool? We all make a magic, magician; the illusion is the loving. I am a freak, she is a freak, he is a freak, you are a freak—ugly little man—I hate you, Mischa Dramov! I hate you."

Ace of spades, jack of diamonds, queen of hearts, joker. Play, hands, play with the cards.

ALL PASSENGERS DISEMBARKING ON LYR REPORT WITH HAND LUGGAGE TO THE LOUNGE.

("Hey, Mama, look at that funny little man!"—"Ssh! It's rude to point. Remember him—that's the magician!")

Don't look at me, say Mischa Dramov's hands, don't look at me, look at the cards, look at *this*, don't look at *me*. DON'T LOOK AT ME!

●

R.A. Lafferty is the result of the ecstatic union of a power shovel and a moonbeam. One of his eyes is a laser and the other an x-ray, and he has a little silver anvil on which, warmed by laughter, he shapes logic to his own ends. For breakfast he eats pomposity, for lunch he nibbles on the improbable, and he dines on fixed ideas (yours and mine) which he finds about him in great abundance. He disjoints and broils them. He has educated every school he ever attended and left when they wouldn't learn. He got his outside, by talking to people like you. Nobody knows where he really came from.

As for his stories: some time ago I wrote in *The New York Times* that some day the taxonomists, those tireless obsessives who put labels on everything, will have to categorize literature as Westerns, fantasies, romances, lafferties, science fiction, mysteries....

—Theodore Sturgeon
Los Angeles, 1978

QUIZ SHIP LOOSE
by R. A. Lafferty

There were five persons on Quiz Ship. The ship's interior is shown as a functional lounge and wardroom, with food center, game center, navigation center, and problem and project center. There are three doors in the back bulkhead of this functional lounge: the triangle-sign door of the Crags, the circle-sign door of the Bloods, and the square-sign door of Questor Shannon. At back left is the "Instant Chute."

The five persons are Manbreaker and Bodicea Crag with the power of their earthiness (of whatever earth they are down on); George and Jingo Blood with their "movement-as-power"; and Questor Shannon, a slight man who expresses an oceanic massiveness and depth. Four of these people seem completely relaxed, but one of them, Questor Shannon, does not.

"Each time we go into an adventure, we go

relaxed," Questor was saying. "Some day we're going to get smeared when going in so relaxed. I feel we should go tensed on this one."

"Relax, Questor," the other four said, as they said so often.

"This is an easy one," Bodicea Crag (Queen Bodicea) gave the relaxed opinion. "Paleder World has no reputation for danger. Two other parties have been here, and they have left it unscathed."

"The logs of both parties show them to have been a bit scathed," Questor still argued. "Persons of both those parties have sworn that Paleder is a murderous world behind its smiling and open face. And their own words have been contradictory. 'The most open of all the worlds,' one of them said. Well, why does it remain a closed world then? What has been the obstacle? Why have we come here to solve, in relaxed fashion, an enigma that some have called murderous? Coming to any other world that has been called murderous, even in minority report, we would come with much greater caution."

"Murderous it does not seem to be," Manbreaker Crag spoke with assurance. "No one of either previous party was killed. Well, yes, it is a puzzle. I like puzzles. The John Chancel Party—Chancel was always essentially a one-man party, but he did have three companions with him here—recorded that Paleder World was an absolute puzzle, that they did not know what they had seen after they had seen it, that they did not remember what they had been told after it had been explained to them. Chancel was good at puzzles, but he did not solve the puzzle here. He said that this world had the most advanced technology of any world known, so advanced that the world seemed to deprecate it a bit and keep it in the background."

"I know what Chancel wrote in his ship's log," Questor said tensely. " 'It has a rich hoard,' he wrote. 'Like every hoard, it is guarded by a sleeping dragon. Unlike most cases, this is a corporate dragon. And unlike other corporate dragons, this one has a sting in its tail. It can murder you with that sting.' So there is something to this puzzle to be tense about."

"Chancel filled his log books with riddles and with enigmatic statements," Jingo Blood (the Empress Jingo) said. "But he didn't solve this riddle. I will."

"How will you solve what John Chancel couldn't, Jingo?" Questor asked. "How will you figure out what Vitus Ambler misfigured? What special attributes do you have for this?"

"I'm smarter than they were," Jingo Blood said. "Relax, Questor."

"But we shoot in just nine seconds."

"So, relax for nine seconds, then," Jingo told him.

The nine-second interval ran its course. The five persons shot into the "Instant Chute" at back left. The Quiz Ship went into a "blank-out hover."

The "Instant Chute" was itself a piece of very advanced technology. Much of the technology of Gaea—also known as Eretz or Earth—was quite advanced. The chute brought the five Quiz Ship persons down through ten thousand meters of space instantly, and it set them onto Paleder World. The requirements set into the chute in this case were simple: "That the persons be brought down within Paleder City, on solid footing, in an outdoor place near or at the nexus of the most intense intellectual activity of the city." Well, any sufficiently sophisticated "Chute" could do that.

They landed without a jolt. But did they come down safely?

"This is wrong, abysmally wrong!" Questor croaked fearfully as he came to ground in totally unacceptable surroundings. "There is not supposed to be any such jungle or miasma as this in Paleder City. We have overview pictures. It is not supposed to be like this. Something is very wrong." He beat what seemed to be a fanged bird away from his face. And these were not acceptable surroundings. No one could dream of worse.

"There sure are not supposed to be any fer-delance snakes like that one," Manbreaker Crag barked, "not in the middle of the leading city of one of the most civilized planets ever reported." He flipped his swagger stick into a bolo or machete. "We have landed solidly, but barely so. This is quicksand all around us, and all the poisonous-looking flora are floating plants on that quicksand. Ah, look at the jag-rocks protruding from the quagmire! And there is a jag-toothed monster perched on every one of those rocks or snags. A person would lose a hand or an arm if he reached for *anything* to keep from sinking in this bog. What went wrong with our landing anyhow? Is this even Paleder World at all? The Chute has goofed. But there cannot be any such outrageous malfunction as this!"

"It isn't my idea of beautiful downtown Paleder City either," George Blood growled. "There hasn't been such a miasmal landscape anywhere since the Devonian period on Gaea. And we were exactly over central Paleder City. Neither the Chancel nor the Ambler expeditions mentioned anything like this, and there are no such extensive, endless, I might say, areas of desolation in our photographs, not in the rougher sections of this world, certainly not in Paleder City. This is a very sticky malfunction. Let's back out of it. Let's go back and do it again."

"Let's go back and *not* do it again," Bodicea Crag said. "Let's not do it again till we find out what went wrong with our Chute. This is deplorable."

The firm land "island" that they were on was hardly big enough for the five of them to stand on even with extreme crowding; and the snouts and serrate mouths that broke the surface of the quicksand were murderous. The whole thing was a churning soup-bowl of death-dealing monsters.

"The best place to attack a problem is where it is," Jingo Blood stated firmly. "It may be that we have been handed, quite by accident, entrée into the underlying mystery and puzzle of Paleder. Hey, this is a puzzle that can really get its teeth into you! That was a new boot too! Let's attack the puzzle where it sprawls about us here. I do not believe that the Chute malfunctioned at all, but some phrase of our instructions to it may have led it to give us this unusual opportunity. Let's use it, let's use it! How real is this, Questor? There will never be a better time to test the latest of the latest, the new portable instrument. What does the gadget say?"

Questor Shannon had the small reference instrument out and in the palm of his hand. It read "fact and depth and intensity of illusion." But immediately, a sleek head on a long neck came out of the quicksand, gobbled the reference instrument, took three of Questor's fingers and a part of the palm of his hand with it, and withdrew into the quagmire again. It had a neat and precise operation for something so large, for that head could as easily have taken Questor himself entire in one gulp. And

Shannon sniffled and whimpered and shook with the pain of it.

"Ah, reality, along with the reality discerner, has been swallowed by a swamp dragon," Jingo Blood said. "So now, reality is to be found in the dragons and not in ourselves. We can use your lost fingers for a reality meter now though, Questor. If you find that your fingers are back on your hand, after a bit, that will mean that the present scene is a little less than real. But, if the fingers stay gone, that means that points are scored against all of us."

Jingo Blood seemed to be enjoying the situation a bit more than the other four were, but she was surely not leaping with joy about it. They couldn't move from there without being done to death by the huge and slashing creatures. And they couldn't stay there very long, as their "island" was beginning to crumble under them.

"At the present moment, there is no sun in the sky over Paleder World," George Blood remarked in what was supposed to be an even-toned conversational voice. "And yet it was at Paleder City noon that we shot the Chute and came down. The sky should now be full of the Sun Proxima (the Grian Sun) which is also the sun of Kentauron-Mikron, Camiroi, and Astrobe. Why, by the way, have the people of those three worlds not sufficiently explored Paleder, or Dahae as some of them call it? Why have not the inhabitants of the planets of Sun Alpha and Sun Beta explored it? A mystery. There is no sun in the sky over us, and yet there is sufficient shocking gray and orange, lurid and garish light. No sun, and no real cloud-cover either. Dull daytime stars are above us; but instead of clouds there are globs of gloop drifting in the very low air. And one of them is coming upon us now at an unnatural speed."

The glob came upon them and swallowed them in its fetid breath. It was sharp with teeth in it, and these were quickly identified as belonging to aerial snakes. The glob brought with it a saturating mental and emotional depression, a stark consternation, an unbearable fearfulness and unpleasantness. It brought dread. It brought hallucination and contradiction, fear of falling, and fear of ultimate fire. It brought ravening ghosts and ghost-animals. It brought flying foxes that fastened onto throats with hollow and life-draining teeth. It brought violent small creatures who sometimes seemed to be human children and sometimes tearing monsters.

But a voice came from one of the small and possibly human monsters. It was a boy's voice speaking in Demotic or Low Galactic:

"Hang in there, Gaea guys! Some of us are on your side. Don't let this whip you. It's only a little psychic storm."

What sort of stuff was that?

And then came the abomination of total despair. This corroding despair entered into the organs and entrails of all the Quiz Ship people. It entered the streets and alleys of their brains and the avenues of their notochords. It entered all the bags and vessels of their bodies. It suffused their glands and seeped into the marrow interiors of their hollow bones. This was complete despair.

"If this is not the ultimate damnation, then I'd gladly choose the ultimate damnation in place of it," Bodicea Crag gave a sharp-voiced value judgment. "Whatever we are in, it cannot get any worse than this."

It got worse suddenly. The "island" they were

crowded onto, the island in the midst of the endless quicksand-quagmire, erupted and cast them all into the noisome and poisonous morass.

They were struck and gobbled and slashed. They were torn apart by tides and concussions. They were drowning in hot, searing, vividly inhabited and attacking mud; and they had limbs lopped off by swamp dragons. They screamed, and their screams were choked off in mouths full of mud.

"I'm not a cowardly man," the huge and pompous Manbreaker Crag sounded then, managing to get his mouth, but nothing else, above the surface of the erupting and devouring mud, "but we have to make our peril known to somebody, somewhere. Loudness is called for, and my own loudest voice is rather unpleasant and piercing."

It was indeed. But everything else that remained in that world was likewise unpleasant and piercing. All of the persons of this expedition had, under test conditions, endured as much as fourteen megapangs of pain. They could not have qualified for the expedition elsewise. But here, in the ravening bog, there was multitudinous pain dozens of times more intense, and there was no way they could endure it.

But how does one not endure things that are at the same time beyond endurance and beyond escape? The five screamed, screamed with their mouths and their eyes full of blood and mud and offal. They were being eviscerated by dragons, and they were being boiled alive like lobsters. Things were literally eating the brains in their heads and the organs in their bodies. Things had already devoured their minds and their souls.

The five of them screamed, underwater and under mud, mindlessly and soullessly, on and on.

"Oh, stop that exasperating shrilling," adult voices were saying to them in High Galactic. "And stand up! And stop fouling yourselves in the mud! Are all the people where you come from as frivolous and silly as you are?"

The five persons from Quiz Ship stood up. There was something about the silliness of their situation that was almost more horrible than the pain they had thought they were suffering.

They were standing somewhat less than ankle-deep in little puddles of tacky mud. They stepped out of it and tried to cleanse themselves of flecks and spotches of mire. There really wasn't too much of it on them. They were smeared somewhat, but they weren't mortally dirty.

"We were in a horrible quagmire-jungle," Questor Shannon was saying. He felt that they owed some sort of explanation to someone. "We were overwhelmed with despondency, and we were being killed by swamp-dragons and fire-snakes and frenzied foxes. We were in the abomination of total despair."

But it was plain that these people didn't believe him at all.

"You were where you are now," one of those Paleder adults said. "We are sorry if we fail your expectations, but we do not have any swamp-dragons or fire-snakes or frenzied foxes on our world. You landed in this little spot where you are now. This was less than a minute ago. Then you began to scream and carry on."

"What? What is—what was this place?" Jingo Blood was asking. "What a double-dealing monstrosity of a place it was! And where has it gone?"

"It was, and it is, as even you should be able to see, a very small amusement park for very small children," one of those adults said. "As you can see, it is no more than twenty meters across, and nowhere is the growth, the 'jungle' as you call it, more than one meter high."

That was true. The fearful flora did not now come to the waists of any of the Quiz Ship people; but, just a moment ago, it had seemed to reach all the way to the sunless sky, sunless no more.

For the Grian Sun was strong in the noontime sky now. What, it had been less than a minute since the Quiz Ship people had landed? All that confusion had taken place in less than a minute?

"The snakes, the dragons, the sea-serpents, the air serpents, the flying devil foxes—" Bodicea Crag was pleading as though for justification.

"Oh, you mean the little rubber creatures," one of the Paleder adults said. "The small children like to make them and to play with them. And they make jangles of noises when they play here, but not so discordant noises as you yourselves make. Do you like to play with the little rubber animals also? Perhaps you will be allowed to make some of them. The small children have dragon-making contests, but these are the failed constructions that you find here. The children. Ugh, the children! They are tedious when they are uncontrolled. Where are the adults of your own party?"

"*We* are the adults. *We* are all the party there is," Manbreaker Crag affirmed with a touch of sad arrogance.

"You—are—the—adults?" the Paleder people asked in apparent disbelief. "The way you were carrying on, we thought that you were simply incredibly loutish children. Now we see that you are, yes, that you are incredibly loutish adults. We will have to take you into custody and to inquire into your awkward arrival here. Yes, and into your grotesque behavior. We are not sure that you are genuine humans or proto-humans at all. You may be what are called 'fiasco humans'. It is likely that you are from Gaea or one of the other very backward worlds."

"It's only one-upmanship," Jingo Blood tried to rationalize it to her companions as the five of them were led away (by moral force, not physical), apparently to some sort of confinement. "The people of Paleder seem to be very good at one-upmanship. But I do not quite understand—"

"We haven't made a very impressive beginning here," Manbreaker Crag said dismally, and they silently all agreed with him. But how had they seemed to be drowning and dying? How had they been doing it in little patches of mud that were no more than five centimeters deep? How had it seemed that they were being broken apart and eaten alive by ravening animals that now turned out to be no bigger than their thumbs, and that moreover were made out of rubber?

"How are your fingers, Questor?" Jingo Blood asked him.

"They hurt terribly," he said, and he showed them.

"Ah, but you still have them," Jingo chortled. "That means that the little scene we just experienced was not real and that it didn't happen."

"Those fingers, they *are* bad," George Blood said. "They're highly infected already. I suspect that they will have to come off. And if you do lose them, that might mean that the little scene we just experienced *was* real to some extent, and it *did* happen, a little bit anyhow."

"Loss of nerve, and loss of our sense of proportion, that's what has been responsible for our fiasco," Manbreaker Crag was rationalizing to his fellow Quiz Ship people. "We let them get the jump on us, and make fools of us."

"Being made a fool of shouldn't matter a lot to an explorer," Jingo Blood told them. "The job of an explorer is to solve problems and to get information. The explorer must be willing to serve as bait if there is no other way to coax the information to strike. Special information is like lightning, and it must be tempted. So, we have been bait. Yeah, live bait."

"It hasn't seemed like a loss of proportion to me," George Blood said. "Maybe it is a finding of a lost sense of proportion on this problem. We lost our sense of proportion as to Paleder World one hundred years ago, when John Chancel first set down here. And no one from our world has been able to see this world in proper proportion from that day till this. Why have we been confused? This isn't an alien planet. This is a world of human or proto-human persons. It is a civilized world where they speak Galactic.

"But there are so many enormities to be solved here! There are so many towering questions to be answered, and none of our people has even had the wit to ask them yet. Why is Paleder permitted to hide its light? That is the question."

"How have the people of Paleder become such master illusionists? That is the main question," Manbreaker Crag stated pompously.

"No, that is not the question at all," Jingo contradicted. "I don't believe that the head of the creature even knows that there are illusions going on. Those things are part of the snap of its tail. But what is the creature itself like if its tail has such a snap to it? That is more like the question. The things to notice aren't the little diversions such as the tiny park that seemed to us to be enormous. What are we being diverted from? That is the question. There must have been many people diverted away from raiding the wonderful technology of Paleder. The people of Paleder seem to set up the illusion that their technology is not worth bothering with. How have they managed *that* illusion? That is much more important than the little tail-flick illusion of the quagmire and its dragons."

They were in a pleasant enough room, large and probably comfortable. They hadn't explored it thoroughly yet, but they had learned one objectionable thing about it: they couldn't get out of it. They couldn't open the doors. They couldn't even *find* the doors.

"If we are not to mind being fools, then let's take the fools' way of getting some action here!" Manbreaker shouted. "Let's make a noise about it."

"*You* make a noise about it, Manbreaker," Bodicea said. "You have a peculiar talent for that."

Manbreaker Crag made howling, roaring, gibbering noises of fearful volume. Possibly he did it for no longer than a quarter of a minute, but it seemed like hours to his four companions. What did it seem like to the Paleder people?

"Simpletons from Gaea, stop that childish racket!" Paleder voices sounded the command to them from outside the room.

"We want out of here!" Manbreaker roared. "Out, out, out!"

"Come out then," said the voices with perhaps a touch of taunting. "The doors aren't locked."

"We don't even know what are doors and what aren't," George Blood howled.

"Intelligent persons would know doors," the voices outside remarked. "The doors can be found by persons with eyes in their heads. They are not locked. They are only intelligence coded. Persons of adequate intelligence can open them easily. Persons with inadequate intelligence had better remain where they are for a while. We will possibly have to locate your keepers and have them come and get you."

"Oh, there's no problem about getting out," Jingo Blood told her companions after a moment. "*You* can get us out of here, Manbreaker. You can get us out of here by another very peculiar talent that you have. But let us first take the blinders off our eyes, now that they are loosened. Let us consider why the Paleder affair has not been properly pursued.

"Why have we people of Gaea not pursued it? Paleder is a gleaming 'goldmine in the sky' with its technology that is beyond any other. But this is only our third acknowledged attempt at it, the other two being one hundred years ago for one of them, and fifty years ago for the other. No, our own is not an acknowledged attempt either, so there have been only two of them. But there may have been several sneaky Pete attempts like our own. And why have the people of the nearer worlds, Camiroi, Astrobe, Kentauron-Mikron, not pursued it? Probably they have, but somehow they were shaken from it or diverted from it.

"Does Paleder really have the most advanced and most sophisticated technology of all the worlds? Likely it has. Then why hasn't that technology been appropriated? Or why haven't there been attempts, with or without force, to appropriate it? Is it the case of 'Yes, it *is* the most advanced technology to be found anywhere; yes, it *is* the most sophisticated technology of all; only—' Well, *only what*? What is it that turns people away from the acquisition, from the follow-up? Is there something phony about this 'most advanced technology to be found anywhere'? Is there something undesirable about it? That is what we have to find out. Now let us get out of here and find it out. Lead us out of here, Manbreaker."

"How?" the ponderous Manbreaker asked.

"By one of the small number of talents that you have. No, not by roaring, by your other main talent."

"Oh, that one!" Manbreaker barked. He was a large and powerful man.

"You can tell the doors, Manbreaker," Bodicea said. "They will be the easiest parts to break open."

Manbreaker Crag broke out of that room, presumably through a door where it should have been the easiest. And the other Quiz Ship people followed him out.

"How novel," said a Paleder person with the only touch of amusement ever noticed in any of those high-brained ones. "We ourselves would never have thought of that solution. And yet it conforms to the requirements, as being an alternate intelligent solution, a solving of the egress problem by using a more spacious interpretation of the framework of the problem. We might be tempted to incorporate such a procedure into our own thinking, were we not beyond the stage of incorporating any new material."

"Certainly we allow visitors to Paleder World," a Paleder person was saying in answer to a question.

"Being the most open of all worlds, by our own claim and covenant, we could hardly bar visitors. No, we do not encourage them to come. Why should we? Visitors are always something of a nuisance. Yes, there have been many parties here from various worlds. No, you are not the third party to arrive here from Gaea. You are more like the thirtieth. Oh, we suppose it's true that the parties who come here on 'unacknowledged' attempts, those who do not file 'Paleder' as their flight destination, do not often return from Paleder, or do not return in good case. Often they have bad luck in leaving. Those who come without filing flight patterns usually have a bit of theft in their hearts, and they must expect retribution. We find that you yourselves have not filed 'Paleder' as your destination. That was thoughtless of you."

The people from Quiz Ship were on Paleder for part of three days. They held conversations with several dozens of the Paleder people in that time. Or else they held several dozen different conversations with a smaller number of these people. Why were the people of Paleder, those people of most surpassing accomplishments, of such undistinguished presence and appearance? Thirty seconds after speaking to one, you would remember only most vaguely what he looked like.

And certainly the science and technology of Paleder was unutterably advanced. Why then did it seem so trivial? Why were the Quiz Ship people so unamazed by it?

Take the weather. One could turn the "manual over-ride" on the weather box at any Paleder City street corner, and the indicated weather would happen at once. One could turn it to "rain," and it would rain instantly. One could turn it to "rain harder" and it would rain harder. But the visitors from Gaea were made to feel that there was something gauche about using the "manual over-rides" on anything. The programmed, automatic way of everything was the best. The "manual over-rides" were there only in case of error in the automatic. But there were no errors.

"After all, we *do* have perfect weather," a Paleder person said. "Perfect weather is weather that is not noticed at all. Perfection is anything that passes absolutely without notice."

"I must disagree with that," Questor Shannon argued. "Perfect weather is that of which one might say 'Ah, this is a beautiful day!'. I can find no fault at all with your controlled and flawless weather of Paleder; but I am *not* impelled to cry out 'This is a beautiful day!'. I wonder why I'm not?"

There was the "hand-of-death" feeling on all things of Paleder. How to explain it? It was as if the people of Paleder had simply decided to stop living, their problems all being solved. And this decision to stop living was reflected in all their handiwork. Dead man stuff, yes. Puzzling.

"Both the impulse and the expression seem a little bit sticky to me," the Paleder person said in answer to Questor's "This is a beautiful day" thesis. "I am glad that our flawless weather does not provoke such jejune outbursts."

Everything on Paleder was flawless. But was that the same thing as being perfect? Maybe. Was it the same thing as being excellent? Maybe. But there were surely some things that it was not. Perhaps it was not inspiring.

There was no impulse to revel in the flawlessness

of things here on Paleder. Why then, on Gaea or most other worlds, was there often the impulse to revel and to hold high celebration for things that were hardly half this good?

The persons of Paleder traveled hardly at all. And this seemed unappreciative of them, since they could travel as much as they wanted, as far as they liked, as comfortably and as instantly as they wanted; and they could do it at no cost at all.

"Your 'Travel Tricks' are something on the line of our 'Instant Chutes', farther up on the same line," Bodicea Crag was saying to a Paleder adult. "And yours are, yes, flawless. Our device uses a staggering amount of power to transport just five of us only ten thousand meters in an instant. But a million times as many of you could go a million times that far with the consumption of hardly any energy. I notice though that you do not use (I get the impression that you *have* the feature but no longer employ it) the 'particular-excellence' factor in selecting destinations. For instance, we instructed our 'Instant Chute' to set us down at the 'nexus of the most intense intellectual activity' of this city. As it happened, the chute goofed and set us down we know not where. It failed or misunderstood, but usually it succeeds with pleasant results. Now, you could have yourselves transported to 'the most pleasurable site and circumstance of this world, at this moment.' You could always have the best of the best. Why don't you?"

"We do, but not by selection. To do that, we would have to accept the view that one thing is ever more pleasurable than another, that one thing is ever better than another. We don't accept that."

"You don't?" Jingo Blood asked in amazement. "But things have to be better or worse than others.

Such differences are what makes the world go around."

"Not this world," the Paleder person said.

"You amaze me," Jingo pursued it. "Don't you believe that one thing may be more interesting than another, that one person may be wittier than another, that one hill may be higher than another, that one song may be more musical than another?"

"No, no," the Paleder person said. "We believed and acted on these things on our way up. But when we got to the top, we saw it all more clearly, so we did away with the top. All these apparent differences are mere illusions, to be cast aside."

"Well, dammit, don't *you*, master illusionists that you are, believe that one illusion may be more illusionary than another?" George Blood demanded in full voice.

"No, no," the person said. "We don't accept illusion even about illusions. On Paleder World, one hill may *not* be higher than another. We no longer have any hills or mountains. They caused elements of randomness in our world, so we did away with them."

"Did you really level your hills and mountains?" Questor asked in amazement.

"No, of course we didn't. That is to look at it backwards. We raised our plains. Everything on Paleder is at highest point. 'Highest and most equal' is our motto," the Paleder person said.

Food on Paleder was, well, flawless. And it was always locally sufficient. But would you ever cry out, in the midst of devouring some of it, "Hey, this is good!"? Well, why wouldn't you?

Most of the consummate technology of Paleder was invisible. And, according to the Paleder persons, this general invisibility of unnoticeability was the sure sign of perfection. It is only imperfect things that draw attention to themselves.

"How does *that* tail belong to *this* animal?" Jingo Blood wailed in sudden frustration early on their last day there. "What is the atrocious imbalance here all about anyhow?"

"My modified love, what are you talking about?" George Blood asked her.

"These citizens of Paleder, these possessors of the highest sophistry and equipment, they are a bunch of sleep-walkers! There is just no other word for them. What sort of animal is Paleder anyhow?"

"As you imply, Jingo, it is the animal whose tail is its most interesting part," George Blood said.

By the "tail" of Paleder, the Quiz Ship people seemed to mean the weird children of that world. Oh, the strange children of Paleder, lurking and flickering and burning, and seldom to be seen straight off!

"These people have their world set up so that no one is permitted to be too cold or too hot," Jingo puzzled, "or too wet or too dry; so that no one is allowed to be hungry or in bad health; where no one—this curdles me—is allowed to be unhappy. No one is permitted to be worried or uneasy, or ill-clad or unintelligent. Isn't that exciting? No, it isn't. *But why isn't it?*"

"Well, these people here will answer us anything we ask," Bodicea said. "Let's ask them more questions then. Yeah, and come to more dead ends."

"With us, of course, there is no division between our psychology and our technology," was the answer that one of the Paleder persons gave to an awkwardly-asked question. "You cannot have our technology without also having our psychology. You cannot have our attainments without being like us. Ours is not a technology for conscious persons."

"It is not a technology for *whom*?" Manbreaker crackled. But the High Galactic word which the person used, "syneidos," "conscious," was unmistakable.

"The 'dragons' with us as with you, though you may not understand it of your own cultus, the 'dragons' are no more than aspects or alternate morpha of our own children. Oh, yes, they are often the murderous aspects of our children. They are often solidly, though unnaturally, fleshed dragons. And they can be mean! The dragon and the child are always one. But the child, given a little time, will usually outgrow its dragon. Or, less frequently, the dragon will outgrow its child and will then become the viable form."

That is what another Paleder person said in answer to another awkwardly-phrased question from one of the Quiz Ship people. But the kid-dragons on Paleder were more often visible than those of Gaea.

"You say that we should control our children better? You say that our children should all be in bed by this hour of night? People of Gaea, we *do* control them, they *are* all in bed right now. I will wager that every child in Paleder City has been in his bed for two hours already tonight," said another Paleder person in answer to another set of questions. "Ah, but you ask who then are those small and savage persons or creatures congregating so murderously in the small parks and stalking so devilishly through the darkened streets? Oh, those are our same children, sleeping in their beds in one of their aspects, and ravening in the tangled night in another. Small children often have more than one aspect to them."

"I thought," Questor said lamely, "that the 'dragons' were really only small rubber devices made by the children."

"There are many ways of looking at it. The little rubber dragons or monsters are entry-points for most of them. They pass through them. They are the talismans or triggers. They are their conceptions of how they will look. And then they *become* those conceptions for a while."

"The reason we get such wraithy answers is that we ask all the wrong questions," Jingo Blood complained to her companions. "Well, on the one end we can only fight dragons with dragons. And on the other end we can only seek the right questions to ask."

So they set up "Project Fight-Dragon-With-Dragon." They implemented it with what talent of that sort they could discover in themselves. And they found that talent to be quite abundant, once it started to flow.

And they asked more, and still more awkward, questions. But it was Bodicea Crag (Queen Bodicea) who finally asked the key question.

"Are you people conscious?" she asked a group of Paleder people, and she was amazed at herself for asking it.

"No, of course not," one of those person said. "We are entirely too civilized for that. Consciousness is a short and awkward interval that many persons and many races pass through. Other persons and races, less fortunate than these, remain in the state of consciousness and do not pass through it. Another group, ourselves, are now able to avoid consciousness entirely in our adult forms. Centuries ago, we passed through it as a race. We still pass through it as small children. But there is no reason for us to repeat that passage in our adult forms."

"If you are not conscious, then you are—unconscious," Jingo Blood said as if pronouncing a great truth.

"That is the silliest attempt at logic that I have ever heard," a Paleder person said. "But how can we explain her silliness to a completely silly person? We are not conscious. We are not unconscious. We are post-conscious. And ours is a post-conscious world."

"If you are post-conscious, then you are not conscious that you are here talking to us," George Blood said. "You don't *know* that you are here. You don't *know* that we are here."

"No, we're not conscious of these things. We don't know that we're talking to you. But there's a 'pattern' on our world that responds to you correctly, through us, or in other ways. That saves us trouble."

"If you don't know that we're here, then we can insult you with impunity," Manbreaker Crag said with a big grin on his big face.

"You can try it," one of the Paleder persons said. "But our 'pattern' may react to your insults, either through ourselves or otherwise. When our 'pattern' reacts, you can get hurt badly."

"Then all your vaunted technology will serve only post-conscious persons," Questor Shannon said.

"Yes, our flawless technology will serve only flawless persons—ourselves."

"Then you are no more than zombies!" Manbreaker chortled.

"No, we went through the zombie phase, in our race, a little while after we went through the conscious phase. But now we are post-zombie as well as post-conscious. Really, now that we have arrived at our destination, we don't much care to remember the roads by which we arrived."

"Will you prevent, or try to prevent, our leaving Paleder World?" George Blood asked.

"No, we will not," one of those post-conscious persons answered. "But *something* may try to prevent your leaving, perhaps the 'pattern,' perhaps the dragon-children."

The Quiz Ship persons withdrew from the post-conscious aggregation. It was late at night of the last (but they did not know that it would be the last) night of their visit to Paleder World.

"There's a psychological imbalance in all this," Jingo Blood said. "Becoming post-conscious is going to have a devastating kick-back through the whole psychic web. It has to be counter-balanced somewhere. What is it that must proceed from such an imbalance?"

"Nothing will proceed from it," George Blood said. "The kick will be a backward one. Nothing will follow. But, oh, what will go before! The seemly adults will throw it all back onto the childhood. The dragon-children are not post-conscious. They are conscious, and murderously pre-conscious. All the psychic lumber cast off by their fastidious parents comes clattering down upon them. It has to land on someone. What power, what twisted power those kids must have!"

So the Quiz Ship people concentrated all their energies on "Project Fight-Dragon-With-Dragon."

"Our 'Instant Chute' did not fail or misunderstand when we came down here," Jingo said now. "The little quagmire park that seemed so large to us, it really was the nexus of the most intellectual activity in town. Wherever the morphic children are concentrating in their psychic monsterness, that will be the nexus of what intellectual activity there is here. Everywhere else, things are post-intense and post-intellectual and post-active."

"Yes," George Blood agreed.

"They got rid of such a lot of clutter when they became post-people," Jingo went on, "and it all comes down upon their children."

"We have the picture now," Manbreaker blasted with his strong voice. "All their brains are in their tail now, and the tail has a murderous flick to it. Let's take the Chute and get to Quiz Ship as soon as possible. And let us get away from this world. The Chancel party got away. The Ambler party got away. A lot of the others must have failed. Let's make a break for it."

"We can try," Bodicea said. "Maybe we can get the ship loose."

The midnight town was lively. And post-people do not usually indulge in night life very much. What was reveling through the town tonight were great numbers of monsters and dragons, and those small creatures who seemed to be human children and also to be tearing monsters. Fanged kids, poisonous kids, mean kids. Aye, and the damnable aspects of them!

Roving ghosts and ghost-animals. Flying foxes attaching with hollow, blood-sucking teeth. Swamp dragons. A sleek head on a very long neck came out of the slimy darkness and took three of Questor's fingers and part of the palm of his hand. This was the same flesh and bone that he had lost on their arrival. And Questor Shannon sniffled and whimpered and shook with the pain of it.

"The unthinkable calm of the post-persons must be paid for in some more jittery coin," a pleasant dragon said. "It is paid for, or recompense is made for it, by this delirious chaos here in the undermind of this world. It is the children who compose the undermind now, and their creatures, and their creatures' creatures. It is the howling irrationality."

"Dragon," George Blood spoke dangerously, "you speak with my wife's voice. Have you devoured my wife?"

"Oh, it's myself, George," the dragon said in the voice of Jingo Blood. "The dragon and I are one. It's part of the 'Project Fight-Dragon-With-Dragon,' but it's a difficult projection when it's done consciously rather than unconsciously. I suspected, while I was still an undergraduate in psychology, that children of our own world were sometimes able to incarnate their dragons, but those one-in-ten-thousand cases of it were always explained away as something else. I can't do it very well yet. I notice that Bodicea is doing it a little bit better, but not really well. And you other three are total busts.

"Oh, by the Great Clamminess, here comes that Glowering Glob again!"

It was much as it had been during that first minute after their arrival. The glob of clammy gloop, drifting in the low air, came upon them and swallowed them with its fetid breath. There were aerial snakes in that glob, and they struck out of it with paralyzing pain. There was the saturation of mental and emotional depression, the stark consternation and unbearable fearfulness and unpleasantness. There was the hallucination and contradiction. There was the dread. There was the fear of falling forever.

"No, no, no, no, I cannot go through this again," Manbreaker Crag yowled.

"It is the end of it all, the dirty end of it," George Blood roared.

There were fer-de-lance snakes. There were swamp-dragons and jag-toothed monsters.

"I do hate a dragged-out death," Jingo keened as her dragonness slipped away from her. "Come quickly, end of it! Oh, come quickly!"

"Be of stout hearts, Gaea guys," a little giggling dragon cried in a clear and boyish voice. "Some of us are with you. We're on your side."

They had heard that voice before.

But the Gaea people were being struck and gobbled and slashed. They were drowning in hot, searing, vividly inhabited and attacking mud.

"I'm Glic," the clear, boyish voice sounded again. "I'm pleased to meet all of you."

"Oh Lord," Manbreaker moaned. "Is it the amenities that we meet again in this our final passion?"

"Voice of Glic, how did the people of the Chancel Expedition escape from this world?" Questor Shannon was imploring. "How did the people of the Ambler Expedition escape?"

"How would I know?" Glic's voice sang. "I'm just a little kid. Move it along though, folks! Don't block the concourse! We're going too. Some of us are going to get on Quiz Ship whether you make it or not. We want loose from here."

But the Gaea people were being torn apart by tides and concussions. They were drowning in boiling mud, in boiling air. Then there was a horrible constriction. They were being forced through the suffocating gullet of the most dread dragon of them all. Yes, swallowed up.

"It's nothing but a psychic storm, people," said the boyish voice of Glic. "Don't they have them on Gaea too? Keep saying to yourselves 'This is fun, this is fun.' We might make it through and get loose yet."

Then they were through the gullet and into the very maw of the devouring dragon. And the maw heaved and launched. It was moving through space!

No, it was a dragon's maw only in a manner of speaking. The Chute had been a very tight gullet to go through, but it had been the Chute that swallowed them up. Now they were inside Quiz Ship and it was in acceleration away from Paleder World.

"We're loose, we're loose,
 And Paleder's the Goose," eight little dragons were chanting.

Little dragons or not, they *were* loose and in flight. Four of the Quiz Ship people were there. And there were *nine* dragons who had begun to shed their dragonness. Some of them were becoming approximately human children. One of the fastest-shedding of them was Glic, who was recognized by his voice.

"You sure are lucky we wanted to go with you, or you'd never have made it," Glic chirped. He was a red-headed little boy with a bit of dragon spirit still abiding in him.

"One of us is missing," Manbreaker Crag grumbled. "There are only four of us now and there are supposed to be five. Does anybody know which one of us is missing?"

Questor Shannon was at the controls of Quiz Ship now, though the only direction he was able to give it was "Away from here! Get us loose!"

Then they were loose, and Questor was singing a glum ditty, but his voice was a little more cheerful than usual:

"After the world is over,
After the minds are gone."

"It was a bust, of course," Jingo Blood was saying. "Their famed technology was wonderful, I suppose. But it was not wonderful for us. And it was not for export."

"Oh, you are wrong, lady!" eight children with tatters of dragonness still clinging to them cried out.

"You are still sick from the psychic storm, people," Glic cried. "But look at the bright side— us. I am here, and with me are seven companions more witty than myself. We know a lot of that technology, but we don't lock ourselves inside it. That's why we wanted loose from Paleder, so we wouldn't become post-people too. They had become post-space-flight, and where would that leave an adventurous person like me? We know the gadgets and technologies, though. Eight brainfuls of technologies you're getting with us."

"One of us is missing," Manbreaker insisted. "Bodicea, which one of us is missing? Oh, it's Bodicea who isn't here."

"I'm here," she said.

"Bodicea, get out of that dragon suit!" Manbreaker roared.

"It isn't a dragon suit. It's me," she said. "I wasn't quite ready to grow up anyhow." Nevertheless, the dragoning was falling off her in big pieces, and soon it would be gone.

"We're just little kids," said a little girl who still had her hair full of dragon scales, "but we're unsufferably smart on that technology already. We can't give you enough of it to turn you into post-people with everything completed, but we can sure give you enough to pop your eyes. I bet we can set all the Gaea guys to gaping with what we know."

It wasn't really too difficult to understand the Demotic or Low Galactic that the children spoke.

"We couldn't see any future in that post-people stuff we were supposed to grow into," another of them said, "but we look forward to life with backward people like you."

"I knew we'd stumble on the answer," the Empress Jingo guffawed. " 'Creative Chaos' that was the answer."

"Thank you," Glic said. "You're lucky we met you."

●

Mildred Downey Broxon is a serious lady with an array of well-earned letters after her name, who has twice been vice-president of the Science Fiction Writers of America; yet she answers cheerfully to "Bubbles"—why, deponent knoweth not. She lives in a houseboat in Seattle with Dr. Broxon and some snakes; I visualize the craft nested in froth, like sticklebacks.

Bubbles is a Clarion alumna, and after having sold a number of short stories and two fine novellas, has gone the whole route and written herself a novel: *Too Long a Sacrifice*. I look forward to it.

Here is a most gratifying story, full of compassion and pathos and that special blend of love and intelligence which happens between exceptional mothers and exceptional children.

—Theodore Sturgeon
Los Angeles, 1978

WHERE IS NEXT DOOR?

by Mildred Downey Broxon

Ben was drawing felt-pen butterflies on our daughter's arm, covering the large needle-bruises from her latest transfusions.

"See? All blue and green and yellow. They're pretty colors." Marcy giggled. I stood in the doorway. Ben looked up. "Have a good time, Tina."

"You've got to be kidding." I left the house and walked across to our neighbors' back yard. Voices from the party filtered out and mingled with the song of crickets. I took a deep breath and looked up at the summer sky. The stars were very bright. There was Hercules; below him I traced Ophiuchus, the Serpent Holder, between Serpens Cauda and Serpens Caput. I was proud I could still pick out such dim constellations, blurry as I was from the tranquilizers.

I was stalling. That blasted kitchenware party! But Arka, my new next-door neighbor, had invited me, and I felt obliged to go. She, her husband Sashi, and their son Dov had moved in last week, settling in early for Fall Quarter. Ben was right; I *had* to get out of the house, and he could take care of Marcy; she'd been back from the hospital a week and a half, and was still tolerating the new medicine. It was probably another remission.

I swung open the screen door and entered Arka's house through the kitchen. Many of the neighbors were there, and a few people from the University. Sashi was nowhere in sight, not that I blamed him. Marie, one of my other neighbors, was chatting with the saleswoman; she either enjoys these things or pretends well. Paula and the rest of the wives were exchanging gossip, glad for any excuse to get away from theses, surly graduate-student husbands, and miserable menial jobs.

Arka, our small, vaguely Mid-Eastern hostess, laughed at everyone's jokes and gave the impression of a small child at Disneyland, surrounded by unknown marvels.

At least Marcy hadn't asked for Disneyland. Some of the kids in her terminal group at the Clinic said that was what they wanted, as if it were Valhalla. I could imagine them being wheeled through the crowds, their pale faces trying to smile, fighting fatigue and nausea and disillusion. It's almost as bad as the ones who demand Christmas in August, when the weeping parents haul out the tree and sing carols. Some kids have a sadistic taste for the maudlin.

Not Marcy. She snickers at things like that. She's very grown-up for eight. She used to love school, and she still reads lots of books.

I had to stop thinking and pay attention; we were playing "How many uses can you imagine for this product?"—a hollow plastic rolling pin. Let's see ... it could be filled with lead shot and paraffin, and used as a lethal weapon. No, I didn't want to win the damn thing.

Arka was looking at me with a perfectly straight face, her green eyes squinted in mirth. I shook my head and shrugged, then stared at the picture behind the sofa. What was it? Something blue. My eyes weren't working tonight. Well, Ben *said* those pills might blur my vision.

Marie won the rolling pin, and the saleswoman gave us each a plastic tea strainer as consolation. I closed my eyes and drifted. I'd have to buy something. I could use one of the big containers to store Marcy's cold packs in the freezer. Ice packs helped the swelling in the joints.... I giggled. I ought to tell the saleswoman; she could use it in her pitch.

Shocked, I opened my eyes. Tina, you're getting weird. Those pills have gotten the better of you. I rose, a bit unsteadily, and went in search of the bathroom. Maybe cold water on my face—

I should have asked my hostess, but she was busy, and all the bathrooms in these project houses are in the same place. I opened the typical plywood-panelled door of the downstairs bathroom—in the hall between the kitchen and living room—and was confronted by a sheet of roaring blue light. I blinked; it was still there. Bright blue, with crackling lightning streaks. I shut the door fast and stepped back. This was worse than I thought. I must be having terrible side-effects. I staggered back to the living room and waved to Arka. "Sorry, I've got to go lie down."

She rose. "Are you all right, Tina? May I help you?"

I shook my head. "I'm fine. Just a little under the weather." Was it less socially disgraceful to be on booze or tranquilizers? I couldn't recall, so I didn't explain.

She walked me to the back door. As we passed the downstairs bathroom I swayed and grabbed the knob.

"We're not completely moved in," Arka said, "but I did want to meet my new neighbors."

"Yeah. I'm sorry, Arka. See you soon, but right now it's time for bed."

Ben said if I started hallucinating he'd have to change tranquilizers. I figured I'd best tell him.

It's been rough on Ben, too, Marcy dying. Being a psychiatric resident, he has to listen to problems all day and come home at night to a hysterical wife. He's never said so, but I see it in his eyes. When I started having screaming fits he brought me free samples of tranquilizers.

Ben isn't interested in the interpersonal, clinical aspects of psychiatry, but he needs to finish his residency. There's a research program on the causes and cure of schizophrenia; many people think it's biochemical. They may be right. He's working at the University Hospital now, treating the first human subjects. He can't stop his work just to come home and take care of something personal like a death in the family.

I had to quit my teaching-assistant job when we found out about Marcy. The world needs a lot more psychiatrists than literature profs.

During Marcy's last hospitalization Ben got called away—the night everyone thought she was dying—by a suicide-gesture overdose. He said he almost told the woman to go finish the job, and if she didn't have enough pills he'd write her a prescription.

As soon as he can get out of Clinical and into pure research he figures he'll save the world from mental illness. The research program seems to be working; the patients stop being crazy after a few weeks of intensive enzyme therapy—all they lose is a little imagination. Nothing like the dullness after being on back wards for thirty years, or, in the old days, having a pre-frontal lobotomy. They just end up a little—straight. I believe in what he's doing, of course; schizophrenia is a very serious problem, and if he can help solve it, it will be worth all the things I never got to do. He's going to have a place in history.

Some day I'll get what I want. I want to go back to work, or maybe back to school. I want to learn about everything: languages, astronomy—I used to love astronomy, but the math slowed me down, and I had to change majors. If I'd studied something else, at some other college, I might never have met Ben. Maybe, after all, that would have been best. We didn't know about the recessive gene. Even the researchers at University Hospital didn't catch on for a long time; there have been only a few reports in the literature. Not that it makes any difference to Marcy, but doctors love to diagnose. We'll never have another child, of course. I couldn't face the prospect of an abortion. I wished sometimes this was already over.

I put Marcy out in the yard, on a sheepskin—it prevents bruising and skin breakdown—and watch her from the kitchen or the back porch. As soon as he moved in, Dov, the little boy next door, started bringing her things. I used to worry about Dov, because you had to be so gentle with Marcy. I told him right away that she was breakable, and after that he was fine.

Unusual for kids that age, they'd sit and talk for hours. Marcy, of course, wasn't up to roughhousing like she used to, and Dov was as serious as a very small adult. He had this thing about animals: he was terrified of anything that flew, but snakes and worms and turtles were all friends of his. He'd find them somewhere and carry them over to introduce to Marcy. All we have around here is garter snakes, thank God.

The other day a butterfly landed on Marcy's arm. She laughed and called Dov to see it; he turned pale and knocked it fluttering to the ground. One wing was broken, and it crawled in circles. He stamped it and wiped his shoe on the grass. Marcy started to cry.

"No," Dov said, "never touch flyers. They are poison, they bite—"

I'd had enough. I marched into the back yard. Marcy may not be around much longer, but she didn't need a phobia. "Where did you hear that, Dov? They're perfectly harmless, the poor little things."

Dov shook his head. "They come from the sky and kill. The small ones, and the larger ones—" He pointed to a far-off robin—"they try to kill anything."

"But Dov," I said, "I've lived around here all my life, and have never been bitten by a butterfly or a bird."

"Mrs. McGinnis, please, back home they bite, they sting—" He was very earnest.

"Well, bees and wasps sting, sure." Was the poor

kid allergic?

"No, the color-wings." He pointed to the shattered insect.

"That may be back home, Dov," I said, "but here they're safe." I tried to remember where on earth there were poisonous butterflies. Somewhere in the jungles, maybe, or in Asia? I walked over to where a large Monarch was fanning its wings. "Look, Dov, I'll touch it, and it won't hurt me." I held out one finger, not wanting to brush off the dust. "See?" It fluttered away.

Dov had covered his eyes. The sides of his hands, I noticed, were oddly scarred, white against the brown. He put down his hands, took one panic-stricken look at the butterfly, Marcy, and me, and bolted. I heard his screen door slam.

Ben called to say he'd be late that night. After a quick supper—Marcy only eats soft food, now—I went to see Arka, in case she thought I'd been trying to scare her kid.

I knocked on the screen door; Sashi opened it. He was shorter than Ben, and darker, with his son's green eyes. "Tina?" He held the door open.

"I came over to see Arka." I didn't know Sashi very well, and didn't want to go into his house alone.

"She is not here. Was it about Dov, this afternoon?" He stepped backward into the kitchen, and I held the door.

"I'm sorry if I frightened him, but he's usually such a sensible little boy, except for this thing about butterflies. He said there were poison ones back home." I regained my courage and looked at him. "Where *is* back home, anyhow?"

"Come on in," he said, "it's getting cool." I

shivered. He preceded me into the dim living room, switching on lamps to cover the soft blue glow, and closed a magazine. How could he have been reading in that light? I sat on the sofa, and he occupied the easy chair across the room.

"Dov will be fine. His training was incomplete, and he is being re-instructed."

Re-instructed? It sounded ominous. "Dov is such a nice little boy," I said. "He's so good to Marcy. I couldn't trust most children, you know. They don't have much sense, or they get impatient."

He nodded. "Dov is very patient. Was Marcy injured?"

"Oh, a tiny bruise, not enough to hurt much—it wouldn't make any difference, but, you know—" I wasn't sure he did know. After all, it isn't the sort of thing you tell your new neighbors. There's an etiquette of death; it's supposed to happen quietly, so everyone is surprised. "Marcy, ah, bruises easily, she has this problem." I couldn't let it all out to a stranger, even a neighbor, not with those strange green eyes looking right through me.

"Sometime this autumn, then?" He sighed. "And she always liked the bright fall colors."

Where did he learn that? I didn't think he'd ever talked to Ben—Sashi was faculty, and they didn't work in the same department. Did Dov get it from Marcy? Is that what Marcy wanted to see? Not Disneyland, not Christmas, but autumn?

Marcy, jumping into brilliant piles of leaves; bringing home her new books (gee, Mom, they smell so good) so I could wrap them in brown paper—then coming home that day with a nose-bleed (honest, Mom, I wasn't fighting)—

I closed my eyes and went limp, as I've learned. It would be all right in a few minutes. *Against the*

Universe, what does it all matter? There. I was better. I took a deep breath and opened my eyes. "I'm sorry. I've been under a great deal of strain lately. I'm glad Dov is okay. He's such a nice little boy." I rose from the sofa and, for some reason, turned toward the wall. I could see more clearly, since I quit the tranquilizers. The picture above the sofa showed stars. A photo, or a painting? The representation was excellent. "Are you interested in astronomy, Sashi?" It was time for polite chat.

"No, not especially." He murmured something else I didn't catch.

"I've got to go now," I said. In the hall I noticed a new knob on the downstairs-bathroom door—not the standard tract-house coppertone, but large, and mirror-shiny. It looked difficult to grasp.

I paused outside and glanced at the night sky, but it was cloud-streaked and dim. Sashi was watching. I hurried into my house.

Marcy's arm was purple where Dov had brushed it, defending her from the butterfly. I put on a cold pack and sat with her a while, administered her medicine, and went to bed.

Ben woke me in the middle of the night; he said I was crying in my sleep. All I remembered was a huge butterfly carrying Marcy off, and it had teeth. . . .

The next day was rainy, so I didn't put Marcy outside. Her bruise was dark. I thought of that casual flick and shuddered. She was close, very close, to another hospital admission.

Arka and Dov came over to visit. I was sitting in the living room, and Marcy was reading from her overhead projector.

Dov was formal. "I am sorry, Mrs. McGinnis, about yesterday. It has been explained to me that I was wrong, that the small flyers are not poison here, and that I should have listened when you told me."

There it was again. Not poison *here*. The calm assurance that they were, indeed, terribly poisonous elsewhere. Arka nodded in approval. "I understand," she said, "there was a bruise?"

I shrugged, embarrassed. Marcy hated to be fussed over; she'd accepted the cheerful, uncomplaining role that society seemed to demand. To my surprise, she switched off her projector and held out her arm. Arka clucked. "Dov, you did that. You fix it."

"He doesn't have to apologize," I said. "It wasn't really his fault. There's no way to keep these things from happening, in the long run."

Dov touched Marcy's arm. I expected her to flinch, but either she was brave or her bruises didn't hurt that much; perhaps both.

"I don't think you should—" No one was listening to me. Marcy's eyes were closed, Dov was staring at her arm, and Arka was watching them both. After all, what harm could they do? I went into the kitchen to make tea.

Of course I didn't see that bruise go away. It got better by itself; that's what Ben told me when he came home. He hadn't seen it the night before; I hadn't wanted to depress him, and he left early in the morning. There was no point in discussing it.

Ben wouldn't admit he thought I was cracking up, but he kept asking me how I was sleeping, and if the new pills he brought were helping. (I took one of them and it knocked me out, so I threw them all away.) He kept our conversations very concrete: what the Chief of Staff said at lunch, what happened on the six o'clock news, the weather. Next, I supposed, he'd be asking me the date and who was President, like they do in mental-status exams. He used to do that for a joke, when I indulged in wild flights of fancy, back in our early years.

I knew perfectly well it sounded crazy, so I kept quiet about the folks next door. I heard Dov telling Marcy stories about mythical animals, and about camping trips where the trees sang and the sky crackled blue at night. Ben, I knew, would think I was so worried about Marcy that I was grasping at straws, and had invented the whole thing. I told him once about the blue light and the stories; the next day he brought me some different medicine, which I also threw away. It was frightening not to be able to talk to my own husband because he thought I'd cracked under strain. I kept quiet, then, and went back next door.

Sashi was there alone, and again I was reluctant to go into his house. This time he sat on the sofa, so I chose the easy chair facing it. The picture was still on the wall. It showed a thick star-field, far brighter than even our winter sky, with a red/blue binary next to three blue-white star clusters. The effect was spectacular, and I would have remembered, had I ever seen it.

I had to begin somewhere. "That picture is interesting." Oh, subtle, I was. But not a single recognizable constellation? It must have been taken with a large telescope, and the sky was so cluttered with the fainter stars—of course, that was it. But it didn't have the reflector-distorted foreground stars I'd seen in deep-space telephotos.

Sashi spoke. "No, it is not a telescopic photograph."

I hadn't said a word. One of the symptoms of impending madness is the impression that others can read your thoughts.

"We, too, get homesick. We are going home on vacation Friday, and will return in two weeks."

I swallowed. "That's a very interesting picture. Once, at a public astronomy lecture, I saw a computer-generated slide of the sky from Tau Ceti. The constellations were all moved around; I couldn't identify them." I looked back at the picture. "Scrambled." Like my brain.

"That is not from a planet of Tau Ceti."

"Well, no, of course not, how could it be? I mean, no one's ever been there. It's a very good painting."

"It is similar to a photograph," he said. "We have been meaning to ask if Marcy might accompany us. She would enjoy it, and it would do her good."

"Go with you? On vacation? Marcy? She can't go anywhere—"

"She would need nothing but her sleeping bag and personal articles," Sashi said. "She would be back in two weeks."

"You don't understand. She's sick, a terminal illness. She could have her final relapse any day. She needs medicine, and has to be watched—she bruises so easily. Anything could start another hemorrhage—she couldn't possibly go camping."

"Some children," he said, "ask for amusement parks. Others want Christmas early. Marcy would like to accompany us. If she does, I promise she will live to see the autumn leaves."

All right. I really have gone crazy. It all looked so real, even when Arka stepped out of the downstairs bathroom. The lock clicked open with a smooth, heavy sound, like a bank vault. Reflected on the wall I saw a moment of bright shining blue.

"The connection is set," Arka said, "and our supplies are ready." Sashi nodded.

"Where would you take her?" I said. "Why would you want to?"

"She is a friend of Dov's," said Arka. "She is a bright child, with great potential."

I rose. "I'll have to think about it." My gaze lingered on the picture. Where were those stars from? So many, and so bright.

"We leave Friday afternoon," Sashi said.

This was Wednesday.

I sat on my back porch for a long time. It was late afternoon; I couldn't see the stars, but I knew they were up there. It was hard to think of them as suns, they were so small and so far away—suns with planets, maybe, and people of some sort living on those planets, sitting in the warmth of their own afternoon. Were they, too, wondering if there was anyone out there? What constellation would our Sun be in? It was probably too dim to notice.

Even in the warmth I had goose pimples. *There really are other people out there, and I've met three of them.* No, that didn't make sense. It's just because I've always hoped there was someone else in the Universe. How are they the same, and how different from us? In the end, what does it mean to be human?

I was letting my imagination run away with me, of course. Or it was a joke. But why? None of them was laughing, and it wasn't funny, unless—aliens— had a different sense of humor.

I wouldn't pick on someone whose kid was dying. I didn't think they would, either. Not anyone who could have Dov for a son.

I sat there, getting freckled, until the Sun set. I watched the first stars sprinkling the sky, until they grew thicker and it was full night. I could see Ophiuchus, the Serpent-Bearer, between Serpens Caput and Serpens Cauda. Mythologically, the Serpent-Bearer was associated with Aesculapius, god of healing. But that was our mythology, not theirs.

If the Sun was in anyone else's constellation, did they have a myth about it too? Constellations are all a projective test anyhow. What needs of theirs were spread across the sky?

Finally I rose and went into the house.

Marcy had fallen asleep reading; I switched off her overhead projector. What could I say to Ben? If anyone came to me with a story like that—

Marcy stirred in her sleep, then sat up. "Mom? Are you going to let me go with them, Mom? Please?"

"Do you know where they're going, Marcy?"

She lay back down, still sleepy. "No, but it sounds neat, and Dov says I don't have to worry about being sick. Please, Mom, make Dad let me go."

"I'll see, hon. Go back to sleep now."

Well, Marcy had heard it too, but children will believe anything. What would they want her for? I shuddered. *Aliens.* I sounded like all the flying-saucer nuts in the world.

I was sitting in the living room staring into a glass of sherry when Ben came home.

"Tina! You know you shouldn't drink when you're taking tranquilizers!"

It was an inauspicious start. "I'm not taking tranquilizers."

"Why not?"

"I don't need them. The side effects were terrible. I don't feel nervous or depressed."

He frowned. "I think you need them." He put down his briefcase and fell back into his chair. "God, what a day. Up all night on call, then today there's a suicide on the unit. Everyone's blaming everyone else. Don't know how, but she got out a window." He wiped an arm across his eyes.

"Have you eaten?"

"They sneaked me an extra tray." He laughed without mirth. "Hers. She did it in mid-afternoon, and no one thought to call Dietary." He closed his eyes, then opened them and stood up. "If I don't get to bed now I'll sit here all night. How's Marcy?"

"She's okay. Wants to go away on vacation."

He smiled. "Well, she's no quitter. It's out of the question, of course, even if I could get the time off. Gotta get to bed."

It did not seem the optimum moment to mention my suspicions.

The next day, Thursday, Ben was on call again.

I was still wondering. I went to see Arka, but she was not home. Dov answered the door. I was surprised he was left alone, but their ways must be different from ours.

"Hello, Mrs. McGinnis," Dov said. "Have you decided?"

"Dov, I can't just send her off, sick as she is, and not know where she's going."

"It isn't the same name you'd give it," he said. "It's the second planet of a little star. It just has a Greek letter in your books. We looked it up once, but I forgot."

"What's it like?"

"Home. Your planet is brighter, and greener. And

the animals are different. I told Marcy; she wants to see it. We would spend a short time in the city, first, to fix Marcy, of course, or she would be sick all the time we were camping."

"How can anyone fix Marcy?"

He held out his scarred, brown hands. "I fixed her bruise, but I am only learning. I have more to study. Other ones, who have lived longer, some of them have studied very well."

"You don't even know what's the matter with Marcy."

"Oh, I do. Her body is fighting itself, that's why she bruises so easy. She is very tired now, Marcy is." He looked at me, sad. "You know that Marcy always had this, that she did not catch it, it was part of her?"

I nodded.

"But you did not know before you made Marcy? You would not have done that to her, would you?"

"No, Dov, we would not."

He held out his hand. "I did not trust you, because of that. I thought you people might be different. But if you truly did not know—"

I shook my head.

Dov looked at his hands. "Maybe I'll never be good enough to fix people like Marcy. But I'm studying. Marcy will be worth the trouble when she grows up."

"Dov, Marcy's alone. I've got to go home."

Back in the house I looked at my new pills, but didn't take any. Friday noon Marcy had another hemorrhage.

I found her stretched out on a blood-soaked pillow. She was scarcely conscious.

Oh, God, what am I going to do? I called Ben at

the hospital. "Marcy's had another hemorrhage."

"Not just a nosebleed?"

"No, this one's from the mouth. Her gums, I think."

"Well, call the Clinic and bring her in." He sounded frightened and cross. "I'll get down there as soon as I can."

"Ben?"

"Yes?"

"She isn't going to make it this time. I'm sure of it. She wants to go on vacation with the people next door, and they're leaving today, and she won't be able to if I take her to the Clinic. And what can the Clinic do anyway? They've tried everything."

"Tina, get hold of yourself. I know this is difficult. How in hell could you even *think* of sending her on vacation in her condition? You know it's touch-and-go. And with a bunch of almost-strangers?"

"I've talked to them more than you have."

"Get her in to the Clinic, or bring her in a taxi if you can't drive. But *get her in here.*"

"She's going to die if I do. I think if I send her away they can cure her, they know things we don't—"

"Tina, stop it. Marcy has an incurable genetic disease. Is this some foreign quackery bit like the cancer clinics in Mexico?"

I began to giggle. "It's foreign, all right, Ben. Really foreign. That's why I think they might be able to help. They're aliens. From another planet, I mean. They're going home on vacation. They want to take Marcy, and she wants to go. You know how she hates the Clinic. She never asked for Christmas or anything—"

"Tina, why don't you stay right there. I'm coming

home now, and I'll take care of everything." His voice was dangerously calm. "Now don't do anything, just wait. I should be there in twenty minutes to a half hour. Everything will be all right. I'll be there as soon as I can, Tina." He hung up. I stared at the phone, then bundled up Marcy in a quilt.

Sleeping bag. They wanted a sleeping bag, and her personal gear. I couldn't carry all those things and Marcy too, and I had to get her next door and out of the house before Ben came home and stopped me.

She'd lost a lot of weight, so I could lift her. She woke from her daze. "Mom? Are you gonna let me go?"

"Yes, Marcy, I am. I'm taking you next door now, and I'll be back for your stuff, jeans and all, but I want to make sure I get you next door first."

I could push our screen door open, but, carrying Marcy, I couldn't open the door in the other house. "Arka? Sashi? Dov?"

It was Dov who opened the door for me. "Oh, she's worse," he said. "Good thing we're going soon."

"Where are your parents?"

"They are coming back soon."

"I have to get her stuff. Can I leave her with you?"

"Yes. What is the matter?"

"Where can I put her? My husband's coming home and he thinks I'm crazy and he'll stop me if he can. He'll take her to the Clinic and this time she'll die, I know."

"Follow me," Dov said. He led the way into the hall and paused outside the bathroom door. He palmed the lock, which snicked open, revealing the curtain of blue flame. "Put her in there, Mrs.

McGinnis," he said. "I can't carry her. I'll try to wait for Arka and Sashi, but—"

I reached through the shining blue light; my arms tingled.

"It's going to be all right soon, Marcy," said Dov. "It doesn't take long once they get started. I watched them once, when I was studying back home."

She nodded. "It hurts some, now."

I set her on the—floor?—I couldn't see. "Goodbye, Marcy." The hissing drowned out her answer. "I'll get her things, Dov." Halfway through the kitchen, I stopped. "Is the weather cold where she's going? Will she need a jacket?"

He considered. "Maybe. It's about like here, right now."

I nodded and ran across my back yard into the house. Marcy's clothes were clean and folded in her drawers—she hadn't been able to wear them for some time. I gathered three pairs of jeans, a few T-shirts, underwear, pajamas, a comb and toothbrush, and rolled them into her sleeping bag. Shoes. That's right. And socks. I put her newest pair of sneakers into the bundle and sprinted across the yard.

I found Dov crouched by the bathroom door, waiting. I put down Marcy's sleeping bag. "All her things are in here, Dov. I'll get back to the house and delay Ben as long as I can." He nodded.

"Thank you, Mrs. McGinnis."

I went home and sat in the living room. I did not have long to wait.

Ben burst through the front door. He had a determined expression, and his hand was in his jacket pocket. He saw me and tried to sound casual. "Hi, Tina. I came to help get Marcy to the Clinic. Want to come along?"

I shook my head.

"How is she, by the way? I'd like to see for myself." He headed toward her room and stopped at the doorway. "Where is she?" He spun back and grabbed my shoulders. "Tina, what have you done with my daughter?"

I met his gaze. "I sent her away on vacation. They said she'll be all better when she comes home."

"Where did you take her? Next door?"

"Farther than that, by now."

"Show me where you took her, Tina. I need to know."

I knew what he had in his pocket: a syringe of Thorazine. It would knock me flat, and I'd wake up on his ward, for my own good, of course. I twisted free. Maybe I, too, could escape. By the time we came back, Marcy and me, he'd know I wasn't crazy. I ran out of the house, into the kitchen next door, and down the hallway. It was deserted, and the bathroom door was closed.

"Dov? Arka? Sashi? *Marcy?*"

I grabbed for the door-handle. It was slippery, and I could not grasp it. Of course. It wasn't keyed for my hand. *Oh, please, let them have gotten Marcy away.*

I slid to the floor and was crouched, sobbing, when Ben reached me. He held my wrists, and I felt the syringe sting my thigh. So be it, then.

"All right, Ben, I'll go along. But you won't find Marcy. And when she comes back in two weeks, I'll tell you one thing."

She's got to come back in two weeks, or they might never let me out. But they wouldn't put me in Ben's schizophrenic program, would they? Not in two weeks. Ben wouldn't do that to his own wife, even if he thought—Marcy's got to come back and be all right.

Ben raised me to my feet. "What one thing do you want to tell me?"

It all seemed very funny. I began laughing, and couldn't stop. Finally I choked out, "Marcy's never going to feel the same about butterflies."

●

Imagine Clarion, and the hardest-working class I have ever seen anywhere, slogging through damp heaps of manuscripts in the middle of a ferocious Michigan summer. A visitor arrives, and maybe the students took advantage of the interruption to rise and stretch, but it looks to me like a standing ovation. For this is Bob Thurston, only last year a Clarion alumnus, now a Real Writer Selling Stories. This, to the kids, struck a great deal more awe than any of us faculty. It was, somehow, more real to them; and, impossible as it might seem, when he left they worked even harder.

So has he. There are a couple of dozen Thurston stories in print now, and no less than six introductions in the prestigious Gregg Press books. He has sold his first novel to Berkley/Putnam (*Alicia II*) and a novelization of the pilot of NBC's "Galactica" series.

This story was actually begun at Clarion, then abandoned, then dragged out, retreaded, shined up and sold. It's a strange little piece full of very strange people indeed.

—Theodore Sturgeon
Los Angeles, 1978

THE BULLDOG NUTCRACKER
by Robert Thurston

Not many people know that John Keats is still alive. They think he died of TB or reviews or syphilis. All the great writers who did die died of syphilis, but not John Keats. His death was a P.R. thing—he knew it would be good press, so he faked it. Thomas Chatterton is still alive, too, but he's a prick.

Keats reads all the biographies of himself several times each. He marks every section that is not true with a Flair pen and charts all the inaccuracies chronologically on his bathroom wall. He plans to collect all the inaccuracies into a book labeled the definitive biography. He spends thirty minutes of each day thinking up possible titles for the book:

Keats!; John Keats's Literary Debts: Owed to a Nightingale; Lashes to Lashes, Lust to Lust; Snails to Thee, Escargot: An Autobiographical Cookbook; Errant Rod; I Never Promised You A Rod Hard-

ened; One Hundred and Fifty Years of Solitude; Similes Are Like Life; Metaphors Are Not Like Life; Metonymies Are Life!

None of us thinks he'll ever write the book.

John Keats lives in a modern apartment on the twenty-fourth floor of a high rise apartment building in the middle of an unnamable city. The apartment's rooms are sort of strung together, like the prepositional phrases in the previous sentence. And furnished, similarly, with redundancies.

Nobody ever drops in on Keats. We only come when he calls us. On the phone he never says hello or addresses us by name. He says, "Come over," and hangs up. He usually spaces his calls so that his guests arrive at half-hour intervals.

The first thing you do when you get to his apartment is go to the dining room, where Keats sits at the table drinking coffee, his left hand resting on the tail of his bulldog nutcracker. An antique iron nutcracker in the shape of a bulldog. The following words describe the sitting Keats: balding, furrowed, sallow, pursed, jowled, scraggly, slouching, plump.

"Sit down," he usually says, smiling. He has a fine smile.

He pushes the bulldog nutcracker at you. The nut would be placed between the bulldog jaws while the user, the cracker, pressed down on the tail. But Keats never uses it to crack nuts. You place a finger in the bulldog's mouth while Keats slowly applies pressure to the iron tail. The bulldog's mouth feels like the business end of a pair of pliers.

"Hurts, does it?"

"No, not a bit."

"Now?"

"A little."

"Now?"

"Yes."

"Like it?"

"Yes."

You must say yes, or he'll press harder.

Each guest (there are usually only four or five, he detests large gatherings) comes to the dining room, sits, and places his finger in the mouth of the bulldog nutcracker. Then we talk. Normally we talk about the people who were not invited this time. We are a very closed circle, and so always know immediately who's missing. Although Keats presides, he does not actually say very much. He sips and rests his left hand on the tail of the bulldog nutcracker.

Sometimes we talk about Keats, but never about *Keats*. We have rarely been able to elicit old information about him, and then only when he's drunk. But we all know that he lies a lot, so we don't know what's true even then. Whether or not he really hacked verse for Tennyson, smuggled bootleg whisky over the Canadian border, or is briefly seen as a longshoreman extra in *On the Waterfront*.

He is even more evasive about his former contemporaries. Try asking him.

"What do you remember about Shelley?"

"Not too much. Good actress, but a bit too plump for my tastes. One time she and I—"

"No, no, not her. I mean the writer Shelley, the—"

"Oh, right. Good old Mary Wollstonecraft Godwin Shelley, 1797-1851, a winsome creature that, wrote *Franken*—"

"No, no, no. Percy Bysshe Shelley. Her husband. The romantic poet."

"Romantic? Well, you might talk to good old Mary Wollstonecraft Godwin about that. She told me, in secret mind you, he had only one—"

"But you *must* remember him as a poet, as a man, as a radical."

"He didn't make much of an impression on me that I can recall."

"But surely—"

"I can never remember whether he was the dandy or the clubfooted one. Here, put your finger there. My bulldog's hungry."

On each one of his responses he looks at those of us who are observing, and winks. We smile and chuckle on cue. Personally, I think his humor is a bit crude, but being in his presence is worth playing up to him according to his rules.

Around eight-thirty Linda arrives. Linda is Keats's mistress. Or at least we think so. She is a tall pretty girl with black hair and a likable figure. Standing beside her, Keats comes up to her vaccination scar.

We are not supposed to comment on the difference in their heights. Therefore, on some nights, when we have settled into the living room for drinks and snacks, Keats goes around the room and says to each of us:

"You think that Linda is too tall for me, don't you?"

"Of course not."

"You answer too quickly, with too much obvious sincerity. I look like a shrimp beside her, don't I?"

"I've never noticed."

"Like a softshelled crab. Like a condemned skyscraper next to the World Trade Center. Like a raisin bran flake next to a shredded wheat biscuit."

"No, no. Height's not important."

"I'm not asking if it's important. I'm asking what it looks like. Like a bent straw next to a giant soda glass. Like a demolished 1952 VW next to a brand new Mercedes. Like the exhaust from a steel plant chimney, rising brightly but reluctantly into the sky, next to the fluffy and lovely cloud it will soon merge with."

If you continue protesting or tell him that he is indeed rather short, at least in comparison to the willowy tallness of Linda, he brings out the bulldog nutcracker. He tends to finish his conversational exchanges with the nutcracker. If he does not use it on you, he simply sits in an armchair holding it like a real animal, or lies on his back on the couch, the bulldog perched on his stomach. He is rarely without it. I have thought of stealing it, all of us have I suppose, but somehow it seems petty to steal from John Keats.

At some point in the evening Linda tells us about her day. First, her work, which is some kind of civil service office job. Her narrative is another chapter in the intense and suspenseful maneuvering for position between two minor bureaucrats, whom I've always imagined to be short and fat, although Linda is careful not to use these two words in Keats's presence. Then, her lunch, another battle inside her as her stomach turns sour at the sight of the dietary foods so necessary to maintain her shaky hold on slimness, and her eyes become tearful at passing views of the delicacies her cultivated tastes long for. (When she and Keats go out to dinner, which is a relatively rare occasion, they go only to the finest places.) Then, her adventures after work, where the element of unpredictability operates. Today she went shopping in the downtown mall.

"And I tried on seventeen separate different dresses. I just kept slipping them on, and looking, then slipping them off and handing them to one of those sourfaced old women who are always in charge of dressing rooms. She just lined them up on a rack with a horrible look of distaste on her face. Once, I asked her how a certain dress looked on me—a horrendous pink and black checkered thing with a ridiculous belt with a heartshaped buckle—and she said, 'It looks darling, as if it was made specially for you.' And I said to her, 'You ought to have your big nose put in the mouth of John's bulldog nutcracker,' and strode back to the dressing room. I sneaked a look in the mirror, the old bitch looked quite astonished. Finally I chose this one."

She stands up and swirls around displaying her new dress, a modest but delicately attractive yellow and black check with a belt buckle designed to resemble the beast Cerberus.

"Do you like it, John?"

"Like what?"

"My new dress. Look."

"Is that new?"

"It looks old."

"Everything looks old to you. Don't you even like it?"

"No."

"Doesn't anybody like it?"

She is asking all of us. She does this on purpose. There is a long silence, interrupted only by the creak of the bulldog tail being lowered. Finally I say:

"It looks very nice, Linda."

Keats leaps off the couch.

"Do you really mean that?"

"Sure."

"You think that dress is beautiful?"

"It's quite pretty."

"But not beautiful?"

"Pretty seems more appropriate to me."
"Are you settled on that? Pretty?"
"Well, yes, sure, I guess so."
"You guess so. But *is* it pretty?"
"It quite positively definitely absolutely is pretty."
"I just wanted to be sure you knew what you were saying."

He jumps back onto the couch. Now Linda may begin pouring drinks. She knows what each of us likes and prepares it without asking. Keats drinks hot toddies. Linda drinks triple Scotches. I drink Scotch and 7Up. Most of us talk about local art and culture. We hope that somewhere along the line Keats will grunt while we are talking, then we know he approves of what we just said. Later, when we have all had a few drinks, we play frisbee, throwing it across the spacious living room. Linda runs around the room protecting antique vases. Keats always throws the frisbee as hard as he can. If he throws it at you, you are to catch it with one hand. If you drop it, or catch it with both hands, he sneers. If he sneers at you enough, you usually throw it back to him as hard as you can. He usually catches it.

After that, we fall back into our respective chairs and drink some more. Conversation trails off as we wait for it to be time to go. Occasionally Keats directs a question at somebody.

"Do you really like Antonioni?"
"One must like Antonioni. He has achieved existential piquancy."
"But can you really like all those long shots on electric fans, billboards, street litter, Death Valley for God's sake!"
"They speak of the loneliness and alienation of

contemporary man who—"

"Rocks don't speak. Garbage doesn't speak. No, I take that back. Garbage does speak. When you open your mouth. But objects don't speak. They just sit there and slurp up film footage. Objects do not speak."

"Well, then, if you like, they represent—"

"They do not represent. Nothing represents. Everything is what it is. Objects that do not speak, also do not represent."

We know that Keats is tired and drunk. The corners of his eyes strain at whatever weights pull at them. When he makes a point, he has to stop to aim his finger. He will fall asleep any minute now and then we may go. We know that he is in the last stages of awareness when he puts his own finger into the mouth of the bulldog nutcracker and begins to press down on the tail. He seems to apply just as much pressure on his own finger as he does on ours. Then he lies back on the couch, settling into the cushions, and carefully places the nutcracker on the peak of his stomach. The rest of us sit forward, ready to mobilize at the onset of heavy breathing. Once or twice he snorts. At our movement he opens his eyes and says, "You all look like graverobbers who've just opened the lid on something moving." He readjusts the nutcracker and makes himself more comfortable. The next set of heavy breathing sounds like genuine snoring and we, creatures of habit, make the same moves. Without opening his eyes he says, "Or morticians closing the lid and encountering resistance." A minute or two later Linda, who has the best sense of whether Keats's sleep is real or feigned, tiptoes to him. His left arm, which had held the nutcracker, has dropped away from it and now hangs over the side of the couch, the hand resting on the floor like a delicately woven five-fingered rug. Linda whispers, "Are you asleep, John?" He mutters, "We never sleep." She waits a long suspenseful minute. We all stare at her. A couple more times he tries to answer her. Later he mumbles. Then he does not respond. Linda gently removes the bulldog nutcracker from his stomach and, cradling it in her arms, carries it to her chair. We each go through our ritual of time-to-leave remarks.

"Well, the old clock on the wall..."

"Got to be up at dawn..."

"I'm for hitting the sack..."

"Busy day tomorrow..."

We all file by Linda and say our goodbyes. She sips at her triple Scotch and idly strokes the bulldog's iron back. Keats's snoring fills the room, seems to come from more than one direction. It is monumental snoring. As we speak to Linda, we try not to look at her eyes or, rather, at the tears in them.

When I am home, I try to force myself to sleep by watching the Tom Snyder Show, by slipping in cassettes of soothing Baroque music, by reading *Love Story* again, by staring at my reflection in the glass covering my Carzou lithograph, by mentally listing the cast of *Casablanca*, by smoking an ashtray's worth of Gauloises cigarettes, by gulping boorishly a glass of Harvey's Bristol Cream Sherry, by thinking of what it might be like to have Jeanne Moreau living with me, by mentally composing a letter I will write tomorrow to the editor of *The New York Review of Books* on the subject of *Saul Bellow: Literary Titan or the Troll Beneath the Bridge?* But none of the methods works. I remain awake, worrying, reconstructing the evening with

Keats, cursing myself for having to be the one to tell Linda that her dress was pretty. I didn't have to say anything, I didn't have to take a stupid risk like that, a risk that might blow my chances of being invited again. It is ridiculous worry, unnecessary heart strain. I will be invited again. Keats will phone tomorrow. Or the next day. They couldn't do without me, I am sure.

•

Craig Gardner comes out of Rochester, New York, where a fifth-grade teacher infected him with science fiction (incurable, you know, though not lethal) by reading Wells's *The Time Machine* and where, according to him, he later earned a college degree by watching movies for four years. A couple of years ago he was unearthed by *Unearth,* that extraordinary little magazine which discovers and displays previously unpublished writers, and in which Gardner discharges his passions—film and sf—in a movie review column. It's a good one, and only one of the many reasons for finding and keeping all issues of *Unearth,* which will certainly be regarded in the future as the jewel-case for early gems of literature. Craig Gardner may well be one of these literary lapidaries.

"One More Song" is a bitter whimsy with a light heart and a sting in its tail, with which it will jab you for the rest of your life every time you find yourself in a movie musical.

—Theodore Sturgeon
Los Angeles, 1978

ONE MORE SONG BEFORE I GO
by Craig Shaw Gardner

He slammed the door behind him. This was no way to live.

"Jerry, wait!" came from the other side. The door opened. Susan stood there, holding the baby. "I didn't mean—"

"You said get out! So I'm out!" Jerry called over his shoulder as he took the stairs down two at a time.

"Jerry!"

He was through the front door and beyond her call. That was the last argument he was going through with her.

He could still see her standing in the middle of the one big room they called home. She held the baby in front of her, as she always did when they fought. Held as her eternal burden. Offered for worship at the same time. The baby. The reason we live.

He'd had enough of it. He'd done enough sleeping, eating, living, cooking, fighting in the one room. He wasn't going back.

A fine drizzle had begun to fall from a sky that was grayer than his apartment building. He started to walk. Down one street, around a corner, down a couple blocks and another corner. He kicked his foot through a curbside puddle. The puddle responded by dampening his pants leg to the knee. Jerry brushed back the hair that was sticking wet to his forehead. He wasn't dressed for this kind of weather. He'd have to find shelter of some sort.

There was a movie theater halfway up the street. Big green letters above the marquee read THE PALACE, except that the first A was burned out. Jerry walked towards it. *The Hollywood Musical*, not-quite-so-large black letters said against white. A revival house? Jerry had always liked old musicals. He couldn't believe his luck.

Underneath the first line on the marquee, in smaller red letters, was NOW SHOWING: *Brighter Days* AND *A Circus of Song*.

Jerry hadn't heard of either one of those. But what the hell, he needed to get out of the rain. Besides, he could watch any movie once.

There was no one inside the ticket window. Jerry looked around. Dull red light spread out from an open door that led into the theater.

He looked inside the door and stopped breathing for a minute. The place was huge. It was one of those movie houses built fifty years ago to impress. It still did its job fifty years later. The lobby looked like a grand ballroom. At the far end of the place was a refreshment stand, with someone sitting behind it.

Jerry went inside.

Up close, the room didn't look quite so elegant. The rug he walked across was worn in spots, and paint peeled here and there, especially from the faces of the angels carved on the pillars that supported the huge curved ceiling. It made the angels look sunburned.

Jerry smiled at the thought. The old place wasn't what it used to be. But then, who was?

The man behind the counter looked up as Jerry approached.

"Yes sir. Like to see the films?"

"Please." Jerry reached for his wallet. He glanced over the refreshment counter. "And a small popcorn, too."

"Yes sir. That'll be one dollar."

Jerry must have looked surprised. The old man smiled, adding "Bargain matinee. You like musicals?" the man asked as he retrieved the popcorn.

"Yea, I see them whenever I can. They cheer me up."

"That they do." The man turned to look at Jerry. His eyes were as gray as his hair. "Tell you what. Go up that passageway on your left. Best seats in the house. You'll think you're in the movie."

Jerry nodded, taking the popcorn and ticket stub. The popcorn box was red, white and blue, with pictures of circus animals, baseball players, a movie screen; a different scene on each side. Jerry hadn't seen a box like this in years. Goes well with the movie, he told himself. He walked up the corridor, into darkness.

And into light.

What was this? He was outside. This was why the movie was so cheap. The old man was playing a joke on the world.

To make matters worse, he had lost the popcorn.

He must have dropped it somewhere.

But the rain had stopped. It was quite sunny, actually. And green. Trees were everywhere. Jerry hadn't known there was this much green in the city.

Somebody ran up a gravel path toward him, the gravel path on which he stood. As the newcomer got closer, Jerry noticed how oddly he was dressed; striped shirt and pants, a straw hat and a dark blond mustache drawn into elaborate handlebars. Maybe he was part of a barbershop quartet.

As if to confirm Jerry's suspicions, the man began to sing:

"Howdy, neighbor!
Why you standing there?
Don't you know it's time,
Know it's time, know it's time,
Time to go to the fair?"

A fair? Well, why not? It sounded like fun. To heck with the musicals. Jerry waved at the newcomer.

"Where's the fair?" he asked.

"It's over there!" The man in the striped suit pointed and pranced away. Jerry had to run to keep up.

They followed the path around a bend, where it opened into a large clearing filled with brightly colored tents and even brighter signs inviting you within. In front of the tents were easily a hundred people, dancing as fervently as his stripe-suited guide. They all sang as one:

"You can sample jams and jellies,
You can see a horse race there.
C'mon all you Neds and Nellies,
Are you going to the fair?"

Jerry found himself in a line of newcomers, marching in front of the dancing crowd. His line began to sing cheerily. It was so infectious that Jerry started to sing along.

"Yes we're coming. *You bet*! Yes we're coming to the fair! Yes we're coming. *You bet*! Yes we're coming to the fair!"

Fiddle music carried through the air. Women swirled around in bright calico, long pigtailed hair flying away from their faces as they danced. Jerry stepped forward, and a woman was in his arms. They whirled around in time to the music. Jerry found it easy to pick up the steps. As he circled, he saw that the other newcomers had gained partners too. Everybody began to sing:

"Come on to the county seat.
You can court a lady fair,
Dancin' to a Dixie beat.
Are you comin' to the fair?"

The music's tempo increased. Jerry took his partner in an allemande left, circling faster and faster. Then, with a flourish of horns, it was over.

Jerry stood there for a moment, trying to catch his breath. Remarkably, he was hardly perspiring at all. He turned to his dancing partner, who was still by him but smiled off past the group of dancers to the front of the clearing, where a couple still sang.

Jerry glanced around. It was the first quiet moment he had had since leaving the theater.

Something was strange about the colors out here. They were too dazzling. Some trick of the autumn sun, perhaps, coming out of the clouds after the rain. Something that deepened the blues and greens, and made the reds so dark they verged on purple.

He had seen these colors somewhere before.

His partner grasped his hand. He turned to see her inviting smile, perfect white teeth beneath those deep red lips. The music began again. Where did it come from?

Everybody began to sing. Jerry found himself caught up in the infectious song again.

"C'mon, you don't have to roam.
Here's a place without a care.
Leave your worries back at home.
We're all going to the fair!"

He took his partner in his arms and they danced, part of a great circle of dancers. How light she was! She threw her head back, laughing to the music. As if dancing for her was life. The opposite of Susan, to whom life was one room, and the baby, and slowly getting older.

The music stopped and the world went gray.

At first Jerry thought it was the rain clouds coming back. He knew this was too good to last.

Some of the dancers began to move toward the tents, a few in other directions. They moved without sound. All the shouting, singing, stomping revellers of a moment before slid away like ghosts.

Jerry ran to his former partner. "Wait!" he called, touching her shoulder. She didn't seem to notice.

Jerry pushed in front of her. "Wait! What's going on?"

She looked past him toward the tents. "We have to get to the next number." The statement was made flatly. Her once glowing face showed no trace of emotion.

He let her go past him. Number? Where was he? Nothing made sense. He stood in the middle of some gray limbo that a moment before had been full of music and color and movement, almost too full of life to be real. It was like a scene out of something.

Like a musical.

It was too funny to be frightening, too strange to be laughable. Too obvious for him not to have seen it before. Except he wasn't seeing it. He was living it.

He hadn't been cheated by the old man; he had received a gift. Joy, not bounced at him off a flat screen, but experienced directly. Jerry smiled as he thought of the dance a few minutes before. He could think of few moments to compare with it. A couple of times with Susan, maybe, but those had sunk beneath a sea of grief.

The action of the musical must have moved someplace else. That would explain this hazy landscape; it was like walking through a memory. But the light and action would come back. Nearby, if not here. From the dancers' movements, Jerry guessed the music would soon start again down among the tents.

He stood there for a minute, uncertain what to do. He was somewhere that had shown him pleasure and promised him more. But it was far from his apartment, his city, his world. He didn't know the rules here.

He shook his head and started toward the heart of the fair, and the next number. He looked inside a tent and the colors came back.

A line of women smiled expectantly at him. Each one stood next to a table laden with baked goods. They sang:

"Hiya, judge,
Nice day, judge.
Won't you sit down?
Have a taste.
Eat a slice.
Best pie around!"

He seemed to have been granted a character

part. Jerry smiled. Why not? This could be interesting. He walked to the first table. A tall blonde in a bright red apron handed him a piece of pie. He cut off a bit with a fork and chewed it thoughtfully.

"Texture good, taste is sweet,
A good looking slice.
And this here is my verdict:
This apple pie is—nice!"

The blonde's smile fell a bit as he moved on to the next table. The women sang again:

"Hiya, judge.
Nice day, judge.
Won't you sit down?
Have a taste,
Eat a slice,
Best pie around!"

He was presented with another piece of pie, this time by a redhead with a green apron. He chewed.

"Apples plump, crust is crisp,
Looks just like it should.
My verdict on this piece of pie
Is an undeniable—good!"

The redhead made a worried "oh" with her pretty mouth. Jerry handed back her plate and moved on as the women sang the chorus again.

The next woman, to his surprise, was his former dancing partner. Brunette, with a blue apron, she smiled pertly at him. Jerry was surprised how happy he was to see her again.

He dug his fork into her piece of pie. It was a pie with a difference. He began to sing:

"This here pie is butter rich
And sweeter than the rest.
In my considered judgment now,
This here pie is—best!"

The woman cried in delight and kissed Jerry on the cheek. A small thrill went through his body, the kind of thrill he'd had with Susan, years ago, before they were married.

Music was still playing, but the tempo had changed. Instead of jaunty fiddles, there were mellow violins. The crowd looked expectantly at him.

He'd gone this far, he might as well go the rest of the way. Jerry took a dark blue ribbon someone had thoughtfully given him and pinned it to the lighter blue of the girl's apron. She glanced at the ribbon, then looked in Jerry's eyes. Jerry began to sing to the violin melody.

"Well, I thought I'd eaten pie before,
But now every other pie's a bore
Compared with this delight.
I savor every bite.
And I long for more."

He took her hand then, and sang the second verse.

"Well, I thought I'd seen the sky before,
But with you the sky is something more.
It has a deeper hue
When I walk with you,
And I long for more."

She was in his arms and they danced. Their shoes made tapping sounds on a floor remarkably hard for the inside of a tent. She was as light as a dream, or the memory of a dream, and he spun her around the tables. He put her down at last and sang again:

"Yes, I thought I'd eaten pie,
And I thought I'd seen the sky,
But now neither one will do,
'Cause I've got my apple pie
In the sky with you."

They held each other as the strings faded away. But the music didn't stop. It changed, filling with a chorus underlined by ominous tubas.

A tall man in full cowboy regalia, from his ten-gallon hat to his mud-stained boots, stepped into the tent. The other women stared at him with naked lust and grabbed at his arms, chorusing "Howdy, Clem! Howdy, Clem!" Clem just tipped his hat and pushed his way through until he came to Jerry and the girl. And he wasn't interested in Jerry.

"Well, Emmy Lou," he drawled. "Comin' to the horse race?"

Emmy Lou looked uncertainly from Jerry to Clem and back again.

"I'll be riding Diablo." The cowboy began to sing something about "Be a rodeo rider with me, gal." Jerry considered it rather tasteless. Not even half as good as the one he sang.

"Well, okay," Emmy Lou said, and left Jerry with only a smile. Jerry couldn't believe it. His arms went out toward the retreating couple, but the two of them left the tent and the world went gray.

Jerry shivered as he realized what had happened to him. He was getting too close to the musical, caught up in the surface pleasures of this all-too-bright world. A world that always returned to this, silent shadows gliding away toward their next rendezvous with life.

Where had all these shadows come from? He had stepped into this world and immediately been offered a part in it. Had others wandered in from somewhere, and chosen to perform again and again in some small part of the film? Maybe when they first arrived, they had each been given a romantic lead, too, until someone else entered the film. They'd be shifted then to smaller and smaller parts; a villain perhaps, or comedy relief, eventually ending up as just another anonymous face in the chorus. Is that where it all ended? Jerry didn't know. Standing in the gray, he decided he didn't want to know. It had been a pleasant visit, but it was time to leave. He stepped out of the tent.

Which way had he come in? The world looked different devoid of color. He squinted, trying to remember greens, blues and browns. A path toward his left looked familiar. He walked to it, out of the clearing and toward the woods.

There—ahead—was the bend from which he had first seen the tents. Jerry walked faster. It was time to get away from this gray, even with its splashes of color. Back to the city, where colors mixed with the rain, and people did more than just laugh. He wanted to see Susan. And the baby.

Color came back as he ran around the bend.

"I'm not that kind of girl!" Emmy Lou cried.

"What?" was the incredulous reply. "Every woman loves Cowboy Clem. Why, there's dozens of gals who would jump at the chance...."

"Well, let them! And—and—you can jump, too, for all I care!"

Emmy Lou ran away from the stunned cowboy, straight into Jerry's arms.

Wait! a part of Jerry cried in alarm. This wasn't right! He had to leave.

Clem strode toward the couple. Jerry looked up from the weeping woman to give him a level stare. Clem, coward that he was, skulked away.

Jerry looked at the trees bordering the path. This was very close to where he came in. Just a few more steps and he would leave all this behind.

Emmy Lou looked at him, eyes filled with love. Her hands took his. She began to sing, her voice a sweet soprano.

"Yes, I thought I'd eaten pie,
And I thought I'd seen the sky,
But now neither one will do.
'Cause I've got my apple pie
In the sky with you."

Jerry smiled as he heard his song again; a simple happiness. He'd stay for just a minute more. The dancers appeared around the bend, frolicking down the path four abreast. They surrounded Jerry and Emmy Lou and swept them back toward the fair grounds.

Jerry tried to push his way back toward the woods, but there were too many of them. They began to sing.

"C'mon, you don't have to roam.
Here's a place without a care.
Leave your worries back at home.
We're all going to the fair."

The world was getting dark. Not the off-scene gray that Jerry had seen before. This was an all-consuming blackness, enveloping the landscape.

The unseen orchestra rose to crescendo. The dancers all held one long final note. Jerry realized then that the movie was over.

This was the end.

Or was it?

Everything was dark and quiet. But there was a breeze—wind moving against his body. Or perhaps his body was moving in the wind. Jerry got a picture of forms passing through the blackness, being set up for their first entrance when the musical began again.

He took a step and felt gravel beneath his feet. He was back on the path! Now, if he could only remember where he came in. He took another step. It was hard to walk. The air was thick and he had to fight against it—like walking through soup.

Two, three, four steps off the path. Was that right? He swung his hands in front of him. Nothing. He took another step. His knuckles struck something hard. He felt it with his palm. It was flat. A wall? A door frame? He took another step. And fell down four stairs to a landing. Around a corner, another dozen steps led to the lobby.

He was out! He could get home, to his wife. Susan and the kid. And he'd never leave them again.

He stood up, a little bruised but nothing broken. There was a red EXIT sign on the wall opposite the lobby. Jerry squinted into the dark and saw a long bar and the outline of a metal door. He'd go out this way. He didn't want to have to go through the lobby and meet the old man again. Cautiously, he pressed the bar across the door to open it. It jerked open, pulling Jerry out with it onto a fire escape, with rain falling from a gray sky. He climbed down to an alley, and walked to the street that would take him to his apartment.

It was raining. So what? He was so happy, he could sing. A melody filled his head. "Are you coming to the fair?" Jerry smiled at the song. Was the rain letting up? The whole world seemed brighter, the colors more vibrant. Perhaps, Jerry thought, there was a healing power in those old films even the old man in the lobby didn't know about.

He took the steps leading to his apartment two at a time. He knocked twice on the door, then flung it open.

"Honey!" he cried. "I've come back!"

Susan looked up from where she had been feeding the baby. Behind her, the sun had broken through the clouds, and the clear yellow light streamed through an open window to frame her face in a soft halo. Jerry couldn't remember when she had looked prettier. Those long lashes, those inviting lips. They seemed very red, dark against her face. The baby's cheeks and lips were red, too; a trick of the autumn light.

"Da-da," the baby said.

His wife turned and smiled at the child. "Da-da," the baby cried. "Da-da. Da-da. Da-da." Over and over.

His wife turned to Jerry and sang in time to the baby's rhythm:

"Gee, Jerry, it's good to see you,
Though a man may have to roam,
And seek adventure. Oh bold defender,
Gee, it's good to have you home."

Jerry didn't notice the small box of popcorn—red, white and blue, with a different picture on each side—that he knocked over as he ran down the stairs, out onto the bright streets.

●

Since 1972, this amazing young writer has sold more than thirty short stories and six novels, and edited an anthology. He has been a finalist for the John W. Campbell Award (which is given to the best new writer) and a two-time finalist for the Nebula (given by his peers in the Science Fiction Writers of America). He writes plays, performs on the guitar, and enjoys photography, bicycling, carpentry, leather-work and playing around with audio equipment. Otherwise he just lies around in Columbia, Maryland.

He says of this story that it's basically a spoof on that kind of time-travel tale regarded as a pillar of the science fiction estate. "I know that logically the story does not make sense," he says, "but then of course, logically, time travel *can't* make sense . . . I think."

—Theodore Sturgeon
Los Angeles, 1978

JUST IN THE NICHE OF TIME

by Thomas F. Monteleone

Frank Vecchio's life was getting too complicated, and he wanted to end it.

But not completely. Just temporarily.

Frank sat at his desk nervously drumming his fingers on its oiled walnut surface. Out his window stretched a fortieth-floor view of the creaking city of Baltimore. His digital clock said 2:01. Callabrese would be calling soon, thought Frank. And that was not good. Not good at all.

No sooner had he finished the thought than the intercom buzzed and he heard Ms. Walker, his receptionist, nasal-toning: "Excuse me, Mr. Vecchio, but I have a call for you. Says his name is Callabrese."

"Shit."

"What was that, Mr. Vecchio?"

"I said 'shit', Ms. Walker," said Frank. God, I'm tired of all this. He exhaled dramatically. "All right, put him on."

The phone lit up and rang briefly. Vecchio picked it up. He noticed that Callabrese had left his camera off and the screen was ominously dark. "I take it you've thought over our proposal, Mr. Vecchio," said the voice.

"Actually, if you want to know the truth, I haven't thought about it much at all," said Frank, feeling as if he had just drawn a straight razor across his carotids.

"Hey, you tryin' to be funny, Vecchio?"

"Funny? No, I wouldn't *think* of it. It's just that I'm not crazy about the whole idea, that's all."

"Well, listen, Vecchio. It's like this. Either you accept the front money or start payin' the protection fees. That simple."

"Look," said Frank. "I don't think I want to get involved in any illegal trafficking of—"

"Hey, whadya some kine a asshole or somethin'? Don' talk like that on a Public Utility, Mr. Vecchio. Might be tapped, you know? As a matter of fact, Mr. Vecchio, I think I'm gonna have to send some of my associates down to have a talk with you."

"A talk?"

"Yeah, and you know what, Mr. Vecchio? I feel sorry for you. Bye-bye."

Frank opened his mouth to reply, but the phone was dead. Hanging up, he mused calmly to himself, Well, that just about seals it up. No turning back now. He pressed the intercom. "Ms. Walker, get me Mr. Howe, right away, will you?"

Picking up the receiver, Vecchio listened as his receptionist punched in his lawyer's number. A pretty female answered at the other end. "Dewey, Cheetum, and Howe," she said sweetly.

"Mr. Howe, please. Tell him it's Frank Vecchio."

"Oh, yessir, Mr. Vecchio. One moment please."

Frank waited several seconds, wondering how long it would be until Callabrese's goon squad showed up. Probably have twenty-four hours, anyway. Goons are pretty busy these days. Suddenly the screen and the receiver crackled into life. Maury Howe burst into life, resplendent in the garish clothing that had become his trademark. "Frank, baby! How're you doing?"

"Not so good, Maury. Now listen, I have to ask you about something. Remember when you were telling me about that other client of yours, I forget his name, had cancer and got himself frozen?"

"Oh, you mean Wilbur Heatherton, the solar furnace manufacturer? Sure, Frank, what about him?"

"You set that thing up, right? Well, I been thinking, and I think I want to do the same thing."

"You *what*! Frank, are you nuts? You're in perfect health! You're a successful businessman— Frank 'the Cannoli King' Vecchio! You got a beautiful home, everything a man could want. What the hell would you want to go and do a crazy thing like that for?"

"I got my reasons," said Frank, but I ain't telling you, you jerk.

"Frank, I don't know if I can approve of such—"

"How much, Maury?"

"To draw up the papers? Oh, about thirty thousand?"

"I knew you'd see it my way," said Frank. "Now how long would it take?"

"Well, there's only a few places in the area that I'd recommend, and the best of the lot just happens to be run by an old buddy of mine. Name's Herman Bluthkalt—a real nice guy if you ever saw one."

"All right, call him. You take care of everything, Maury. I just don't feel like fooling with it."

"Sure, Frank, sure. Now, say, when do you want to be . . . ah, 'placed in remission', as they say?"

"Tomorrow morning."

"That's kind of soon, isn't it?"

"For thirty thousand? I wouldn't say so."

"Hmmm," said Maury. "No, I suppose it isn't. All right Frank, I'll get on the horn and set things up. Call you at home and let you know the hour, right?"

"Yeah, right, Maury. Okay, see you later." Frank hung up the phone, wondering if he should call Jay, and tell him about the decision. No, better wait, he thought, as he got up, pulled on his suit jacket and left the office. Passing Ms. Walker in the outer office, he paused to give her the rest of the day off. After she had disappeared, Frank locked up the office and stopped to read the lettering on the door for perhaps the last time. *VECCHIO'S*, it read, *Home of the World's Finest Italian Pastries.* Frank shook his head. Hell, even that was probably a lie. He had never tasted anybody else's pastries except his own—and his grandfather's, but that was a long, long time ago.

Down forty floors of the old U.S.F. & G. Building and out on the street towards the parking garage. Frank looked down Baltimore Street to the east and saw the signs for the city's famous "Block"—a tawdry stretch of show bars, burlesque houses, and porno shops. The place always had a special allure for Frank, although he had not been there in many years. He remembered his salad days when he used to haunt the "adult bookstores" in search of that mythical piece of pornography that you would never get tired of.

He never found it. None of us ever did.

Just about reaching the corner of his garage, Frank paused, and regarded the sleazy lure of Baltimore Street. What the hell, he didn't have anything better to do.

And so he payed a visit to *The Jewel Box Lounge*, *The Oasis*, *The 2 O'Clock Club*, *The Pink Pussy*, and a host of other bars where the beer sold for $7 a bottle. He also visited the "bookstores."

The sun had set by the time he reached his penthouse atop a sleek glass tower on Saint Paul Street. Dinner at the *Chesapeake* had been a bland, tasteless affair, and he had already forgotten the overflow of young flesh he had seen earlier. Nostalgia certainly was no condolence, and he was feeling low.

Picking up the phone, he called Jay.

"Hello," said an old man's voice, tainted by a Holland Tunnel accent. There was no picture; Jay had an old phone.

"Jay, it's me, Frank."

"Hey, Frank, how are you? What's up?"

"I gotta talk to you," said Frank, and he told his friend about all his troubles and his plans to leave the scene for a while.

"Wow, are you sure this is what you want to do? It certainly has an air of finality about it."

"Yeah, I guess it does," said Frank. He did not sound happy.

"Well, it's awfully sudden, anyway. Look, why don't you stop out at the farm tomorrow. We can talk, and besides, the new crop's just about ready. I'm sure I could get a little early stuff ready for us."

Vecchio brightened. "Yeah, that sounds good. I'm supposed to see my lawyer tomorrow, but I can squeeze it in. I'll be there for breakfast."

They exchanged warm goodbyes and Frank hung

up feeling somewhat content. When he went out to Jay's farm, he always felt good. Maybe it was the clean air or something, but there was a distinct difference between the pleasures of the farm and the urban pastimes of fine food, women, clothing, cars, cultural events—all the things that Frank's wealth had provided him. But none of those things held much attraction for him any more. In fact, when Frank was being brutally honest with himself, he knew that none of that crap ever did satisfy him very much at all.

Then why, Frank asked himself, was he planning to freeze down and preserve himself for more of the same, even if it was in some future time?

He did not know the answer to that one, but he had an intuitive streak that seemed to insist that the future *had* to be better than the life he had carved out for himself in 1992. Frank looked about his opulent trappings and saw that it was an empty place. There would be no answers there. He turned off the lights and went to bed.

But he did not fall asleep for a long time.

After a shower and a shave, Frank was in his Mercedes, squeezing through the workday throngs, fighting the familiar images of the seething port city—slidewalks jammed with workers, teardrop-shaped Rapids sliding in and out of all the terminals, the columns of gray concrete that looked like row upon row of gravestones. He pushed his petrochem vehicle through it all and entered an expressway. There was little passenger traffic since there were few people who could afford the astronomical taxes levied on petrochems, but the other lanes were packed with bustrains, Rapids, and trucks. Frank punched in the coordinates for the closest exit to Jay's farm, sat back in his seat, and let the computer drive him along at 160 kays.

With nothing to do for the next hour, Frank let his mind wander over the clutch of years and memories, especially those concerning Jay. Frank had met Jay Leshnefsky in college; they became room-mates, then best friends who eventually grew old together, even though their lives took different forks in the road. After college, Jay had married Maggie, a lithe, blonde farm-girl from northern Maryland, and had settled down to live off the land. Subdividers chased him farther north and to the western part of the state where he acquired a farm of great peacefulness. Jay dedicated his life to working the land, reading philosophy, and loving Maggie. Maggie was gone now, but Jay stayed out on the farm alone, cultivating his crops and his mind. Frank had spent many pleasant evenings out on the farm, sitting on the front porch swing, talking and sharing a few pipefuls of Jay's homegrown marijuana.

Frank, on the other hand, had decided he was going to make himself some money. So back in the early days, he hooked up with various shysters, and got taken to the cleaners a few times, before cashing in on the Italian pastry business. Frank did not know the first thing about baking, but he brought over some old Italian bakers with faces like sun-parched Sicilian almonds and flour under their fingernails. Along with Maury's machinations, those old men had built Frank an empire. His lawyer initiated corporate proceedings and soon there were *VECCHIO'S* franchises all over the country—lots of fancy glass-and-steel with giant plastic *cannoli* on the roofs. The money was coming in faster than (to use one of Frank's favorite expressions) "shit through a tin horn." Everything was smooth until the mob tried to cut into the action.

Diverse as their lives had become though, Frank and Jay remained close. Even if they did not see each other for months at a time, they were always able to talk as if they had seen each other yesterday.

The warning buzzer on the dash cut through his thoughts. Frank's exit was coming up and it was time to switch over to manual. He transpared the window and took over the control stick, gliding off the expressway and trundling onto an old asphalt four-lane. It was late summer outside and the first traces of orange-flecked autumn had begun to appear. Frank ticked off the kays until he spotted the cutoff to Jay's place up on the left, wheeled up the dirt path past a modest cornfield, and neat rows of lettuce and artichokes.

Up ahead was the stone house with the nut-brown shutters and the wrap-around front porch. Jay was standing on it, his gnarled hands thumbed into his belt loops, waiting. Although he and Frank were the same age, Jay still looked lean and strong. His thick hair and full beard were pepper-and-salt, and his complexion was tanned evenly by work in the sun.

Parking the car, Frank eased out of the Mercedes, shook hands with his friend. Jay smiled and took him into the house for a breakfast of flapjacks and freshly-picked blueberries.

Afterwards, they sat on the porch swing, looking down into the slight depression in the land which Jay wistfully referred to as "the valley." Beyond it, the tilled land rubbed edges with thick forest.

"You don't look good, Frank," said Jay, reloading his hand-carved pipe. "What's going through that head of yours?"

"You know the whole story. I guess this thing with the Mob's just the capper. Seems like all the things I've worked for are turning to shit."

"And you're going to run away from everything?" said Jay, pausing to light the pipe, take in a lung-filling toke, and pass it to Frank. "That's not the answer."

"Maybe not, but it's all I've got," said Frank drawing a pipeful into his lungs, holding it for a moment before exhaling. "I figure things can't be any worse in the future. Besides, it's exciting. I mean, wouldn't you like to see what it's like hundreds of years from now?"

Jay shrugged. "Oh I guess so. But you know, Frank, there's always been enough to keep me occupied right here and now."

"Nothing seems to be worth the effort any more."

"Few things are," said Jay.

"You don't believe that." Frank passed the pipe back to his friend.

"Well, not exactly, but think about it Frank—maybe that's why I only concern myself with a few things." Jay sucked in a lungful, coughed and harrumphed.

Frank smiled. It was just like Jay to say something like that. Ever since he had become a farmer, he had mixed his metaphysics with fertilizer, becoming a real bucolic philosopher. Looking at the old man in the coveralls, Frank would never have guessed, if he did not know it already, that Jay had started out as a 5'7" basketball player from Weehawken, New Jersey. But that had been a long time ago ... and people were shorter then.

Finally Frank broke the contented silence. "Well listen, Jay ... what about me? Have I been worth your time?"

"Well," said Jay, giving the swing a new push with his dirt-caked boot, "of course you have, Frank. I mean, after all this time, we're still friends, aren't we?"

"You're the only friend I got, Jay."

"Well, there you are then. Look Frank, you're a good man, I know that. We've both been searching the same things in life. I just found mine a little sooner, that's all."

Frank laughed just as he was exhaling from a short pull on the pipe. He was quite stoned yet. "Sure, like about fifty years sooner. Hell, Jay! I don't think I ever found what I was looking for. Maybe I never even knew what it was! That's why I came up with this freezing thing. But to hear Maury talk about it, you'd think I was taking a trip to Barbados or something. Everything's such bullshit. The whole thing's a mess, but I gotta give myself another crack at it."

"Recognition," said Jay nodding his head with eyes closed, as if he were recalling something he had read, "recognition is the key to knowing one's true self. Time and place lose significance when one has discovered who he really is. Maybe things will truly be better in the future, Frank."

"Now I know you don't believe that," said Frank.

Jay smiled. "You got me that time."

Neither man spoke for a while. Frank had driven out there thinking that there were a whole lot of "last things" he would have to get off his chest, but with his old friend sitting beside him, swinging on the porch in the clean mountain air, he felt as if he did not have to say much at all. That's the way with close friends, real friends.

Ten minutes must have passed. Frank cleared his

throat, then spoke. "You know, I guess I won't be seeing you any more."

Jay nodded, as if he could accept the fact, like any of the other natural events he understood so well.

"Well," said Frank, "doesn't it bother you?"

"Oh, I guess you could say it bothers me, but I've got to look at it the way I regard everything else. Let me explain, Frank. Look out there, down by the cornfield. See? It's all husks now, not green any more. But next year, some more will be coming up to take its place. Everything, Frank, that's worth renewing itself, will eventually do so."

"C'mon, Jay! I'm no cornstalk. I'm me! I'm not gonna grow back next spring!"

Jay shook his head. "Yes you will. You'll be waking up in a new world. You'll be getting another crack at it. Don't you see? It's not like when Maggie died," he said, closing his eyes, as if the memory still carried its special pain. "A human death is something different."

"What about you, Jay? You ever think about freezing down?"

"I'm happy, healthy. No, Frank. It's not for me."

"You're not gonna live forever."

"Well, when that time comes, I think I'll just accept it, flow with it. Besides, I'll still be around somewhere: in your memory, in the earth, and eventually who knows... maybe my atoms will return to starstuff. Maybe I'll get started all over again. There just might be a cyclic cosmology, you know."

"Oh yeah, sure," said Frank. There was no use talking to Jay about such things. All Frank wanted was a little support for what he was about to do, and he had inadvertently launched Jay into one of his philosophical musings.

So they just sat and swung some more, enjoying the quiet lassitude of late summer and *cannabis sativa*. After a while, they took a walk through some of Jay's timberland, pausing to examine a curious species of flower or some moss, but mostly just kicking through dead-leaf paths and talking about wind-borne subjects of little real importance.

After lunch, Maury called, and Frank cursed the efficiency of his lawyer for intruding upon his peace. Maury had him scheduled for "processing" late that afternoon, and he told him that Mr. Bluthkalt would be expecting him. Maury gave him directions to the cryogenic parlor and hung up.

Having told Jay about the sudden new plans and his appointment, Frank walked down to the car. Jay was by his side.

"It *is* almost like dying, though," he said as he struggled through the gull-wing opening.

"At least we have a chance to say good-bye," said Jay, shaking his hand. "And listen, Frank, I hope you find it, what you're looking for, up there in the future."

Frank closed the door and fired the ignition. Jay waved to him as he backed down the driveway, waiting until he was almost out of sight before walking back to the house.

The Mercedes whined responsively as Frank depressed the accelerator. It was hard to imagine that he was not going to see Jay any more. Automatically, he punched for a map on the dashboard grid, checking the location of the cryogenic center—it was across the Pennsylvania line in the foothills of the mountains. When he reached the electric highway, he keyed in the coordinates, switched to autodrive, and reclined the seat to get some sleep.

The buzzer awakened him and he sat up to see the Mercedes slipping down an exit ramp. Smoothly he regained control, snaking the car down open, rolling country roads that headed toward grey-blue rounded peaks in the distance. Several miles and turns later he saw signs giving notice to FROZEN ASSETS CRYOGENIC REMISSION CENTER. When he reached the entrance, there was a long driveway leading to a monstrous black steel-and-concrete building that squatted on the landscape like a great ugly bug. It was an enormous pillbox that would probably survive a nuclear strike. It might have to, someday, thought Frank as he slipped into the almost empty parking lot. A few spaces down he saw Maury's gilt-edged sports car huddling restively on the asphalt—a fitting machine to match Maury's gaudy and mildly offensive personality.

Once inside, the receptionist guided Frank down a corridor lined with plastic models of cryogenic capsules, till he reached a door at the end of the hall. Passing through it, Frank saw a skinny jaundiced little man wearing over-sized glasses and a rumpled black suit that looked like it still had the hanger in the shoulders. Maury was seated by the skinny man's desk, and he brightened as he saw Frank.

"Frank! Good to see you. This is Herman Bluthkalt, founder and president of Frozen Assets."

"Pleased to meet you, Mr. Vecchio," said Bluthkalt, his voice creaking like a rusty hinge. He extended a hand that looked like an anemic spider with some of its legs missing. Frank grasped and shook the hand, fearing that it might crumble like pie crust in his grip.

"Thanks to some quick preparations by Mr. Howe, I think I will be able to accommodate you this afternoon," said Bluthkalt, who cast a knowing glance at Maury. Frank looked over at Maury, who flashed him a quick O.K. sign with his right hand, winking, and making the whole thing seem like one of his Grade-A swindles. Frank just grimaced.

"Now, I suppose you would like to know something about our operation here..." said Bluthkalt, steepling his long fingers on the edge of the desk.

"Not really, I just want to get it—"

"Frozen Assets is one of the oldest cryogenic centers of its kind," said Bluthkalt, ignoring Frank's words. "Its staff of technicians and specialists are second to none throughout the world, and we pride ourselves in keeping abreast of the state-of-the-art in both cybernetic and cryogenic technology. The capsules are made of the finest 10-point steel and molybdenum alloys and are cast right here in the good old United States of America. No foreign ingredients here at Frozen Assets, Mr. Vecchio."

"Hey look, I really don't give flyin'—"

"In addition, you will, as one of our preferred customers, be able to choose between several of our most spacious, luxurious capsule models. Starting with the SQ-887HG with a subliminal quadruplex sound system ... all the way up to the top-of-the-line CGA-1001 which features a hand-painted mural of one of your favorite scenes on the interior roof of the capsule. Now, if you'll just spend a few moments paging through this brochure..."

"Hey, wait a minute!" cried Frank, slamming his fist on the desk and looking at his attorney. "Maury, do something, will you?"

"I don't think Mr. Vecchio is interested in the ... ah, particulars, Herman. Let's get on with it."

"I see," said Bluthkalt gravely, as he folded up the four-color brochure. "Very well then, just sign these papers and our staff will take care of the rest."

Bluthkalt passed a stack of papers across the desk which looked like a novel manuscript and Maury chimed in with: "This is all the legal stuff that will take care of your holdings and your estate until you wake up." Then he ran through the pages, showing Frank where to sign on each line.

Frank did this, many times, until finished. Then passing them back, said: "All right, Maury, let's get this over with."

Bluthkalt stood up and led them to a door where a cadre of white-clad young men with waxen expressions were waiting for him. They guided Frank into an elevator, which took him down three levels into the depths of the building. There he was stripped naked and ran through a series of rooms where they removed all the hair from his body, cleaned his fingernails, flushed his gastrointestinal tract, de-plaqued his teeth, gave pleasant relief to his sinuses, shrunk his hemorrhoids, and relaxed his muscles to the point where he felt like an *al dente* piece of fetuccini. After that, they wrapped his body in fine linen, then in what looked like aluminum foil, and placed the whole package on a waiting hospital wagon-bed. As he was wheeled down another bright white corridor, he consoled himself with the knowledge that at least he would be safe from the rampaging orders for cannoli, the ubiquitous investment schemes of Maury, and phone calls from people like Callabrese. Perhaps he was doing the right thing after all.

He was vaguely aware of hands lifting him from the cart and into an object that looked like an overgrown Contac capsule. Someone said "Sweet dreams," and things started to get hazy. They must have given him some kind of drug amid all those preparations. Things grew darker and darker; there was nothing but silence and ...

... a thrumming sound filled his ears, which he soon realized was his own blood coursing past the auricular canal. He fluttered his eyelids open but perceived only darkness. He wiggled his toes. But he was trapped within the black-as-night capsule. *Poe. Premature burial and all that.* His heart leaped in his chest and he thought he might suffocate from fear, just as he heard the sound of groaning metal and felt bright light suddenly wash over him. Frank squinted as his eyes adjusted to the illumination; an image of someone leaning over him slowly came into focus.

"Goddamn!" cried Frank as he saw the creature looking down at him. It looked like a man, but where its left eye should have been, there was something like a TV camera hung up in some tiny girders and struts around the socket. Its left shoulder and arm were a mass of steel rods and wires ending in a claw-like appendage.

"Hey, here's one!" the thing said in a normal human voice.

Frank heard a clatter of other footsteps and soon there were three other faces staring down at him, smiling and nodding with approval. Each one sported a variety of spare parts: artificial larynx, another camera-eye, a mechanical mandible, claw hands.

Someone extended Frank a hand, a real one, thankfully, and helped him up and out of the capsule. The room around them was mostly concealed under mounds of dirt which had been recently overturned during excavations.

"Welcome, sir," said the one with the weird eye and hand.

"Who're you guys?" Frank looked at them suspiciously.

"I am Dr. Jonz," said the man. "And these are my assistants. You must be Frank Vecchio."

"Yeah, how'd you know that?"

"It says so on this plaque right here on the side of your capsule, but it doesn't mention your disease or cause of interment."

"Oh, there wasn't any. I just did it because I wanted to see if things were any better in the future. Are they?"

"Well, we like it, don't we boys?"

There was a chorus of yeses behind the man.

"What's that supposed to mean? Wouldn't *I* like it?" Frank stepped back from them and nervously picked at his aluminum foil.

"Well, there's a bit of a problem as to what we should do with you. If there's anything wrong with you, we can probably fix you up. But after that . . ."

"Yeah, and after that, what?"

"Well, it's quite involved, but to put it as simply as possible, you will not be allowed to live here—in this time era. Over-population and that sort of thing, you know? We have very strict regulations to control the number of people in the world. You must realize that there is a limited number of jobs, foodstores, accommodations, etc. I'm sure you understand."

"Oh sure," said Frank. "Say, what year is this,

anyhow?"

"By your dating system, it's around 2580, I'd figure."

Frank rubbed his chin. "No kidding? You mean I've been in here sleeping all that time?"

The man nodded.

"Well what about other people? What have you done with the other guys you've found like me?"

"Nothing. You're the only one we ever found that was still alive."

"What?"

"That's right. Most of these systems just didn't account for all the geologic, climatic, and sociological changes that would take place over the centuries. Your capsule seems to have survived through a series of freak, but very beneficial, events. You are a lucky man, Mr. Vecchio."

"Oh, I'm sure I am," said Frank more than a little bit facetiously. "But, say... uh, what are you gonna do with me?"

Jonz shrugged. "Well, there have been contingencies proposed for occasions such as this by the Archeological Institute. The most popular idea has been to send any cryogenic survivors back to their original time span. So that they could live out their lives in their proper timestream."

"Back in time!" Frank boggled at the very thought. "You mean to tell me that you guys can travel in time?"

"Oh certainly, but we don't do it much. It's a bit dangerous, you know."

"Dangerous! What're you talking about, dangerous?"

"Well, it's like this Mr. Vecchio.... There's kind of a cosmic ecological balance at work all the time. Everything, in other words, has its own special temporal niche in the overall...uh, scheme of things, you know?"

"I'll take your word for it."

"Very well. At any rate, your niche is back in the late Twentieth Century—1992, if this plaque is correct."

Frank could only nod his head dumbly. Baking cannoli crusts was never this bad.

"Well then, we'll just get you out of that foil, get you checked out for any defects, and get you shipped back to the...how do you say it?...good ole U. S. of R.?"

"It's an 'A'," said Frank.

But Jonz did not hear him. The archeologist had begun signaling to his associates to help Frank along.

The next few days were spent traveling through darkened corridors buried beneath massive buildings of this far future, which Frank was not allowed to know anything about. His discoverers had said something about his knowledge of the future causing some sort of temporal pollution, which could have adverse affects on the future. Frank did not really understand all that, but he had no choice but to believe them.

They checked him out on a series of machines, found a few things out of order, then hooked him up to give him a three-second jolt on what looked like a pin-baller's wet dream. They even replaced some of his worn out visceral parts with prosthetic devices that seemed to be the rage in their culture. They wanted to give him new telescopic eyes, and he begged off, but he did let them rejuvenate some of his tissue so that he regained some of the appearance of younger days. Of course, that pleased him.

Then, just before they took him to the time machine, Dr. Jonz gave him a short lecture. "About this dangerous business, let me tell you what I meant," said Jonz. "Traveling in the timestream is not physically dangerous."

"What do you mean, physically?" Frank said, as he sat on what looked like a bicycle frame with blinking colored lights. He felt foolish and awkward, bent over like a Olympic racer.

"Well, it's like this: the time-space continuum is like a giant piece of fabric," said Jonz, nervously stroking some of the exposed wires of his mechanical arm. "And each individual, and his perceptions, are like threads running through the fabric. When one of those threads—or individuals, if you will—goes back or forward in time, subtle differences are wrought within the overall fabric."

"Oh yeah? How subtle?"

"Quite subtle, I assure you. For instance, when you re-enter your own time period, you may notice some slight difference in your own life, in the things around you, in the things that involve your own life-thread. But don't worry. There can be no drastic changes. You could not go back and find that you had killed say . . . ah, what's-his-name? That maniac political character—Adolph Shirer? . . ."

"Shirer? You mean Hitler!"

Jonz clicked his tongue. "Well, whatever his name is. You couldn't have killed him anyway. No, no. The fabric of time-space is much too vast for one individual to wreak such changes upon it. Any great tears in the fabric are eventually self-repairing, you see. But what your own time traveling along your own thread-line does is put a few little wrinkles in the fabric. Do you understand?"

"I guess so. Does it really matter?"

Jonz shrugged. "No, I suppose it doesn't. We're going to send you back anyway."

"That's what I figured. All right, so send me back already."

"I fully intend to, Mr. Vecchio. Hang on tight, enjoy the past... I mean your present, and good luck."

"Yeah, right. And thanks for—"

Frank stopped, since Jonz had already pushed a button, causing everything to dissolve into haziness. Frank sat frozen in timelessness as the centuries were rolled back like an old carpet.

Suddenly the bicycle-like machine was gone and he was standing in the parking lot outside Frozen Assets. He was wearing a brown pin-stripe suit that he didn't recognize, and when he looked around for his car, he could not see any Mercedes. There were only three cars in the lot: a boxy clunker from the Seventies that almost assuredly had to be Bluthkalt's, a sleek-looking teardrop, and a fairly new Chevrolet that looked like... well, a Chevrolet. Frank walked over to the Chevrolet and placed his palm against the lock. To his surprise, the I.D. plate registered positive and the car door opened. It was Frank's car—and this was one of those little wrinkles Jonz had spoken about.

As he sunk into the less-than-luxurious front seat, he wondered what to do first. It suddenly occured to him that he had returned to basically the same set of problems he thought he was escaping from. He turned on the radio and soon discovered that it was Tuesday—the same day he left originally.

Frank sighed, thinking about Callabrese's "boys"

who would be paying him a visit. He shrugged his shoulders, fired the ignition, and drove back toward Baltimore.

After parking underneath the U.S.F. & G. Building, Frank took the elevator up to the floor where his suite of offices were located. And he discovered another little wrinkle.

The suite of offices was gone.

The name on the door of what had been his private quarters read: DINDLESTIFF'S SURGICAL SUPPLIES. He thought of asking the secretary inside what had happened, but that was useless. So down the elevator he went to check the plaque in the lobby. Maybe he had been moved to a different location.

But VECCHIO'S wasn't listed anywhere.

Maybe a different location altogether?

Walking into the street, he found a phone cube, slid through and checked the directory. The only listings for VECCHIO'S were two bakeries—one on Charles Street, the other on Reed.

Now that was quite a wrinkle, thought Frank. One sweep of time and my franchising operation is out the window. Suddenly an idea occurred to him. He dialed the secret number for Callabrese.

"Yeah?" said a voice at the other end.

"Mr. Callabrese, please."

"He ain't heah. Who's calling?"

"This is Mr. Vecchio calling. Can you leave a message?"

"Mr. who?"

"Vecchio?" asked Frank tentatively.

"Never heard of you," said the voice. Then: "Say, who is this, anyway?"

Frank smiled. "Oh, just nobody, I guess. Sorry, I must have called the wrong number. Bye now." He hung up before the voice could reply.

Not being connected with those creeps certainly was an added treat in this newly-wrinkled timestream. He decided, however, that before doing anything else, he must make a thorough check of his "new" life.

Hours later, Frank had filled in most of the missing gaps and the situation looked like this: In addition to the changes in his corporate image, the penthouse apartment had been replaced by a modest split-level in Towson; his association with Maury was far less involved; and his bank account was five figures instead of seven.

When he thought about it, that was not all bad. After he had stopped at his main bakery on Charles Street (where the nicely-made Ms. Walker now worked behind the cash register) and sampled a few of his *sfogliatelle* (which still tasted the same), he decided to ride out to Jay's farm for a surprise visit.

"Frank, how're you doing? What brings—?"

He looked at Jay and smiled sheepishly, waving a hand to cut him off. "Look, sit down, I have to explain a few things," said Frank.

So he told his friend the whole story.

Afterward, Jay shook his head and whistled appreciatively. "It's incredible, that's all I can say. What about that lawyer? Told him yet?"

"Naw! Let him sit awhile. I never liked him much anyway. He'll know soon enough."

Gradually, however, their conversation drifted away from the momentous news, and Jay brought out the old pipe of homegrown. Marijuana had been legal for a good ten years now, but Jay still preferred his own organically grown stuff to all the commercial brands. So they lit up and had a quiet smoke on the porch swing.

Yessir, thought Frank. Maybe things would be a little different now. Fewer worries, less pressure, more fun out of life.

But as the weeks rolled by, Frank realized that would not be the case.

He was being invited to lots of barbecues in his split-level neighborhood; he got talked into buying aluminum siding and a set of encyclopedias from a door-to-door salesperson; his neighbor's wife took to dressing up like Carmen Miranda and parading back and forth across her bedroom window dropping pieces of fruit seductively while Frank was out mowing the lawn, which was why it was starting to resemble the Serengeti Plain. But the most awful part was when he told Maury about his franchising operation in his previous timestream. Maury, flashy mover that he was, started making plans and drawing up papers for a big deal. Frank, of course, wanted no part of it, and, of course, there was the chance of attracting the Mob again. All those old headaches back again. No, he couldn't do it. In fact, he was worrying about the little things more and more: making sure the flour shipments were on time, making up payrolls, figuring taxes, feeling guilty about not wearing a suit to work when he left in the morning with all his well-suited neighbors—all of it was getting him down.

Then Frank had an idea.

The drive out to Frozen Assets passed quickly. He parked in the lot beside the grim-looking building, and entered through the front doors. The receptionist made him wait almost two hours to see Bluthkalt because he had no appointment. Finally, though, Bluthkalt came into the room.

Fifteen minutes passed as Frank patiently told the whole story to wan-faced Bluthkalt, who all the while drummed stick-like fingers on his desk-top. At the end of the tale, Frank came to the point: "Now here's what I want you to do. I want you to freeze me again."

"What?" Bluthkalt's complexion turned a lighter shade of pale.

"You heard me. I want to go on ice again. And I want you to put me in the same place that the original was downstairs."

"But what about the first you? The body that's in the capsule now?"

"Oh yeah, there *is* another me, isn't there?"

"I would think so," said Bluthkalt, regaining some of his composure, his face now brimming with his usual other-than-vibrant marble complexion.

"Well, just put it somewhere else. But it's imperative that I be placed in the original spot."

Bluthkalt sighed. "Very well, Mr. Vecchio. If this is sincerely what you want, I will, of course, accommodate you. There will be, of course, a substantial fee necessary and—"

"Of course," said Frank, pulling out his checkbook.

Later that week, after they had once more prepped his body, Frank was wheeled down the corridor again to the vault-like room. Somewhere in there was another Frank Vecchio. *Crazy,* he thought. It was the last thing he remembered before the swirling darkness came...

Awakening came gradually but he was aware of it and waited patiently. The lid of the capsule had been opened and he heard movement.

"Hey! Here's one!" the voice said.

The camera-eye of Dr. Jonz, the scurrying of the others, the crumbled surroundings, everything was the same. It was perfect; it had worked.

"What're you doing here? Vecchio, right?" said Jonz.

Frank smiled. "The one and only . . . " He paused, realizing that maybe that wasn't quite right anymore. Well, it did not matter, anyway.

"I don't get it," said Jonz. "Why did you do it?"

"It's hard to explain, but I want to wrinkle up my timestream a little more. I liked most of the subtle—even though they weren't so subtle—changes, but there's still a few things I'd like to change."

Jonz smiled and gestured to his colleagues, who laughed when he explained Frank's story. After they had peeled off his aluminum foil, he was taken through the underground corridors to the Institute where preparations were made for the return trip to 1992.

As Frank mounted the machine, Jonz smiled and said: "Good luck, Vecchio. I certainly hope everything works out."

"Thanks," said Frank. "That makes two of us. Or is it three? Four, maybe?"

But by that time, Jonz had disappeared, replaced by the swirling ectoplasm of time itself. Frank blinked his eyes and he was once again standing in front of Frozen Assets. This time he was wearing an old corduroy jacket and a pair of faded blue jeans. The Chevrolet wasn't there either. Just steady old Bluthkalt's old Matador and a 350 Yamaha-Ford. Frank walked over to the bike just as he felt something jingling in his right pants pocket. Reaching in, he felt a set of keys.

They fit the bike just as he knew they would, and soon he was wheeling windily down the country roads toward Baltimore...

...where he discovered: (1) no VECCHIO'S bakeries on Charles Street, Reed Street, or any street, (2) no split-level in Towson, and best of all, (3) no—wait, let me tell you:

After Frank had found Wrinkle No. 2, he went to his new address in Highlandtown, and he decided to call Maury to tell him what had happened.

"Dewey, Cheetum, and Howe," said the receptionist.

"Let me speak to Mr. Howe, please."

"May I tell him who's calling, please?"

"Yeah, c'mon, Clarisse, it's me—Frank Vecchio."

But Clarisse did not acknowledge, only saying: "Hold on, please..."

Seconds passed, then she returned to the connection. "Ah, I'm sorry, Mr. Velcachio—"

"That's Vecchio," corrected Frank.

"Yes, of course, I'm sorry. At any rate, Mr. Howe is busy with a client at the moment. Would you like to schedule an appointment? I have an opening three months from now on the 12th at 3:30."

"What're you kidding me? This is Frank Vecchio! Now you tell him I gotta talk to him *now*. Like immediately."

"I'm sorry, Mr. Velcro...but Mr. Howe claims that he has never made your acquaintance. He is a very busy man, and I'm rather pressed myself. Now would you like to make that appointment or not?"

"Ah, no, I think I've changed my mind. Thank you very much," said Frank, smiling as he hung up the phone. Now there's a wrinkle, he thought. What a relief to have Maury off his back! There was something to be said for this time-traveling business.

So after doing some checking, Frank found that it was *still* Tuesday, that his bank account had dropped to four figures, and that he was now employed as a rehabilitation therapist at a maximum security mental institution for the criminally insane. He rode the Yamaha-Ford down into Eastern Baltimore to his 3-room apartment which he found decorated spartanly, but was crammed with books and magazines. It reminded him of the apartment he had back when he had first graduated from college and hadn't found a job yet. It was kind of comfortable.

He fixed himself a simple meal from the refrigerator—some leftover stew and some fried eggs—before calling Jay to report on the latest developments.

"You mean you were actually a successful businessman, before?" asked Jay, laughing. "*You*, Frank?"

"That's right. Wild, isn't it?"

"Well, what's going on? Are we in a different timetrack? I don't get it."

"Well, I'm not really sure. It could be an alternate universe that I start each time I return from the future, but there's no way of telling. Anyway, here I am, and things are looking better already."

"If you say so," said Jay.

"Well, time will tell, right?" asked Frank.

And it did.

The job at the mental institution was abysmal. Frank's assignment there was to supervise, as he had for the last 26 years, the patients' library, which was located in a converted storage closet just off a corridor leading to the gymnasium. In addition, there was a door by his desk which led to the patients' lavatory, and which must always be kept locked. So Frank's days were filled with the never-ending tasks of locking and unlocking the lavatory door, lighting patients' cigarettes, and checking out books—the most recent of which was *The Jungle Adventures of Captain Farquhar* written by that literary immortal, Marvin Ainsworth, back in 1932.

It was not, as they say, a good gig.

And this was compounded on the home front by a romantic "relationship" Frank found himself tied up in. It concerned a woman named Frieda Pound, who bore a strong resemblance to *Pithecanthropus*. Frieda had been "waiting for him" for almost 16 years, and her idea of a good time was sitting around her apartment eating chocolates and listening to old Neil Sedaka records.

Quite simply, this was no way his kind of life, thought Frank, and he drove his little bike back out the country roads to Frozen Assets.

Bluthkalt was very snotty and negative, but he finally acceded to having Frank frozen. The cost was exhorbitant, reducing his bank account to a mere two figures—$41 to be exact—but anything would have been worth it just to get away from Frieda and her "charms." He made the now familiar trip down the white corridor and waited while they wrapped him up for encapsulation. Drowsiness washed over him as he settled in for his appointment with Dr. Jonz.

"You again!" cried Jonz. "This is getting kind of ridiculous, isn't it?"

"If you say so," said Frank, grinning self-consciously behind the peeled-back edges of aluminum foil.

"This is the third time today, Mr. Vecchio. It's getting to be a drag."

"But you'll still send me back, won't you?"

"Do you think we'd want a jerk like you hanging around?"

Frank just laughed and let them pull him from the capsule.

Time passed and soon he was sitting on the time machine once again. Jonz was again at the switch, a haggard look on his mechanical features. "And please, Mr. Vecchio... don't do this again. My Director's going to have me demoted if I use the time facilities any more this week. It's kind of expensive, you know?"

"Gotcha," said Frank, giving the thumbs-up signal with his right hand.

"Okay then, no offense, Mr. Vecchio, but I hope I never see you again." Jonz pushed the buttons and the lights started blinking.

Frank yelled "Contact!" like they did in the old WWI movies and was enveloped by the grey nothingness of inter-time.

Even the Yamaha-Ford was gone this time. Frank's boots were cracked with age and the soles were falling off at the seams as he scarped across Frozen Asset's parking lot. The work-jacket and pants were in great need of a cleaning, and he had about a week's worth of beard on his face. This time there was no mistaking it—maybe several wrinkles too many had been added. Perhaps he had taken one trip too many, Frieda notwithstanding.

Walking into Frozen Assets, he heard the receptionist tell him: "We take all deliveries at the rear door."

"I'm not delivering anything," said Frank. "I just want to use the phone."

"There's a pay cube in the lobby," said the receptionist—an officious-looking man of perhaps middle-age.

Frank checked his pockets. "Yeah, I know that but I don't have any mon—er, ah, change."

The receptionist looked at him as if he had just crawled out from beneath a flat rock. "Well, this is most irregular. Mr. Bluthkalt would be annoyed if I let you—"

Frank grabbed the receptionist by his shirt front. "Look, I don't want a sermon, I just want to make a call. Yes or no?"

As the man blanched, Frank thought: Earlier in the day (damn, was it still only Tuesday?) I could have bought and sold Bluthkalt without batting an eye.

"Well, all right," said the receptionist pursing his lips. "If you insist. But, please, make it quick."

Frank took the receiver and punched in Jay's number.

"Hello?"

"Jay? It's Frank! Listen, you're not going to believe this, but I did it again."

"Frank, what are you talking about? Where are you anyhow? I've been waiting all day for you to bring back those finishing nails."

"Huh? Finishing nails?"

"Don't tell me you forgot them? Oh, the hell with it. It'll wait till tomorrow," said Jay. "You can just finish varnishing the porch swing."

"What are you talking about, Jay? Why should I be varnishing your porch swing?"

"C'mon Frank. You built the swing years ago,

when we first bought this place. You know that. You always varnish it, every year."

Frank smiled. "Oh...oh yeah," he said as the pieces fell into place. "Yeah, right, Jay. I'll be there as soon as I can. See you then."

Hanging up the receiver, Frank thanked the receptionist and walked out into the country air of the northern foothills. The walk down the driveway passed quickly as he turned over the salient points of his phone conversation. *My* porch swing, he thought. That certainly was reassuring.

And he hitch-hiked back to the old farm, back to his *home*, and the only happiness that he had ever known.

●

Alan Ryan hails from New York, and began writing when he was fourteen. Onward and upward: at sixteen he won a fifty-dollar prize in a literary contest, and had an essay published in the *New York Sunday News*; another twenty-five dollars and a Schaeffer pen in there somewhere. Next ... well, it was twenty years later, and he sold a sort of parody essay piece to *The New York Times Book Review*. They liked it. I like it—I've read it and it's absolutely delightful. Now he's reviewing books for them regularly. He has sold other pieces, but the first actual sale was the parody, and this is the second.

And it is utterly and completely different from any story you or I have ever read in all our lives. It is not (in my cosmos) as trivial as it might seem initially. Among a good many other things it has done is to make me, unsuspectedly and not altogether willingly, responsible for his damn dragon. I mean, Dragon. I mean, *our* damn Dragon.

—Theodore Sturgeon
Los Angeles, 1978

DRAGON STORY
by Alan Ryan

There's this dragon.

I was going to start this with "Once upon a time there was a dragon," but then you would have thought this was a made-up story. It is and it isn't.

Even as it stands, that beginning is not quite correct. You see, dragons, being creatures of the imagination, in this case mine, both exist and don't exist so to speak, being granted all powers of existence of any sort whatsoever solely by the exercise of the human imagination, in this case, as I said, mine, and therefore live only when somebody, me for example, or you, thinks about them, and don't when I don't or, rather, *she* does because this particular dragon I have in mind is a female dragon, and if that, for some terrible dark reason of your own strikes you as odd, it's just too bad and you'll have to learn to live with it because she's my dragon and I can make her anything I want her to be, in this case female because that's the way I like my relationships and, what's more you, by virtue of the fact that you have consented to read this, thereby, as the process is known, willingly suspending your disbelief, also contribute your powers of imagination to the life-giving process although, of course I, as the creator or principal imaginer, get to make up the rules, even changing them as we go along, in whatever way I see fit, just so long as the whole thing is consistent, not necessarily to some preconceived notion of yours or, for that matter of mine, but rather consistent with itself as a total imagined object which, to be brief, is why her name is Florence.

Florence.

Florence the dragon.

No, Florence the Dragon.

That's better.

Now, I'm calling her Florence for a special reason, because of something I know about her. It's a nice, soft, liquid sort of name and I think it suits her. You'll see why.

You don't know Florence yet, really, but I'm going to tell you about her. I'm going to share her with you. Because, of course, even though Florence is mine and mine alone, with every word I write she becomes yours too. Which, in a sense, is really why I'm telling you all this instead of just keeping it in my head, but that's another matter, not another matter entirely, but another matter nevertheless, and too complicated for us to go into in any great depth just at the moment.

So.

Florence is a very gentle dragon. Oh, a very gentle dragon indeed.

You can't imagine that? Sure you can. Just go

ahead and imagine it. Go on. Oh, sure, you're saying, that's easy enough for you to imagine, you're the Writer and all and, besides, she's your dragon isn't she, but I can't.

Yes you can.

Oh, I see. You're thinking of a fire-breathing dragon. That's the problem. How, you ask, can a fire-breathing dragon be so gentle?

Did I say "fire-breathing?" No. Not a word about it. Not even a suggestion. Remember that business earlier about preconceived notions? Right.

So, Florence is not a fire-breathing dragon. Just a dragon. A gentle dragon. Now, if I may, I'd like to remind you of just one thing, the business about who's in charge. I'm the Writer and I'm in charge. It's true, of course, oh, so true, that I need your help, can't manage this whole thing by myself, but we both have to realize that I'm in charge and we both have to respect that. Both of us.

Okay, then, here we go. The dragon is a she and she's very gentle. That's all we have so far.

No.

No, she's not smiling. Gentle, yes; smiling, no. You'll have to be very careful about distinctions like that. Florence is definitely not smiling. In fact, she ... Well, I'll tell you about that in just a minute. That's what all this is leading up to.

The only other thing we need right away is a picture of Florence, a picture in our minds. Here goes.

Big. No, I don't think quite that big, but big.

And green. You can have some freedom here. I prefer a bright green, maybe even emerald, but you can do her up any way you like just so long as there's green in it.

For the rest, let's say four legs, front ones longer

than back ones, sloping back, fairly long neck, smallish head. And a tail. I guess it has to be pretty thick and long, but it shouldn't look heavy or clumsy. Graceful, maybe, if you can manage it, would be right.

Yes, I know, rather like a dinosaur, but remember our agreement.

Now the next part is tricky.

Sad eyes.

I know, I know, but work on it for a minute and get it as close as you can.

Sad eyes, then. Now you see why we couldn't have that smile.

And there we are.

Our own dragon. Florence the Dragon. Sad-eyed, gentle, Florence the Dragon.

I know. Just a minute, you're saying, hold up there just a minute. Why is she sad? Why is Florence the Dragon sad?

Ah.

She's sad because that's the way I imagined her and I wanted to be sure that you would imagine her that way too and, most important, care about her too the same as I do. And if you're upset because she's sad, well, so am I. But that's the way I imagined her and sad she must therefore be.

At least for the moment.

Let's go back just a bit. I imagined this dragon. Florence. And I imagined her with these big sad eyes, dark and large and sort of wistful, longing almost. And they troubled me, kept me awake at night, until finally I figured out the why and the wherefore of it. Dragons in your mind are like that sometimes. They'll just keep at you until you have no choice but to get them down on paper, tell the Reader about them, get the Reader's help, and figure them out. Maybe not figure them out once and for all, but figure them out at least for the moment. As I said.

So, then, why is Florence the Dragon sad?

Florence the Dragon is sad because she's lonely.

That's okay. We can go with that. It's consistent, it fits, and it accounts for the sad eyes.

But why is she lonely?

That's the tough one.

Now, of course, you realize or, at the very least, assume, that I know why Florence is lonely. And I do. And I'm going to tell you about it.

Florence is lonely because she grew up and spent most of her life in the Middle Ages being quested after, hunted, chased, longed for, by splendidly daring knights in dazzlingly shining armor who devoted all or at least the better parts of their lives to the chase, but the Middle Ages are gone now, and good riddance to them, and so are the knights, which in some ways is really too bad, but that left our Florence high and dry with nobody to quest after her or even hardly think about her, and that's why she's lonely.

Okay?

That's why she's lonely!

Excuse me. I've been living with this for some while now.

That's why she's lonely. And sad.

But, you remember, I said before, twice in fact, that she's sad, at least for the moment. At least for the moment. That's the operative phrase now, the one we're going to work with.

At least for the moment.

Please follow me carefully now. Because some things are going on here that are, let's say, in a very delicate state of balance. But we've already accomplished a great deal. Oh, a very great deal. So let's just be careful with the rest of it. Just follow me.

Now I have a confession to make.

I concealed something from you. Deliberately but, I think, with good cause. Here it is.

When I first saw Florence, there was a tear in her eye.

I didn't tell you about the tear because I wanted you to know Florence before you saw it.

So there's a tear in her eye.

And now you see it too.

And that tear, trembling, shimmering, welling up, about to run out of the corner of her eye, is the tangible, the touchable, result of her problem, her sadness, her loneliness.

But Florence's problem, obviously, is not hers to face alone. Not any more. Not since we started thinking about her. You and me. Both of us.

She's our dragon.

And that tear is still hanging there, still shimmering, still trembling.

Reach out and touch it.

Go ahead.

Wipe it away with the tip of your finger. Gently. Right.

That's right, gently.

There.

You feel better.

I know I do.

And so does Florence. As you can tell.

Just look at her.

Because Florence is being quested after once again. By us. Just as she wanted and needed.

We'll never catch her, of course, we know that. Dragons won't let themselves be caught. But I've made my attempt to capture her. And you've made

hours. So the chase is on, and that's all that really matters.
For Florence.
For you.
For me.

●

impossible for an observer to place his finger upon the exact nature of the defect, yet it was plain that something was frighteningly wrong with many of the boys and girls born in the Miskatonic Valley.

Yet, as the years turned slowly, the pale, faded folk of Dunwich continued to raise their thin crops, to tend their dull-eyed and stringy cattle, and to wring their hard existence from the poor, farmed-out earth of their farms.

Events of interest were few and petty; the columns of the *Aylesbury Transcript*, the *Arkham Advertiser*, and even the imposing *Boston Globe* were scanned for items of diversion. Dunwich itself supported no regular newspaper, not even the slim weekly sheet that subsists in many such semi-rural communities.

It was therefore a source of much local gossip and a delight to the scandal-mongers when Earl Sawyer abandoned Mamie Bishop, his common-law wife of twenty years' standing, and took up instead with Zenia Whateley. Sawyer was an uncouth dirt farmer of some fifty years of age. His cheeks covered perpetually with a stubble that gave him the appearance of not having shaved for a week, his nose and eyes marked with the red lines of broken minor blood vessels, and his stoop-shouldered, shuffling gait marked him as a typical denizen of Dunwich's hilly environs.

Zenia Whateley was a thin, pallid creature, the daughter of old Zebulon Whateley and a wife so retiring in her lifetime and so thoroughly forgotten since her death that none could recall the details of her countenance or even her given name. The latter had been painted carelessly on the oblong wooden marker that indicated the place of her burial, but the cold rains and watery sunlight of the round of Dunwich's seasons had obliterated even this trace of the dead woman's individuality.

Zenia must have taken after her mother, for her own appearance was unprepossessing, her manner cringing, and her speech so infrequent and so diffident that few could recall ever having heard her voice.

The loafers and gossips at Osborn's General Store in Dunwich were hard put to understand Earl Sawyer's motives in abandoning Mamie Bishop for Zenia Whateley. Not that Mamie was noted for her great beauty or scintillating personality; on the contrary: she was known as a meddler and a snoop, and her sharp tongue had stung many a denizen hoping to see some misdemeanor pass unnoted. Still, Mamie had within her that spark of vitality so seldom found in the folk of the upper Miskatonic, that trait of personality known in the rural argot as gumption, so that it was puzzling to see her perched beside Earl on the front seat of his rattling Model T Ford, her few belongings tied in slovenly bundles behind her, as Sawyer drove her over the dust-blowing turnpike to Aylesbury where she took quarters in the town's sole, dilapidated rooming house.

The year was 1938 when Earl Sawyer and Mamie Bishop parted ways. It had been a decade since the death of the poor, malformed giant Wilbur Whateley and the dissolution—for this word, rather than *death*, best characterizes the end of that monster— of his even more gigantic and even more shockingly made twin brother. But now it was the end of May, and the spring thaw had come late and grudgingly to the hard-pressed farmlands of the Miskatonic Valley this year.

When Earl Sawyer returned, alone, to Dunwich

he stopped in the center of the town, such as it was, parking his Model T opposite Osborn's. He crossed the dirty thoroughfare and climbed onto the porch of old Zebulon Whateley's house, pounding once upon the grey, peeling door while the loafers at Osborn's stared and commented behind his back.

The door opened and Earl Sawyer disappeared inside for a minute. The loafers puzzled over what business Earl might have with Zebulon Whateley, and their curiosity was rewarded shortly when Sawyer reappeared leading Zenia Whateley by one flaccid hand. Zenia wore a thin cotton dress, and through its threadbare covering it was obvious even from the distance of Osborn's that she was with child.

Earl Sawyer drove home to his dusty farm, bringing Zenia with him, and proceeded to install her in place of Mamie Bishop. There was little noticeable change in the routine at Sawyer's farm with the change in its female occupant. Each morning Earl and Zenia would rise, Zenia would prepare and serve a meagre repast for them, and they would breakfast in grim silence. Earl would thereafter leave the house, carefully locking the door behind him with Zenia left inside to tend to the chores of housekeeping, and Earl would spend the entire day working out-of-doors.

The Sawyer farm contained just enough arable land to raise a meager crop of foodstuffs and to support a thin herd of the poor cattle common to the Miskatonic region. The bleak hillside known as the Devil's Hop Yard was also located on his holdings. Here had grown no tree, shrub or blade of grass for as far back as the oldest archives of Dunwich recorded, and despite Earl Sawyer's repeated attempts to raise a crop on its unpleasant slopes, the Hop Yard resisted and remained barren. Even so there persisted reports of vague, unpleasant rumblings and cracklings from beneath the Hop Yard, and occasionally shocking odors were carried from it to adjoining farms when the wind was right.

On the first Sunday of June, 1938, Earl Sawyer and Zenia Whateley were seen to leave the farmhouse and climb into Sawyer's Model T. They drove together into Dunwich village, and, leaving the Model T in front of old Zebulon Whateley's drab house, walked across the churchyard, pausing to read such grave markers as remained there standing and legible, then entered the Dunwich Congregational Church that had been founded by the Reverend Abijah Hoadley in 1747. The pulpit of the Dunwich Congregational Church had been vacant since the unexplained disappearance of the Reverend Isaiah Ashton in the summer of 1912, but a circuit-riding Congregational minister from the city of Arkham conducted services in Dunwich from time to time.

This was the first occasion of Earl Sawyer's attendance at services within memory, and there was a nodding of heads and a hissing of whispers up and down the pews as Earl and Zenia entered the frame building. Earl and Zenia took a pew to themselves at the rear of the congregation and when the order of service had reached its conclusion they remained behind to speak with the minister. No witness was present, of course, to overhear the conversation that took place, but later the minister volunteered his recollection of Sawyer's request and his own responses.

Sawyer, the minister reported, had asked him to perform a marriage. The couple to be united were himself (Sawyer) and Zenia Whateley. The minister had at first agreed, especially in view of Zenia's obvious condition, and the desirability of providing for a legitimate birth for her expected child. But Sawyer had refused to permit the minister to perform the usual marriage ceremony of the Congregational Church, insisting instead upon a ceremony involving certain foreign terms to be provided from some ancient documents handed down through the family of the bride.

Nor would Sawyer permit the minister to read the original documents, providing in their place crudely rendered transcripts written by a clumsy hand on tattered, filthy scraps of paper. Unfortunately the minister did not have even these scraps. They had been retained by Sawyer, and the minister could recall only vaguely a few words of the strange and almost unpronounceable incantations he had been requested to utter: *N'gai, n'gha'ghaa, bugg-shoggog,* he remembered. And a reference to a lost city "Between the Yr and the Nhhngr."

The minister had refused to perform the blasphemous ceremony requested by Sawyer, holding that it would be ecclesiastically improper and possibly even heretical of him to do so, but he renewed his offer to perform an orthodox Congregational marriage, and possibly to include certain additional materials provided by the couple *if he were shown a translation also,* so as to convince himself of the propriety of the ceremony.

Earl Sawyer refused vehemently, warning the minister that he stood in far greater peril should he ever learn the meaning of the words than if he remained in ignorance of them. At length Sawyer stalked angrily from the church, pulling the passive

Zenia Whateley behind him, and returned with her to his farm.

A few nights later the couple were visited by Zenia's father, old Zebulon Whateley, and also by Squire Sawyer Whateley, of the semi-undecayed Whateleys, a man who held the unusual distinction of claiming cousinship to both Earl Sawyer and Zenia Whateley. At midnight the four figures, Earl, Zenia, old Zebulon, and Squire Whateley, climbed slowly to the top of the Devil's Hop Yard. What acts they performed at the crest of the hill are not known with certainty, but Luther Brown, now a fully-grown man and engaged to be married to George Corey's daughter Olivia, stated later that he had been searching for a lost heifer near the boundary between Corey's farm and Sawyer's, and saw the four figures silhouetted against the night constellations as they stood atop the hill.

As Luther Brown watched, all four disrobed; he was fairly certain of the identification of the three men, and completely sure of that of Zenia because of her obvious pregnancy. Completely naked they set fire to an altar of wood apparently set up in advance on the peak of the Hop Yard. What rites they performed before Luther fled in terror and disgust he refused to divulge, but later that night loud cracking sounds were heard coming from the vicinity of the Sawyer farm, and an earthquake was reported to have shaken the entire Miskatonic Valley, registering on the seismographic instruments of Harvard College and causing swells in the harbor at Innsmouth.

The next day Squire Sawyer Whateley registered a wedding on the official rolls of Dunwich village. He claimed to be qualified to perform the civil ceremony by virtue of his standing as Chairman of the local Selective Service Board. This claim must surely be regarded as most dubious, but while the Whateleys were not highly regarded in Dunwich, their critics considered it the better part of valor to hold their criticism to private circumstances, and the marriage of Earl Sawyer and Zenia Whateley was thus officially recognized.

Mamie Bishop, in the meanwhile, had settled into her new home in Aylesbury and began spreading malign reports about her former lover Earl Sawyer and his new wife. Earl, she claimed, had been in league with the Whateleys all along. Her own displacement by Zenia had been only one step in the plot of Earl Sawyer and the Whateley clan to revive the evil activities that had culminated in the events of 1928. Earl and Zenia, with the collaboration of Squire Sawyer Whateley and old Zebulon Whateley, would bring about the ruination of the entire Miskatonic Valley, if left to their own devices, and perhaps might bring about a blight that would cover a far greater region.

No one paid any attention to Mamie, however. Even the other Bishops, a clan almost as numerous and widespread as the Whateleys, tended to discount Mamie's warnings as the spiteful outpourings of a woman scorned. And in any case, Mamie's dire words were pushed from the public consciousness in the month of August, 1938, when Earl Sawyer rang up Dr. Houghton on the party line telephone and summoned him to the Sawyer farm.

Zenia was in labor, and Earl, in a rare moment of concern, had decided that medical assistance was in order.

Zenia's labor was a long and difficult one. Dr. Houghton later commented that first childbirths tended to be more protracted than later deliveries, but Zenia remained in labor for 72 consecutive hours, and barely survived the delivery of the child. Throughout the period of her labor there were small earth temblors centering on the Devil's Hop Yard, and Zenia, by means of a series of frantic hand motions and incoherent mewling sounds, indicated that she wished the curtains drawn back from her window so that she could see the crown of the hill from her bed.

On the third night of her labor, while Zenia lay panting and spent near to death between futile contractions, a storm rose. Clouds swept up the valley from the Atlantic, great winds roared over the houses and through the trees of Dunwich, bolts of lightning flashed from thunderhead to hilltop.

Dr. Houghton, despairing of saving the life of either Zenia or her unborn child, began preparations for a caesarian section. With Earl Sawyer hovering in the background, mumbling semi-incoherent incantations of the sort that had caused the Congregational minister to refuse a church wedding to the couple, the doctor set to work.

With sharpened instruments sterilized over the woodstove that served for both cooking and heat for the Sawyer farmhouse, he made the incision in Zenia's abdomen. As he removed the fetus from her womb there was a terrific crash of thunder. A blinding bolt of lightning struck at the peak of the Devil's Hop Yard. From a small grove of twisted and deformed maple trees behind the Sawyer house, a flock of nesting whippoorwills took wing, setting up a cacophony of sound audible over even the loud rushings and pounding of the rainstorm.

All of Dr. Houghton's efforts failed to preserve the poor, limited life of Zenia Whateley Sawyer, but her child survived the ordeal of birth. The next day old Zebulon Whateley and Squire Sawyer Whateley made their way to the Sawyer house and joined Earl Sawyer in his efforts. He descended the wooden steps to the dank cellar of the house and returned carrying a plain wooden coffin that he had surreptitiously built himself some time before. The three of them placed Zenia's shrivelled, wasted body in the coffin and Earl nailed its lid in place.

They carried the wooden box to the peak of the Devil's Hop Yard and there, amid fearsome incantations and the making of signs with their hands unlike any seen for a decade in the Miskatonic Valley, they buried Zenia's remains.

Then they returned to the farmhouse where the child lay in a crude wooden cradle. Squire Whateley tended the infant while its father rang up Central on the party line and placed a call to Mamie Bishop at the rooming house in Aylesbury.

After a brief conversation with his former common-law wife, Earl Sawyer nodded to his father-in-law and to the Squire, and left them with the child. He climbed into his Model T and set out along the Aylesbury Pike to fetch Mamie back to Dunwich.

The child of Earl Sawyer and Zenia Whateley Sawyer was a girl. Her father, after consultation with his father-in-law and distant cousin Squire Whateley, named his daughter Hester Sawyer. She was a tiny child at birth, and fear was expressed as to her own survival.

Earl contacted the Congregational minister at Arkham, asking him to baptise the infant according to rites specified by Earl. Once more the dispute as to the use of Earl's strange scriptures—if they could be so defined—erupted, and once more the minister refused to lend his ecclesiastical legitimacy to the ceremony. Instead, Earl, Zebulon and Sawyer Whateley carried the tiny form, wrapped in swaddling cloths, to the peak of the Devil's Hop Yard, and on the very ground of her mother's still-fresh grave conducted a ceremony of consecration best left undescribed.

They then returned her to the Sawyer house and the care of Mamie Bishop.

There were comments in Dunwich and even in Aylesbury about Mamie's surprising willingness to return to Sawyer's menage in the role of nursemaid and guardian to the infant Hester, but Mamie merely said that she had her reasons and refused to discuss the matter further. Under Mamie's ministrations the infant Hester survived the crises of her first days of life, and developed into a child of surprising strength and precocity.

Even as an infant Hester was a child of unusual beauty and—if such a phrase may be used—premature maturity. Her coloring was fair, almost, but not quite, to the point of albinism. Where Hester's distant relative, the long-disappeared Lavinia Whateley, had had crinkly white hair and reddish-pink eyes, little Hester possessed from the day of her birth a glossy poll of the silvery blonde shade known as platinum. Mamie Bishop tried repeatedly to put up the child's hair in little curls or scallops as she thought appropriate for a little girl, but Hester's hair hung straight and gracefully to her shoulders, refusing to lie in any other fashion.

The child's eyes showed a flecked pattern of palest blue and the faint pink of the true albino, giving the appearance of being a pale lavender in tint except at a very close range, when the alternation of blue and pink became visible. Her skin was the shade of new cream and absolutely flawless.

She took her first steps at the age of five months; by this time she had her full complement of baby teeth as well. By the age of eight months, early in the spring of 1939, she began to speak. There was none of the babyish prattle of a normally developing child; Hester spoke with precision, correctness, and a chilling solemnity from the utterance of her first word.

Earl Sawyer did not keep Mamie Bishop imprisoned in his house as he had the dead Zenia Whateley Sawyer. Indeed, Sawyer made it his business to teach Mamie the operation of his Model T, and he encouraged her—nay, he all but commanded her—to drive it into Dunwich village, Dean's Corners, or Aylesbury frequently.

On these occasions Mamie was alleged to be shopping for such necessities for herself, Earl, or little Hester as the farm did not provide. On one occasion Earl directed Mamie to drive the Model T all the way to Arkham, and there to spend three days obtaining certain items which he said were needed for Hester's upbringing. Mamie spent two nights at one of the rundown hotels that still persisted in Arkham, shabby ornate reminders of that city's more prosperous days.

Mamie's sharp tongue had its opportunities during these shopping expeditions, and she was heard frequently to utter harsh comments about Earl, Zebulon, and Squire Whateley. She never made direct reference to the dead Zenia, but made cryptic and unsettling remarks about little Hester Sawyer, her charge, whom she referred to most often as "Zenia's white brat."

As has been mentioned, Dunwich village supported no regular newspaper of its own, but the publications of other communities in the Miskatonic Valley gave space to events in this locale. The *Aylesbury Transcript* in particular devoted a column in its weekly pages to news from Dunwich. This news was provided by Joe Osborn, the proprietor of Osborn's General Store, in return for a regular advertisement of his establishment's wares.

A review of the Dunwich column in the *Aylesbury Transcript* for the period between August of 1938 and the end of April of 1943 shows a series of reports of rumblings, crackings, and unpleasant odors emanating from the area of Sawyer's farm, and particularly from the Devil's Hop Yard. Two features of these reports are worthy of note.

First, the reports of the sounds and odors occur at irregular intervals, but a check of the sales records of the establishments in Dunwich, Aylesbury, Dean's Corners and Arkham where Mamie Bishop traded, will show that the occurrences at the Devil's Hop Yard coincide perfectly with the occasions of Mamie's absence from Sawyer's farm. Second, while the events took place at irregular intervals, ranging from as close together as twice in one week to as far apart as eight months, their severity increased with regularity. The earliest of the series are barely noted in the Dunwich column of the *Transcript*. By the end of 1941 the events receive lead position in Osborn's writings. By the beginning of 1943 they are no longer relegated to the Dunwich column at all, but are treated as regular news, suggesting that they could be detected in Aylesbury itself—a distance of nearly 15 miles from Dunwich!

It was also noted by the loafers at Osborn's store

that on those occasions when Mamie Bishop absented herself from the Sawyer farm, Earl's two favorite in-laws and cronies, Zebulon Whateley and Squire Sawyer Whateley, visited him. There were no further reports of odd goings-on at the Sawyer place such as that given by Luther Brown in 1938. Perhaps Luther's unfortunate demise in an accident on George Corey's silo roof, where he was placing new shingles, had no connection with his seeing the rites atop the Devil's Hop Yard, but after Luther's death and with the new series of rumblings and stenches, others began to shun the Sawyer place from 1939 onward.

In September of 1942 a sad incident transpired. Hester Sawyer, then aged four, had been educated up to that time primarily by her father, with the assistance of the two elder Whateleys and of Mamie Bishop. She had never been away from the Sawyer farm and had never seen another child.

Mamie Bishop's second cousin Elsie, the maiden sister of Silas Bishop (of the undecayed Bishops), caught Mamie's ear on one of Mamie's shopping expeditions away from the Sawyer place. Elsie was the mistress of a nursery school operated under the auspices of the Dunwich Congregational Church, and she somehow convinced Mamie that it was her duty to give little Hester exposure to other children of her own age. Mamie spoke disparagingly of "Zenia's white brat," but following Elsie's insistence Mamie agreed to discuss the matter with Earl Sawyer.

On the first day of the fall term, Mamie drove Earl's Model T into Dunwich village, little Hester perched on the seat beside her. This was the first look that Hester had at Dunwich—and the first that Dunwich had at Hester.

Although Mamie had bundled the child into loose garments that covered her from neck to ankles, it was obvious that something was abnormal about her. Hester was astonishingly small for a child of four. She was hardly taller than a normal infant. It was as if she had remained the same size in the four years since her birth, not increasing an inch in stature.

But that was only half the strangeness of Hester's appearance, for while her size was the same as a new-born infant's, her development was that of a fully mature and breathtakingly beautiful woman! The sun shone brilliantly on the long platinum hair that hung defiantly around the edges of the bonnet Mamie had forced onto Hester's head. Her strange lavender eyes seemed to hold the secrets of an experienced voluptuary. Her face was mature, her lips full and sensual. And when a sudden gust of wind pressed her baggy dress against her torso this showed the configuration of a Grecian eidolon.

The loafers at Osborn's, who had clustered about and craned their necks for a look at the mysterious "white brat" were torn between an impulse to turn away from this unnatural sight and a fascination with the image of what seemed a living manikin, a woman of voluptuous bodily form and astonishing facial beauty, the size of a day-old infant, sitting primly beside Mamie Bishop.

Elsie Bishop welcomed her cousin Mamie and her charge, Hester Sawyer, to the nursery school at the Congregational Church. Elsie chose to make no comment on Hester's unusual appearance, but instead introduced her to the children already present. These included her own nephew Nahum Bishop, Silas's five-year-old son. Nahum was a perfectly normal boy, outgoing and playful, one of the few such to appear in the blighted Miskatonic Valley.

He took one look at Hester Sawyer and fell madly in love with her, with the total, enraptured fascination that only a child can feel when first he discovers the magic of the female sex. He lost all interest in the other children in the school and in their games. He wished only to be with Hester, to gaze at her, to hold her miniature woman's hand in his own pudgy boy's fingers. Any word that Hester spoke was as music to his ears, and any favor she might ask, any task that she might set for him, was his bounden duty and his greatest joy to perform.

In a short while the various children of the nursery school were playing happily, some of them scampering up and down the aisle leading between the two banks of pews in the main body of the church. The two cousins, Mamie and Elsie, retired to the chancel kitchen to prepare a pot of tea for themselves. Although they could not see the school children from this position, they could hear them happily playing in the semi-abandoned church.

Suddenly there was a terrible thump from the roof of the church, then a second similar sound from the burying-ground outside, then a series of panic-stricken and terrified screams from the children. Mamie and Elsie ran from the chancel and found nothing, apparently, amiss in the church itself, but the children were clustered at an open window staring into the churchyard, pointing and exclaiming in distress.

The two women shoved their way through the panic-stricken children until they could see. What they beheld was the body of Elsie's nephew Nahum Bishop, grotesquely broken over an old tombstone upon which it had fallen when it bounced from the roof of the church. There was no question that the child was dead, the sightless eyes apparently gazing upward at the steeple of the church.

Before they could even turn away from the window, the two women were able to hear a light tread, one so light that, except for the total hush that had descended upon the church as the children's screams subsided, it would not have been heard at all, calmly descending the wooden staircase from the steeple. In a moment Hester Sawyer emerged from the stairwell, her manner one of complete self-possession, the expression on her beautiful little face one of mockery and amusement.

When the state police arrived Hester explained, with total self-assurance, that she and Nahum had climbed the steeple together, up the narrow wooden staircase that ran from the church's floor to its belfry. Nahum had averred that he would do anything to prove his love for Hester, and she had asked him to fly from the steeple. In attempting to do so he had fallen to the roof, bounced once, then crashed onto the old grave marker in the yard.

The police report listed Nahum's death as accidental, and Hester was returned to the Sawyer farm in charge of Mamie Bishop. Needless to say, the child did not return to the nursery school at the Dunwich Congregational Church; in fact, she was not seen again in Dunwich, or anywhere else away from her father's holdings.

The final chapter in the tragedy of the Devil's Hop Yard, if indeed tragedy is the proper designation for such a drama, was played out in the spring of 1943. As in so many years past, the warmth of the equinox had given but little of itself to the upper Miskatonic Valley; winter instead still clung to the barren peaks and the infertile bottomlands of the region, and the icy dark waters of the Miskatonic River passed only few meadows on their way southeasterward to Arkham and Innsmouth and the cold Atlantic beyond.

In Dunwich the bereaved Silas Bishop and his maiden sister Elsie had recovered as best they could from the death of young Nahum. Elsie's work with the nursery school continued and only the boarding-up of the stairwell that led to the steeple and belfry of the Congregational Church testified to the accident of the previous September.

Early on the evening of April 30 the telephone rang in the Bishop house in Dunwich village, and Elsie lifted the receiver to hear a furtive whisper on the line. The voice she barely recognized, so distorted it was with terror, belonged to her second cousin Mamie.

"They've locked me in the house naow," Mamie whispered into the telephone. "Earl always sent me away before, but this time they've locked me in and I'm afeared. Help me, Elsie! I daon't knaow what they're a-fixin' ta do up ta the Hop Yard, but I'm afeared!"

Elsie signaled her brother Silas to listen to the conversation. "Who's locked you in, Mamie?" Elsie asked her cousin.

"Earl and Zeb and Sawyer Whateley done it! They've took Zenia's brat and they've clumb the Hop Yard. I kin see 'em from here! They're all stark naked and they've built 'em a bonfire and an altar and they're throwin' powder into the fire and old Zeb he's areadin' things outen some terrible book that they always keep alocked up!

"And now I kin see little Hester, the little white brat o' Zenia's, and she's clumb onto the altar and she's sayin' things to Zeb an' Earl and Squire Whateley an' they've got down on their knees like they's aworshippin' Hester, and she's makin' signs with her hands. Oh, Elsie, I can't describe them signs, they's so awful, they's so awful what she's adoin', Elsie! Get some help out here, oh please get some help!"

Elsie told Mamie to try and be calm, and not to watch what was happening atop the Devil's Hop Yard. Then she hung up the telephone and turned to her brother Silas. "We'll get the state police from Aylesbury," she said. "They'll stop whatever is happening at Sawyer's. We'd best telephone them now, Silas!"

"D'ye think they'll believe ye, Elsie?"

Elsie shook her head in a negative manner.

"Then we'd best git to Aylesbury ourselves," Silas resumed. "If we go there ourselves they'd more like to believe us than if we jest telephoned."

They hitched up their horse and drove by wagon from Dunwich to Aylesbury. Fortunately the state police officer who had investigated the death of young Nahum Bishop was present, and knowing both Elsie and Silas to be citizens of a responsible nature the officer did not laugh at their report of Mamie's frightened telephone call. The officer started an automobile belonging to the state police, and with the two Bishops as passengers set out back along the Aylesbury Pike to Dunwich, and thence to the Sawyer farm beyond the village center.

As the official vehicle neared Sawyer's place, its three occupants were assailed by a most terrible and utterly indescribable stench that turned their stomachs and caused their eyes to run copiously, and that also, inexplicably, filled each of them with a hugely frightening rush of emotions dominated by an amalgam of fear and revulsion. Sounds of thunder filled the air, and the earth trembled repeatedly, threatening to throw the car off the road.

The state police officer swung the automobile from the dirt road fronting the Sawyer farm onto a narrow and rutted track that ran by the decrepit house and led to the foot of the Devil's Hop Yard. The officer pulled the car to a halt and leaped from its seat, charging up the hill with his service revolver drawn, followed by Silas and Elsie Bishop who made the best speed they could despite their years.

Before them they could see the altar and the four figures that Mamie Bishop had described to her cousin Elsie. The night sky was cloudless and a new moon offered no competition to the million brilliantly twinkling stars. Little Hester Sawyer, her body that of a fully formed woman yet not two feet in height, danced and postured on the wooden altar, the starlight and that of the nearby bonfire dancing lasciviously on her gleaming platinum hair and smooth, cream-colored skin. Her lavender eyes caught the firelight and reflected it like the eyes of a wild beast in the woods at night.

Earl and Zebulon and Sawyer Whateley stood in an equilateral triangle about the altar, and around them there had apparently sprung from the earth itself a perfect circle of slimy, tentacled growths, more animal than vegetable, the only things that had ever been known to grow from the soil of the Devil's Hop Yard. Even as the newcomers watched, too awe-stricken and too revolted to act, the horrid tentacled growths began to lengthen, and to sway in time to the awful chanting of the three naked men and the lascivious posturings of the tiny, four-year-old Hester.

There was the sound of a shrill, reedy piping from somewhere in the air, and strange winds rushed back and forth over the scene.

The voice of Hester Sawyer could be heard chanting, *"Ygnaiih ... ygnaiih ... thflthkh'ngha ... Yog-Sothoth ... Y'bthnk ... h'ehye-n'grkdl'lh!"*

There was a single, blinding bolt of lightning—an astonishing occurrence as the night sky was entirely clear of any clouds—and the form of Hester Sawyer was bathed in a greenish-yellow glow of almost supernatural electrical display, sparks dancing over her perfect skin, and balls of St. Elmo's fire tumbling from her lips and hands and rolling across the altar, tumbling to the ground and bounding down the slopes of the Devil's Hop Yard.

The eyes of the watchers were so dazzled by the display that they were never certain, afterwards, of what they had seen. But it appeared, at least, that the bolt of lightning had not descended from the sky to strike Hester, but had originated from her and struck upward, zigzagging into the wind-swept blackness over Dunwich, reaching upward and upward as if it were eventually going to reach the stars themselves.

And before the bolt of lightning had disappeared from before the dazzled eyes of the watchers, the body of Hester Sawyer seemed to rise along its course, posturing and making those terrible shocking signs even as it rose, growing ever smaller as it disappeared above the Hop Yard until the lightning bolt winked out and all sight of Hester Sawyer was lost forever.

With the end of the electrical display the shocked paralysis that had overcome the watchers subsided, and the police officer advanced to stand near the ring of tentacled growths and the three naked men. He ordered them to follow him back to the police vehicle, but instead they launched themselves in snarling, animalistic attacks upon him. The officer stepped back but the three men flew at him growling, clawing, biting at his legs and torso. The police officer's revolver crashed once, again, then a third time, and the three naked men lay thrashing and gesturing on the ground.

They were taken to the general hospital at Arkham, where a medical team headed by Drs. Houghton and Hartwell labored unsuccessfully through the night to save them. By the morning of May 1, all three had expired without uttering a single word.

Meanwhile, back at the Devil's Hop Yard, Silas and Elsie Bishop guided other investigators to the altar that Hester Sawyer had last stood upon. The book that had lain open beside her had been destroyed beyond identification by the lightning bolt of the night of April 30. Agricultural experts summoned from Miskatonic University at Arkham attempted to identify the tentacled growths that had sprung from the ground around the altar. The growths had died within a few hours of their appearance, and only desiccated husks remained. The experts were unable to identify them fully, indicating their complete puzzlement at their apparent resemblance to the tentacles of the giant marine squid of the Pacific Trench near the island of Ponape.

Back at the Sawyer farmhouse, Mamie Bishop was found cowering in a corner, hiding her eyes and refusing to look up or even acknowledge the presence of others when addressed. Her hair had turned completely white, not the platinum white of little Hester Sawyer's hair but the crinkly albino white that had been Lavinia Whateley's so many years before.

Mamie mumbled to herself and shook her head but uttered not a single intelligible word, either then or later, when she too was taken to the general hospital at Arkham. In time she was certified physically sound and transferred to a mental ward where she resides to this day, a harmless, quivering husk, her inward-turned eyes locked forever on whatever shocking sight it was that she beheld that night when she gazed from the window of the Sawyer farmhouse upon the horrid ceremony taking place atop the Devil's Hop Yard.

•

It came to me as a surprise, when I got some biographical information on Evelyn Lief, that there was so much. You see, I met her once, and you don't expect someone the size and shape of a fifteen-year-old to have much of a biography at all. But no—she's a grown-up lady with a B.A. from Queens College in New York. She works in the editorial department of TV Channel 13 in New York. She has been writing for a long time, and finally took the plunge and enrolled at Clarion in that prestigious course. (Almost a quarter of Clarion alumni are now selling writers.) She immediately sold a story to the first Clarion collection, which is where she came to my attention. On reading it, my first impulse was to break my typewriter over my knee. I had never seen any writer shift so deftly from present to past, from real to surreal—a remarkable achievement.

"EMMA" has some of these qualities, and that quantum of compassion one finds so compelling in her whole approach. The underlying warning about computer-control of the individual and of society is worth your careful thought.

—Theodore Sturgeon
Los Angeles, 1978

EMMA

by Evelyn Lief

She sat in a corner of the room. If she leaned forward, past the mahogany colored plastic coffee table cluttered with outdated magazines, she could just barely manage to see the secretary's desk. But, sitting back against the white wall, she had the comfortable feeling that no one could see her or know there was anyone here waiting for an appointment.

She looked around at the blue couch which was made of non-stick plastic, and at the other white plastic chairs in the room that were really empty. All the other students, except Anna, had already been called. Anna's turn would be next.

There were no windows in this part of the waiting room. Serene watercolor abstracts, painted by students in Anna's class, in calming blues and pastels, hung on the white walls.

She looked up at, into, one picture of a lake with

trees surrounding it. She saw herself in the woods, floating above the muddy edge of the lake, wearing a frilly lace sleeveless white nightgown. It was so lonely here by herself. But so beautiful, with the sun low in the sky, making a pink and purple color.

But wait, someone was waving to her across the lake. It looked like a man. Strangely, she wasn't afraid. She knew that he was different, as she was different. Her body floated toward him, over the lake, to meet him.

Somewhere there was a paper-shuffling noise. Better watch out. Been dreaming again. Better not let my mother catch me. Wake up.

She realized she was still in the waiting room. She clasped her hands together and again noticed how thin her fingers had become. With the thumb and forefinger of her left hand she pressed through the thin skin to feel the bone of a finger on her other hand, rolled the bone between her two fingers, feeling the knuckle, feeling the hollow below the knuckle. Then she held both her hands up in front of her face. They were somebody else's fingers. Somebody else was sitting here, waiting her turn, and soon to be late for her Art History class.

Once before Anna had been late, and the teacher, holding the class hour to be sacred, had made Anna sit up in front in a chair far away from everyone else. Like out of an old movie or in an elementary school class. Throughout the hour Anna's back burned from the other students' stares. She didn't hear a word the teacher had said.

It was better not to go at all than to be late to that class.

"Anna Grosse." The voice spoke from behind the wall where she couldn't see.

She stood up, smoothed down the wrinkles in her

jeans, slowly walked around the table toward the secretary's desk.

"Anna Grosse." The voice sounded impatient. A middle-aged plump woman stepped forward. It was Mrs. Mondell. "Where is she?"

"I'm here," Anna said in almost a whisper.

"You'd think she'd come on time," the middle-aged woman said, and turned her back on Anna.

Anna wondered if she had been the first one called, an hour ago, when she'd come in five minutes after the bell had rung. Maybe that was why Mrs. Mondell was angry.

Anna started to follow Mrs. Mondell.

But the older woman walked into her office and slammed the door in Anna's face.

Maybe I am too late, Anna thought. But she wasn't sure. Maybe Mrs. Mondell would come out in a minute to get her. I'd better wait.

Anna sat, perched on the edge of the blue plastic couch.

Mrs. Mondell has to see me. It's mandatory in a case like mine. The Psych people will be really mad if they hear about this.

Anna stood up and walked over to the secretary. She coughed and harumphed in her throat a tiny bit, but the secretary just kept on typing.

"Excuse me," Anna finally said.

The secretary's fingers ran over the keys, her eyes stared down at her papers.

"Excuse me."

The secretary finished her page, stopped typing and turned her head to look out of the window behind her desk.

"Please, I have to talk to you."

There was no answer.

Anna looked at the clock on the wall. If she

didn't leave this minute she'd be late for her class. She didn't know what to do.

The secretary just didn't want to talk to her. Mrs. Mondell didn't want to talk to her. Well, Anna really didn't want to talk to them either.

But Anna had to talk to them. Why didn't EMMA help her? Now was the time. But I shouldn't really need EMMA. I should be strong enough to talk myself, to do what I have to do.

But I can't.

Anna backed away from the secretary and sat down in the chair in the corner of the room where she had been hiding before.

Why doesn't EMMA help me? But I guess you are helping me, Anna thought. I am back in school, after all, which is better than nothing. And I have to expect to have to do some things by myself.

I have to open the door.

Her hand was motionless three inches in front of the doorknob. The fingers, a little thick, almost chubby, but now spread-eagled, were pulled tight, strained, poised in the air, unable to open any wider, unable to close themselves upon the doorknob.

Anna looked down at her right hand that wouldn't obey.

Open the door.

But the hand wouldn't move.

She had to get to her watercolor class. The teacher had really loved her last exercise. He had said, "Your lines are sensitive and well drawn. It's a fine painting."

But she also saw her paintings, on another day, all lined up against the wall. The head of the Art Department was conducting her junior evaluation.

"You have a decorator's eye for color," he said.

"But you can't draw. It's a good thing you're not an Ed minor because I wouldn't let you teach."

Anna stood motionless.

"Well drawn," one had said.

"Can't draw," the other said.

"Well drawn."

I can draw. I have to go to school, open that door and walk outside.

"Can't draw. Can't draw. Can't draw."

Walk outside where

filaments of blue smoky-looking flat threads swarmed at your feet, climbed up your legs, tightened around your stomach, dug their sharp edges slicing into your rubbery soft skin

while red clouds from above came down as fog that filled your throat and shaped as a fist pushed its way down deep inside, filling you, filling you, making you big to burst

The pain throbbed in her temples. Those loud noises, those screaming sounds were too loud to bear. They shook up her insides. Made her quake all over.

It was so dark. She couldn't open her eyes. Her hands were pressed over her eyes. Her fingers were pressing inward. Her eyes hurt. So she took her hands away. Her throat was sore. So she stopped screaming.

A portfolio and pocketbook lay on the cold tiled floor. Anna was too tired to bend down and pick them up.

There was only one thing to do. Go back to bed.

She turned around and went back into her room which was near the hallway. She lay down in bed. Clothes were too tight. She pushed and pulled and kicked. Clothes weren't too tight anymore. Bed was soft. Quilt was safe to crawl under.

She would try to wake up later, before her mother came home from work, so she wouldn't get yelled at for being lazy.

It was a small waiting room, with a soft, muted-gray warm material on the two cushioned chairs.

Anna's hands wanted to shake, but she didn't think her mother would like to see that happen. So Anna sat on her hands, waiting for the doctors to come and get her.

They were going to put a machine into her head! A psychometer! Her mother said she had to have it put in. They called it EMMA, short for E-Motion-Meter-Analog. It was just like a pacemaker, they said. People with heart trouble weren't ashamed and she didn't need to be ashamed either. All EMMA did was to record the physical signs of her emotional state, relay this information back to the central computer, which in turn directed EMMA about how to make the necessary adjustments, how to regulate the glands, how to stimulate or deaden the appropriate brain centers. It would just help her keep an emotional balance, that's all. That's what they said. Maybe someday, when they could make them more cheaply, even normal people would use EMMA to help them function at a higher level.

So she was really a pioneer.

That's what they told her.

But Anna wasn't sure she wanted to be a pioneer. She didn't feel like a pioneer. She knew she didn't look like a pioneer. Her thighs were too fat and she got tired too easily. Clothes were always tight around her stomach. As soon as she got home Anna always undressed into a loose-fitting robe. She liked to eat too much and lie in bed and watch television. Her cheeks were chubby and her skin was too flabby. She knew she didn't look like a pioneer.

Why couldn't they leave her alone? Why couldn't her mother leave her alone? All the time. She had to do this thing or that thing. Wake up early. Don't eat too much. Go to school. Do some exercises. How could other people do these things so easily? She didn't understand.

"What! Are you crazy?" Anna's mother said. "You can't move out. You don't know what you'd be getting into. You've no idea how much it really costs to live. Food, gas, electric. And all the extra expenses. You'd never make it on your own. You never had any common sense."

Maybe EMMA would help, after all. Maybe things wouldn't be so hard to do after the operation.

It wasn't really like having a computer in your brain. It was just a little machine. But the computer controlled the machine. And the computer would control her too. Just like her mother.

Anna would be ordered around by the computer. She wouldn't even know if it was something the computer told her to do or something she herself really wanted to do. She wouldn't know who she was anymore. She'd be Anna-the-computer. Anna-EMMA. EMMA-Anna. EMMA.

There wasn't going to be an Anna anymore.

She was going to disappear and nobody would even know she was gone.

She could scream and scream for help and nobody would hear.

Except EMMA, who would calm the juices and make everything bad go away.

Go away, bad things in Anna.

Go away, Anna.

Wouldn't it be nice if she could really go away somewhere and rest and sleep and there would be

no more trouble.
Nothing would bother her.
Nothing.
To be nothing.
To be nowhere. Emptied of people that can hurt. Emptied of days that bring fear.
Nothing and nowhere and nobody.
Such a dream.
Maybe EMMA could help the dream come true.
No more Anna. Only EMMA.

EMMA was sitting inside Anna's brain. EMMA had to be helping. Anna was back in school. So EMMA had to be working.

Anna still sat in the chair in the corner of the waiting room.

She was hungry, her stomach empty. The cafeteria wasn't far away and it was already too late to go to her Art History class. It seemed silly to just sit here, waiting, forever.

But she couldn't stand up and leave the room. Something inside was stopping her. Her arms and legs wouldn't move. She looked down at herself and again saw how skinny she had become in the last three months since EMMA had been put in. EMMA didn't like her to eat too much. It was a strange feeling. Anna had been afraid she wouldn't know what she really wanted to do. But she did know. I want to eat. She knew. And EMMA always stopped her. Now all the fat had left Anna's body. The bone of her kneecaps protruded. Her pelvic bones jutted out past her concave stomach.

A chocolate chip ice cream cone. A piece of blueberry cheesecake. Even just a giant tuna fish sandwich.

Anything to eat. To stop myself from shrinking

away.

Anna put her arms around her waist. She was so thin. Too thin. Something was wrong. Something's wrong with EMMA. EMMA's starving me to death. That's what's happening.

"Help, I need help," Anna said.

She stumbled over her feet but managed to walk to the secretary's desk.

"Please, I need help," Anna said.

But the secretary still wouldn't answer.

Something's really wrong with EMMA. People don't answer me. She won't let people answer me. Maybe the secretary can't even see me.

She *has* to be able to see me.

"I'm here. I'm here." Anna banged her fist hard down on the desk.

The knuckles of her fingers, her wrist, hurt. She grabbed her hand close to her body, doubled over, crying. Her legs felt too light to carry her weight as she sank to the floor in front of the desk. She wanted to scream for help.

Anna was disappearing and nobody would be able to find her. But no one really wanted to find her. Even her mother would be glad to be rid of her.

Good riddance to my mother too, Anna thought.

Yes, it is so comfortable to sink down into the floor. Deep. Dark. Safe.

Further down, where there is nothing that can hurt.

EMMA is helping me.

EMMA will take care now.

Of me.

Of nothing.

●

I've known Katherine MacLean ever since we all started to write, and that has become a lot of years ago; and d'ye know, I haven't a single bit of what is known as "biographical information" on her? I think you'd have to know her as well as I do to be able to understand that. From the very beginning, she radiated an *is-ness* rather than a *was-ness*. I never asked her where she was born or where she went to school; that was then, and Katie is now, and always has been. I have many good memories of her: Katie, stalking along a country road in Rockland County, N.Y., with a 40-pound bottle of CO_2 on her shoulder; the sudden machine-gunning of Katie's typewriter in the black dark of the back seat of a 70-mile-per-hour Lincoln ... things like that. I can tell you this: she is one of the very few genuine telepaths I have ever met.

There is only one thing about MacLean which displeases me: she hasn't written enough. Securing this one is a real achievement. It's very different from most of her work, which generally starts from a base of hard science, or rationalizes psi phenomena with beautifully finished logic. This one is something else—a troubled and troubling narrative of a man convinced of a new reality.

—Theodore Sturgeon
Los Angeles, 1978

CANARY BIRD

by Katherine MacLean

I went to see the psychiatrist during my lunch hour. He was a little man with a goat beard, and his appearance surprised me. I don't know what I expected to see, God or Satan perhaps. When we go to someone to complain about our souls and the universe we expect to see someone suited to the job, not a skinny little man behind thick glasses.

He said, "You're Mr. Robert Henley?" and looked me over from shoes to hair. I look harmless, physically healthy and well dressed, a person whose problems should be few and easily solved. He almost smiled and pushed some standard question forms across the desk at me. "Please fill these out."

I did not touch them. There was not enough time for that jazz; I stood there and told him the essential information.

"It's bad watching them walk around," I said.

"Everyone is dead. The whole world is dead. A plague wiped us out when we were not noticing and we are all dead and should lie down and rot."

I usually say complicated things, disguise what I mean and try to make it sound like a joke. He did not know how much effort I was putting into forcing out a simple statement.

The psychiatrist took off his glasses and wiped the lenses, looking at me, then swung his chair sideways to the desk. Probably there was a panic button for him to push in case a client came in completely lunatic. With his feet clear of the desk he could bolt for the door.

"Is this true?" he asked. His lips were tight against his teeth and he was paying so much attention to me he was barely breathing.

"This is the way I feel. The world is the way you feel it is. I feel you are dead, rotting." It was such an effort to get the words out I was sweating with it. You try telling someone he is dead when *he* thinks he is alive, and see how hard it is to get the words out. I had been listening to dead men for weeks and trying to smile as if nothing was wrong, and the smile had frozen on. It was hard to break through it. Besides, I did not want to hurt him or scare him.

But the little skinny corpse with the goat beard was relaxing. He took his hand away from the panic button and put his glasses back on, deciding that I would not have to be packed up by the police and shipped to the funny farm, at least not immediately. There was time to talk.

I talked, a dead man explaining to a dead man. "Nothing that anyone does matters any more. I mean all the live things and love and laughter happened last year. This year everyone is dead. Everyone I see, even on television, they are dead and going through the motions of being alive, like some sort of horror movie. No one really feels anything.... Why do they keep going? If I lie down the gravediggers might come along and bury me."

Yorick I thought, and barely restrained a wisecrack. Hamlet was another kook who would start making jokes whenever things were so bad he couldn't stand it. Gravediggers' jokes. But most people think that jokes mean you are happy.

The psychiatrist had been rolling a pencil in his fingers, but when I mentioned gravediggers he read me deeper than I intended, and his fingers stopped moving and he stopped breathing for a moment, holding a freeze while he looked at me. It ruins a psychiatrist's professional reputation to have a patient kill himself. He had two choices now, or three. He could turn me down as a patient or he could get me to declare my intentions more clearly, and then call the police, or he could ignore what I had said and take his chances on being able to stop me.

He cleared his throat, mumbled something, and then thought of a way to change the subject. "What kind of work do you do, Mr. Henley?" Then he apologized. "If you don't mind the question."

"Advertising," I said. The numbness grew from the skin inward and the heart out. I wanted to tell him how I make really good cartoons, people like them, people praise me for how perceptive they are, how they illuminate human nature. I felt sick. Smog formed and thickened in the air between us.

"Ahh," said the psychiatrist, as if I had given him a clue. "What have you been doing at work recently?"

"I've been very successful," I said, and the man behind the desk seemed farther away and dimmer through a thickening fog of nausea. "They've put me on to cigarette advertisements. The big money accounts."

"Aha," muttered the small corpse, rotting far away across the murky distance of a desk like the Mojave desert. "How do you feel now?"

"If the world keeps on like this I won't have to kill myself," I said. "The stench will kill me."

He laughed as if I had said something funny, and pulled open his desk drawer and fumbled among bottles. He brought out a small plastic bottle that said FREE SAMPLE. Doctors are always getting free samples from drug manufacturers. He poured out two giant-sized pills and offered them to me. "Have a couple of new tranquilizers. They'll hold you for a while."

"Tranquilizers don't do anything to cure it, isn't that right?" I asked. "I'm willing to take LSD or anything that's fast."

"LSD starts by making it worse," he said. "Most forms of quick psychotherapy start by making it worse."

"I couldn't stand it getting worse," I said, but it was already getting worse; it had been changing ever since I came in. He poured a glass of water for me and I swallowed the two big pills. I hoped the manufacturers had made a mistake and they would be poison.

He gave me the forms to fill out and I wrote my name, my address, and the usual information. There was a space where it asked if I had ever been committed, put under custodial care, locked up, incarcerated, declared mentally incompetent, or given a psych disability discharge from the services. I wrote NO. He arranged another appointment and the hour was over.

On the way back to work I began to see that the two tranquilizers had done something for me. The streets were still populated by walking dead men, but I didn't care. That was an improvement. It reminded me of those jokes about tranquilizers: "Tranquilizers are wonderful," says the comic. "You know how crazy I was. I used to be scared of little green men following me?" Uh huh. "Well I'm cured now. I'm not scared of them anymore, I've made friends with them. We play poker every night." I wondered if I could work up a cartoon like that.

The little psychiatrist had said "Aha" when I told him I worked in advertising. Did he mean that advertising had done this to me? There was a joke that anyone who worked in advertising had to spend his wages in a psychiatrist's office. A true joke. Face it.

How did I get into advertising? They had seen my cartoons, that I just used to sort of illustrate my life and my friends' lives. They saw them in the newspapers. They offered me money. My friends said that money is worth having, that advertising jobs bring respect. I was surprised that people respect ad men. I thought, they must have some useful purpose.

What is the purpose of ad men? Darwinian selection, I figured out. Advertising wipes out all the people who are fool enough to believe advertising, people fool enough to be affected by emotions; naive, trusting, emotional people. The standard sales pitch is directed to their desire for fresh air and outdoor exercise, courage and adventure and friendship and love, so they buy smoke, lung cancer, high blood pressure, sugar, fat, inaction, installment payments, debt, weakness, spectator living and early old age. My cartoons just bring in a new group of suckers—my friends, the kind of people who like my cartoons.

I walked through the agency, making the usual quips and cracks, showing my teeth like smiling, and somehow got to my desk. I took out a folder of ideas and sketches and spread them to look like work, braced my elbows on my desk, and scribbled on scratch paper. Everyone would respect my concentration.

Making myself enter this place had been making myself the center and heartbeat of whatever made the world hell. People had talked me into it, sounding enthusiastic. My friends told me I would enjoy spending all the money.

I don't spend money on much: books, records, a small, low-rent apartment, two cats, the conversation of friends, a girl friend who married a friend last year and now every Friday they invite me over to dinner and let me play with the baby. I don't have much need for money.

My friends told me I would enjoy the company of other talented people, sharing their skills and talents, with pooled creativity making the final artistic product. I had stayed there long enough to see that artists and writers do not want help. They hate and fear bad help because it will spoil the good work they have done, and they hate and fear good help because it will make the final layout and copy someone else's triumph instead of their own. I had stayed with the agency long enough to feel the hate running underneath the cooperation.

The final artistic product. The office was slowly descending like an elevator into the depth of a huge grave.

The final product was selling what?

Don't make waves.

That kind of thinking made the nausea worse, but I could not bolt for the door; there were too many desks and people in between. I remembered what the little psychiatrist had said. "Most forms of quick psychotherapy start by making it worse." Most of those interesting stories of LSD cures for neuroses started with something similar to a descent into Dante's hell. I sat at the desk and grimly made it worse, like Jean Valjean wading deeper into the sewers of Paris. The shit closed over my head. Everything went black. The human race crowded in on me in the dark, struggling and strangling each other, fornicating and possessing and destroying, a vast insane asylum. We kill each other in war, and in peacetime we try to drown each other in lies. The false smile over the sugared words over the poison. Hatred came white like a blowtorch flame that could have destroyed the human race if it stood in the way.

I don't have to smile.

I have to eat what they eat. I did not have to love the bastards if they did not love each other. Let them die and be mutually hurt, let them warp and kill and poison each other, and good riddance. Let them wipe themselves out as a species and leave the world free of smiles and lies. In my imagination I let the nuclear bombs blow it smooth and I was the desert, empty and free and clean to the far line of the horizon. Winds blew across it, brushing down from a vast and empty sky and curving back into the sky again.

Suddenly I noticed that I was breathing deep breaths of remarkably clean air. I opened my eyes, and the wall in front of me was clean and quiet. The air hummed with the distant sound of an electric typewriter, and the murmur of two people conferring. I looked around and saw that the office was wide and spacious and empty. The people in it were small and took up almost no space. They were alive and mouselike, and unimportant.

This was a better and changed world. But if things could change so suddenly, just by trying to make them worse, the world could change around me again as suddenly as an LSD nightmare, and become something different. If I freaked out I had to be careful to not act strange and frighten the secretaries. Don't step on mice. Though small and far away, the agony of mice is real.

When I tried to grip the clean quiet empty world and hold it from changing the office began to spin, very slightly, and descend again.

I could not remember the psychiatrist's name but then I found his card in my wallet and called the number.

"Doctor Weyland, when did you give me an appointment? I mean, what time?"

"Right after work," he said. "Five thirty. This *is* Mr. Henley, isn't it? You can come over right now if you feel like it. I take a coffee break from two to two thirty. We can talk."

"Thank you."

"How is the—ah—situation?" he asked cautiously. "How does it look to you from where you are now?"

He sounded nervous. How was the situation now? Clean quiet office. Live frightened people working timidly at their desks, mice doing what they were told, faking free will with wisecracks.

"I made it worse, by thinking. It turned empty. Better now. No more—" I remembered the golems, the walking dead, the smell, the far-away, long-ago horror, like the war experiences. "No more corpses," I said with difficulty, getting the word out. "Live people, I guess. Not important now." My throat was closing up and I almost couldn't talk. I found I'd put my right hand into the desk drawer. I pulled it out. It was red and dripping with some sort of filth which did not stain the desk top. My imagination seemed to be inconsistent about small details. The stuff should have stained the desk.

I managed to speak coherently past such waves of mixed terror of being known like this, and belief in myself as something small and vile and far away, that I was surprised to hear myself speak at all. "I have some red crud all over my hands."

There was a moment of silence at the other end of the phone. "Real or imaginary?" he asked. Mentally I could see him reaching for the panic button again or the hot-line phone to the police department. I remembered he thought I would commit suicide.

"No, not real. It can't be; I haven't—" my throat closed again.

"You're making changes," he said soothingly. "That's progress, you know." He did not sound sure.

"But it's true too. If they see it...." I felt they must have seen it already. Everyone knew I was a monster from a horror movie, with fangs, and hands dripping red. I let him imagine how it would be to drip red in public with people watching and drawing conclusions. "I feel that it is real. I think that they see it."

"Don't fight it," he said. "An image can be a message. Feel whatever it makes you feel. Try to let yourself think what it means. Symbols are good."

I put my red dripping hands into the top drawer, out of sight, holding the phone receiver on my shoulder. How would I get out of the office? *There he goes. We always thought there was something wrong about him. Look at his hands.* "Maybe I should wear gloves," I said.

"Come right over," said the doctor, and hung up.

I found I was looking at one of my cartoons. This was the one I like to draw over and over and think up different captions for.

It is of a small naked man in a bird cage, huddled together, balancing himself on the canary bird perch. There is nothing else in the cage. The wire of the cage around him is closing him in without a door or opening.

I took a good black marking pencil and lettered under the picture: MAYBE I SHOULD TAKE UP A HOBBY. The red crud on my hand was horrible but it did not stain the picture and the lettering was big and clear. I left the picture there, put on my jacket and went out to the psychiatrist's office with my hands in my pockets all the way. Try going through a revolving door with your hands in your pockets.

The psychiatrist was still there. He did not mind my hands. He had read up on all the schools of psychotherapy. When there was another theory to explain what was wrong with everyone, he said, people like that would come along to fit the theory. There are different kinds of people and different ways to be wrong. For me there were lots of theories.

There was the chemical one. We looked it up together in the research journals. The glands make adrenalin for courage and energy in fighting and breaking through obstacles and getting your own way. If you don't argue, if you decide not to try to get your own way, the adrenal glands sometimes stop making adrenalin and grow sick and start making instead some kind of poison that goes to the brain.

"Act angry," said Weyland.

I tried frowning. It felt strange. It wrinkled the skin of my forehead. I stopped.

"Punch that foam rubber bolster on the sofa over there," Weyland said. I tried, but I was afraid it would scream and die. I refused, my hands sweating.

I'm glad I don't have to work as a psychiatrist. My little skinny man slapped his hands at me futilely. "Go on, try. Just hit it."

I refused. "I can't do it. I'm sorry."

He paced up and down, looking at the rug and polishing his glasses. Probably trying to think up some technique that would work on me.

"I'm sorry," I said, feeling helpless. I wished I could think for him, but it was his profession. I was not an expert.

He stopped, looked at me and put his glasses back on. "Are you feeling guilty about me?"

He'd caught me thinking. He'd seen into me. Harder to admit to it than to lie, but I made an effort, resisted shame, and nodded.

We decided that I should have a guilt complex. It's my job now to go around feeling guilty, never mind why. Also I am supposed to tell him my nightmares. I tell him nightmares about a man I had strangled. An enemy soldier infiltrating in disguise, a civilian? Did I kill him or not? I can't remember it all when awake, but the nightmares have details. The details are different every time.

Ever since I admitted feeling guilty the world has been in sharp focus. The people are the right size, human, alive. They are nervous and guilty-looking, like me. I see and think with great clarity. I understand history as a gigantic conspiracy, everyone guilty. I draw better cartoons than ever, and more of them.

If I start feeling sick, I concentrate on feeling guilty instead; sometimes I feel guilty about the man I murder in my dreams. No hallucinations any more. Weyland gives me a different tranquilizer but only to stop me from shaking. I'm alive and awake in an alive and nervous world.

I'm afraid to show my cartoons. Art is a way to do something to people. In a sneaky way it makes them see the world the way you see it. They might wind up doing what I do. I put my pictures in a cardboard box on top of the closet.

I quit my job at the agency.

"Quitting was a gesture of self-assertion," said Weyland. "Think up more gestures of self-assertion; it will do you good."

I looked at him, a little wispy man who hides behind thick glasses and waves a pipe in front of his face like a shield. Sometimes he makes me laugh. Quitting is a gesture of self-assertion—in the world of mice-people. I would have to learn to fight mice. The thought was preposterous.

"I won't charge you for sessions when you are out of work," he said. "Keep coming in." He handed me a bigger sample bottle of tranquilizers.

"All right, Weyland."

I put the bottle in my pocket and went out laughing.

People are always glad to see me at intellectual parties, and publishers' cocktail parties, and Greenwich Village non-conformist parties. I say funny things, I pour oil on troubled waters. I find miserable people sitting in corners and introduce them to other miserable people with the same style of thought, so they have company and become happy. People invite me to all their parties.

Party food doesn't usually have enough vitamins, so I buy bottles of multiple vitamin pills to take with the tranquilizers and borrow enough money to buy cans of cat food for the cats.

I sleep during the day and go out at night.

I make no plans to get another job; the last one worked out badly.

I'm watching to see the trends in people's troubles, to see who else is starting to shake.

I'm a weather vane, a canary bird in a mine shaft. I've been ten and twenty years ahead of what happened to other people all of my life. If it was a hobby, an artist, a kind of popular song, or a writer, I liked it first and other people would discover it and like it years later, when I'd already dropped it and forgotten it and gone on to something else.

I get a disease before anyone else. It proves most diseases are psychosomatic. My psyche gives way faster. I'm a normal thinker, not more profound, just faster, twenty years ahead of time, and with weaker nerves. I break down easily and need some new kind of philosophy, art, or music to glue the pieces back together and get me moving again. I like the Greenwich Village far-out parties, they have the crazy people with new ideas that will be popular in twenty years. Whatever I find that will be good for me, it will be good for a lot of other shaking people in twenty years.

I explained it to Doctor Weyland. I said, "Remember the canary birds they put in cages at the bottom of coal mines and submarines? When the poison gas begins to leak into the air and the air gets too bad, they stop singing and die. That is how the people can tell it is time for them to get out. I'm like that. I react faster. Anyone wants to know what will happen, watch me."

Weyland got a big kick out of that idea. He believed it. He calls me Bob Canarybird, and watches me all the time, and takes notes.

He thinks it is funny and interesting to have a weather vane and make prophecies about future trends and tastes from watching one person. Ten years' warning.

But I don't want to be around the year *everyone* decides that everyone else is dead and rotting.

That will be some year.

●

David Drake comes from Iowa. He was well into law school when Viet Nam happened to him, and when that was over (if indeed a thing like that is ever over for the men who had to do it) he finished law school and became Assistant Town Attorney at Chapel Hill in North Carolina.

In 1966, not too long out of high school, Drake visited the legendary Sauk City and its monument, August Derleth, and with the great man's guidance and encouragement, sold him four stories. Derleth's death turned him to other, and other kinds of markets, and war turned him to another kind of writing. He hit all the big ones—*F&SF, Galaxy, Analog*. One day he'll write a novel, and I'll bet it will be a big one.

"Crossfire" is about another war on another planet, but in essence it needn't be. You'll see what I mean when you read it.

—Theodore Sturgeon
Los Angeles, 1978

CAUGHT IN THE CROSSFIRE
by David Drake

Party politics on Pohweil became civil war when the major commercial houses refused to pay the new export tax. The outvoted Trade Cartel had for months been secretly hiring mercenaries through off-planet factors; now three regiments came streaming into the capital's spaceport.

But the Government—the latifundistas of the Northern and Central Districts who worked their fields with machines and gangs of laborers—had not been taken unawares. The export tax, planned for the Farm Block's benefit and not that of the planet as a whole, would have been useful, but there was already enough in the war chest to hire Hammer's Slammers.

War's coarse tongue licked across Pohweil. In the cities and on the great farms, folk talked of victory or defeat; but in the peasant holdings of the Southern District the talk was of Life or Death as it always had been. It was just that Death, always in the past the creeping jungle, now had a myriad of human allies....

Margritte grappled with the nearest soldier in the instant her husband broke for the woods. The man in field-gray cursed and tried to jerk his weapon away from her, but Margritte's muscles were young and taut from shifting bales. Even when the mercenary kicked her ankles from under her, Margritte's clamped hands kept the gun barrel down and harmless.

Neither of the other two soldiers paid any attention to the scuffle. They clicked off the safety catches of their weapons as they swung them to their shoulders. Georg was running hard, fresh blood from his retorn calf muscles staining his bandages. The double slap of automatic fire caught him in mid-stride and whipsawed his slender body. His head and heels scissored to the ground together. They were covered by the mist of blood that settled more slowly.

Sobbing, Margritte loosed her grip and fell back on the ground. The man above her cradled his flechette gun again and looked around the village. "Well, aren't you going to shoot me too?" she screamed.

"Not unless we have to," the mercenary replied quietly. He was sweating despite the stiff breeze, and he wiped his black face with his sleeve. "Helmuth," he ordered, "start setting up in the building. Landschein, you stay out with me, make sure none of these women try the same damned thing." He glanced out to where Georg lay, a bright smear on the stubbled, golden earth. "Best get that out of sight too," he added. "The convoy's due in an hour."

Old Leida had frozen to a statue in ankle-length muslin at the first scream. Now she nodded her head of close ringlets. "Myrie, Della," she called, gesturing to her daughters, "bring brush hooks and come along." She had not lost her dignity even during the shooting.

"Hold it," said Landschein, the shortest of the three soldiers. He was a sharp-featured man who had grinned in satisfaction as he fired. "You two got kids in there?" he asked the younger women. The muzzle of his flechette gun indicated the locked door to the dugout which normally stored the crop out of sun and heat; today it imprisoned the village's 26 children. Della and Myrie nodded, too dry with fear to speak.

"Then you go drag him into the woods," Landschein said, grinning again. "Just remember— you might manage to get away, but you won't much like what you'll find when you come back. I'm sure some true friend'll point your brats out to us quick enough to save her own."

Leida nodded a command, but Landschein's freckled hand clamped her elbow as she turned to follow her daughters. "Not you, old lady. No need for you to get that near to cover."

"Do you think *I* would run and risk—everyone?" Leida demanded.

"Damned if I know what you'd risk," the soldier said. "But we're risking plenty already to ambush one of Hammer's convoys. If anybody gets loose ahead of time to warn them, we can kiss our butts goodbye."

Margritte wiped the tears from her eyes, using her palms because of the gritty dust her thrashings had pounded into her knuckles. The third soldier, the broad-shouldered blond named Helmuth, had leaned his weapon beside the door of the hall and was lifting bulky loads from the nearby air cushion vehicle. The settlement had become used to whining gray columns of military vehicles, cruising the road at random. This truck, however, had eased over the second canopy of the forest itself. It was a flimsy cargo hauler like the one in which Krauder picked up the cotton at season's end, harmless enough to look at. Only Georg, left behind for his sickle-ripped leg when a government van had carried off the other males the week before as "recruits," had realized what it meant that the newcomers wore field-gray instead of khaki.

"Why did you come here?" Margritte asked in a near-normal voice.

The black mercenary glanced at her as she rose, and back at the other women obeying orders by continuing to pick the iridescent boles of Terran cotton grown in Pohweil's soil. "We had the capital under siege," he said, "until Hammer's tanks punched a corridor through. We can't close the corridor, so we got to cut your boys off from supplies some other way. Otherwise the Cartel'll wish it had paid its taxes instead of trying to take over. You grubbers may have been pruning their wallets, but Christ! they'll be flayed alive if your counter-attack works."

He spat a thin, angry stream into the dust. "The traders hired us and four other regiments, and you grubbers sank the whole treasury into bringing in Hammer's armor. Maybe we can prove today those cocky bastards aren't all they're billed as. . . ."

We didn't care," Margritte said. "We're no more the Farm Block than Krauder and his truck is the Trade Cartel. Whatever they do in the capital—we had no choice. I haven't even seen the capital . . . oh dear God, Georg would have taken me there for our honeymoon except that there was fighting all over...."

"How long we got, Sarge?" the blond man demanded from the stark shade of the hall.

"Little enough. Get those fucking sheets set up or we'll have to pop the cork bare-ass naked; and we got enough problems." The big non-com shifted his glance about the narrow clearing, wavering rows of cotton marching to the edge of the forest's dusky green. The road, an unsurfaced track whose ruts were not a serious hindrance to air cushion traffic, was the long axis. Beside it stood the hall, twenty meters by five and the only above-ground structure in the settlement. The battle with the native vegetation made dug-outs beneath the cotton preferable to cleared land wasted for dwellings. The hall became more than a social center and common refectory: it was the gaudiest of luxuries and a proud slap to the face of the forest.

Until that morning, the forest had been the village's only enemy.

"Georg only wanted—"

"God *damn* it!" the sergeant snarled. "Will you shut it off? Every man but your precious husband gone off to the siege—no, shut it off till I finish!—and him running to warn the convoy. If you'd wanted to save his life, you should've grabbed him, not me. Sure, all you grubbers, you don't care about the war—not much! It's all one to you whether you kill us yourselves or your tankers do it, those bastards so high and mighty for the money they've got and the equipment. I tell you, girl, I don't take it personal that people shoot at me, it's just the way we both earn our living. But it's fair, it's even ... and Hammer thinks he's God Incarnate because nobody can bust his tanks."

The sergeant paused and his lips sucked in and out. His thick, gentle fingers rechecked the weapon he held. "We'll just see," he whispered.

"Georg said we'd all be killed in the crossfire if we were out in the fields when you shot at the tanks."

"If Georg had kept his face shut and his ass in bed, he'd have lived longer than he did. Just shut it off!" the non-com ordered. He turned to his blond underling, fighting a section of sponge plating through the door. "Christ, Bornzyk!" he shouted angrily. "Move it!"

Helmuth flung his load down with a hollow clang. "Christ, then lend a hand! The wind catches these and—"

"I'll help him," Margritte offered abruptly. Her eyes blinked away from the young soldier's weapon where he had forgotten it against the wall. Standing, she lacked the bulk of the sergeant beside her, but her frame gave no suggestion of weakness. Golden dust soiled the back and sides of her dress with butterfly scales.

The sergeant gave her a sharp glance, his left hand spreading and closing where it rested on the black barrel-shroud of his weapon. "All right," he said, "you give him a hand and we'll see you under cover with us when the shooting starts. You're smarter than I gave you credit."

They had forgotten Leida was still standing beside them. Her hand struck like a spading fork. Margritte ducked away from the blow, but Leida caught her on the shoulder and gripped. When the mercenary's reversed gun butt cracked the older woman loose, a long strip of Margritte's blue dress tore away with her. "Bitch," Leida mumbled through bruised lips. "You'd help these beasts after they killed your own man?"

Margritte stepped back, tossing her head. For a moment she fumbled at the tear in her dress; then, defiantly, she let it fall open. Landschein turned in time to catch the look in Leida's eyes. "Hey, you'll give your friends more trouble," he stated cheerfully, waggling his gun to indicate Della and Myrie as they returned gray-faced from the forest fringe. "Go on, get out and pick some cotton."

When Margritte moved, the white of her loose shift caught the sun and the small killer's stare. "Landschein!" the black ordered sharply, and Margritte stepped very quickly toward the truck and the third man struggling there.

Helmuth turned and blinked at the girl as he felt her capable muscles take the wind-strain off the panel he was shifting. His eyes were blue and set wide in a face too large-boned to be handsome, too frank to be other than attractive. He accepted the help without question, leading the way into the hall.

The dining tables were hoisted against the rafters. The windows, unshuttered in the warm autumn and unglazed, lined all four walls at chest height. The long wall nearest the road was otherwise unbroken; the one opposite it was pierced in the middle by the single door. In the center of what should have been an empty room squatted the mercenaries' construct. The metal-ceramic panels had been locked into three sides of a square, a pocket of armor open only toward the door. It was hidden beneath the lower sills of the windows; nothing would catch the eye of an oncoming tanker.

"We've got to nest three layers together," the

soldier explained as he swung the load, easily managed within the building, "or they'll cut us apart if they get off a burst in this direction."

Margritte steadied a panel already in place as Helmuth mortised his into it. Each sheet was about five centimeters in thickness, a thin plate of gray metal on either side of a white porcelain sponge. The girl tapped it dubiously with a blunt finger. "This can stop bullets?"

The soldier—he was younger than his size suggested, no more than eighteen—younger even than Georg, and he had a smile like Georg's as he raised his eyes with a blush and said, "P-powerguns, yeah; three layers of it ought to.... It's light, we could carry it in the truck where iridium would have bogged us down. But look, there's another panel and the rockets we still got to bring in."

"You must be very brave to fight tanks with just—this," Margritte prompted as she took one end of the remaining armor sheet.

"Oh, well, Sgt. Counsel says it'll work," the boy said enthusiastically. "They'll come by, two combat cars, then three big trucks, and another combat car. Sarge and Landschein buzzbomb the lead cars before they know what's happening. I reload them and they hit the third car when it swings wide to get a shot. Any shooting the blower jocks get off, they'll spread because they won't know—oh shit...."

"They'll think the women in the fields may be firing, so they'll kill us first," Margritte reasoned aloud.

The boy's neck beneath his helmet turned brick red as he trudged into the building. "Look," he said, but he would not meet her eyes, "we got to do

207

it. It'll be fast—nobody much can get hurt. And your ... the children, they're all safe. Sarge said that with all the men gone, we wouldn't have any trouble with the women if we kept the kids safe and under our thumbs."

"We didn't have time to have children," Margritte said. Her eyes were briefly unfocused. "You didn't give Georg enough time before you killed him."

"He was...," Helmuth began. They were outside again and his hand flicked briefly toward the slight notch Della and Myrie had chopped in the forest wall. "I'm sorry."

"Oh, don't be sorry," she said. "He knew what he was doing."

"He was—I suppose you'd call him a patriot?" Helmuth suggested, jumping easily to the truck's deck to gather up an armload of cylindrical bundles. "He was really against the Cartel?"

"There was never a soul in this village who cared who won the war," Margritte said. "We have our own war with the forest."

"They joined the siege!" the boy retorted. "They cared that m-much, to fight us!"

"They got in the vans when men with guns told them to get in," the girl said. She took the gear Helmuth was forgetting to hand to her and shook a lock of hair out of her eyes. "Should they have run? Like Georg? No, they went off to be soldiers; praying like we did that the war might end before the forest had eaten up the village again. Maybe if we were really lucky, it'd end before this crop had spoiled in the fields because there weren't enough hands left here to pick it in time."

Helmuth cleared the back of the truck with his own load and stepped down. "Well, just the same your, your husband tried to hide and warn the convoy," he argued. "Otherwise why did he run?"

"Oh, he loved me—you know?" said Margritte. "Your sergeant said all of us should be out picking as usual. Georg knew, he *told* you, that the crossfire would kill everybody in the fields as sure as if you shot us deliberately. And when you wouldn't change your plan ... well, if he'd gotten away you would have had to give up your ambush, wouldn't you? You'd have known it was suicide if the tanks learned that you were waiting for them. So Georg ran."

The dark-haired woman stared out at the forest for a moment. "He didn't have a prayer, did he? You could have killed him a hundred times before he got to cover."

"Here, give me those," the soldier said, taking the bundles from her instead of replying. He began to unwrap the cylinders one by one on the wooden floor. "We couldn't let him get away," he said at last. He added, his eyes still down on his work, "Flechettes when they hit ... I mean, sh-shooting at his legs wouldn't, wouldn't have been a kindness, you see?"

Margritte laughed again. "Oh, I saw what they dragged into the forest, yes." She paused, sucking at her lower lip. "That's how we always deal with our dead, give them to the forest. Oh, we have a service; but we wouldn't have buried Georg in the dirt, if he'd died. But you didn't care, did you? A corpse looks bad, maybe your precious ambush, your own lives ... Get it out of the way, toss it in the woods."

"We'd have buried him afterwards," the soldier mumbled as he laid a fourth thigh-thick projectile beside those he had already unwrapped.

"Oh, of course," Margritte said. "And me, and all

the rest of us murdered out there in the cotton. Oh, you're gentlemen, you are."

"Christ!" Helmuth shouted, his flush mottling as at last he lifted his gaze to the girl's. "We'd have b-buried him. *I'd* have buried him. You'll be safe in here with us until it's all over, and by Christ, then you can come back with us too! You don't have to stay here with these hard-faced bitches."

A bitter smile tweaked the left edge of the girl's mouth. "Sure, you're a good boy."

The young mercenary blinked between protest and pleasure, settled on the latter. He had readied all six of the finned, gray missiles; now he lifted one of the pair of launchers. "It'll be really quick," he said shyly, changing the subject. The launcher was an arm-length tube with double handgrips and an optical sight. Helmuth's big hands easily inserted one of the buzzbombs to lock with a faint snick.

"Very simple," Margritte murmured.

"Cheap and easy," the boy agreed with a smile. "You can buy a thousand of these for what a combat car runs—hell, maybe more than a thousand. And it's one for one today, one bomb to one car. Landschein says the crews are just a little extra, like weevils in your biscuit."

He saw her grimace, the angry tensing of a woman who had just seen her husband blasted into a spray of offal. Helmuth grunted with his own pain, his mouth dropping open as his hand stretched to touch her bare shoulder. "Oh, Christ—didn't mean to say...."

She gently detached his fingers. His breath caught and he turned away. Unseen, her look of hatred seared his back. His hand was still stretched toward her and hers toward him, when the door scraped to admit Landschein behind them.

"Cute, oh bloody cute," the little mercenary said. He carried his helmet by its strap. Uncovered, his cropped gray hair made him an older man. "Well, get on with it, boy—don't keep me'n Sarge waiting. He'll be mad enough about getting sloppy thirds."

Helmuth jumped to his feet. Lanschein ignored him, clicking across to a window in three quick strides. "Sarge," he called, "we're all set. Come on, we can watch the women from here."

"I'll run the truck into the woods," Counsel's voice burred in reply. "Anyhow, I can hear better from out here."

That was true. Despite the open windows, the wails of the children were inaudible in the hall. Outside, they formed a thin backdrop to every other sound.

Landschein set down his helmet. He snapped the safety on his gun's sideplate and leaned the weapon carefully against the nest of armor. Then he took up the loaded launcher and ran his hands over its tube and grips. Without changing expression, he reached out to caress Margritte through the tear in her dress.

Margritte screamed and clawed her left hand as she tried to rise. The launcher slipped into Landschein's lap and his arm, far swifter, locked hers and drew her down against him. Then the little mercenary himself was jerked upward. Helmuth's hand on his collar first broke Landschein's grip on Margritte, then flung him against the closed door.

Landschein rolled despite the shock and his glance flicked toward his weapon, but between gun and gunman crouched Helmuth, no longer a red-faced boy but the strongest man in the room. Grinning, Helmuth spread fingers that had crushed ribs in past rough-and-tumbles. "Try it, little man," he said. "Try it and I'll rip your head off your shoulders."

"You'll do wonders!" Landschein spat, but his eyes lost their glaze and his muscles relaxed. He bent his mouth into a smile. "Hey, kid, there's plenty of slots around. We'll work out something afterwards, no need to fight."

Helmuth rocked his head back in a nod of acceptance with nothing of friendship in it. "You lay another hand on her," he said in a normal voice, "and you'd best have killed me first." He turned his back deliberately on the older man and the nearby weapons. Landschein clenched his left fist once, twice, but then began to load the remaining launcher.

Margritte slipped the patching kit from her belt pouch. Her hands trembled, but the steel needle was already threaded. Her whip-stitches tacked the torn piece top and sides to the remaining material, close enough for decency. Pins were a luxury that a cotton settlement could do well without. Landschein glanced back at her once, but at the same time the floor creaked as Helmuth's weight shifted to his other leg. Neither man spoke.

Sgt. Counsel opened the door. His right arm cradled a pair of flechette guns and he handed one to Helmuth. "Best not to leave it in the dust," he said. "You'll be needing it soon."

"They coming, Sarge?" Landschein asked. He touched his tongue to thin, pale lips.

"Not yet." Counsel looked from one man to the other. "You boys get things sorted out?"

"All green here," Lanschein muttered, smiling again but lowering his eyes.

"That's good," the big black said, "because we

got a job to do and we're not going to let anything stop us. Anything."

Margritte was putting away her needle. The sergeant looked at her hard. "You keep your head down, hear?"

"It won't matter," the girl said calmly, tucking the kit away, "The tanks, they won't be surprised to see a woman in here."

"Sure, but they'll shoot your fucking head off," Landschein snorted.

"Do you think I care?" she blazed back. Helmuth winced at the tone; Sgt. Counsel's eyes took on an undesirable shade of interest.

"But you're helping us," the big non-com mused. He tapped his fingertips on the gun in the crook of his arm. "Because you like us so much?" There was no amusement in his words, only a careful mind picking over the idea, all ideas.

She stood and walked to the door, her face as composed as a priest's at gravesite. "Have your ambush," she said. "Would it help us if the convoy came through before you were ready for it?"

"The smoother it goes, the faster..." Counsel agreed quietly, "then the better for all of you."

Margritte swung the door open and stood looking out. Eight women were picking among the rows east of the hall. They would be relatively safe there, not caught between the ambushers' rockets and the raking powerguns of their quarry. Eight of them safe and fourteen sure victims on the other side. Most of them could have been out of the crossfire if they had only let themselves think, only considered the truth that Georg had died to underscore.

"I keep thinking of Georg," Margritte said aloud. "I guess my friends are just thinking about their children, they keep looking at the storage room. But the children, they'll be all right; it's just that most of them are going to be orphans in a few minutes."

"It won't be that bad," Helmuth said. He did not sound as though he believed it either.

The older children had by now ceased the screaming begun when the door shut and darkness closed in on them. The youngest still wailed, and the sound drifted through the open door.

"I told her we'd take her back with us, Sarge," Helmuth said.

Landschein chortled, a flash of instinctive humor he covered with a raised palm. Counsel shook his head in amazement. "You were wrong, boy. Now, keep watching those women or we may not be going back ourselves."

The younger man reddened again in frustration. "Look, we've got women in the outfit now, and I don't mean the rec troops. Capt. Denzil told me there's six in Bravo Company alone—"

"Hoo, little Helmuth wants his own girlie friend to keep his bed warm," Landschein gibed.

"Landschein, I—" Helmuth began, clenching his right hand into a ridge of knuckles.

"Shut it off!"

"But Sarge—"

"Shut it off, boy, or you'll have me to deal with!" roared the black. Helmuth fell back and rubbed his eyes. The non-com went on more quietly, "Landschein, you keep your tongue to yourself, too."

Both big men breathed deeply, their eyes shifting in concert toward Margritte who faced them in silence. "Helmuth," the sergeant continued, "some units take women, some don't. We've got a few, damned few, because not many women have the guts for our line of work."

Margritte's smile flickered. "The hardness, you mean. The callousness."

"Sure, words don't matter," Counsel agreed mildly. He smiled back at her as one equal to another. "This one, yeah; she might just pass. Shit, you don't have to look like Landschein there to be tough. But you're missing the big point, boy."

Helmuth touched his right wrist to his chin. "Well, what?" he demanded.

Counsel laughed. "She wouldn't go with us. Would you, girl?"

Margritte's eyes were flat, and her voice was dead flat. "No," she said, "I wouldn't go with you."

The non-com grinned as he walked back to a window vantage. "You see, Helmuth, you want her to give up a whole lot to gain you a bunkmate."

"It's not like that," Helmuth insisted, thumping his leg in frustration. "I just mean—"

"Oh, Christ!" the girl said loudly. "Can't you just get on with your ambush?"

"Well, not till Hammer's boys come through," chuckled the sergeant. "They're so good, they can't run a convoy to schedule."

"S-sergeant," the young soldier said, "She doesn't understand." He turned to Margritte and gestured with both hands, forgetting the weapon in his left. "They won't take you back, those witches out there. The, the rec girls at Base Denzil don't go home, they can't. And you know damned well that s-somebody's going to catch it out there when it drops in the pot. They'll crucify you for helping us set up, the ones that're left."

"It doesn't matter what they do," she said. "It doesn't matter at all."

"Your life matters!" the boy insisted.

Her laughter hooted through the room. "My life?" Margritte repeated. "You splashed all that across the field an hour ago. You didn't give a damn when you did it, and I don't give one now—but I'd only follow you to hell and hope your road was short."

Helmuth bit his knuckle and turned, pinched over as though he had been kicked. Sgt. Counsel grinned his tight, equals grin. "You're wasted here, you know," he said. "And we could use you. Maybe if—"

"Sarge!" Landschein called from his window. "Here they come."

Counsel scooped up a rocket launcher, probing its breech with his fingers to make sure of its load. "Now you keep down," he repeated to Margritte. "Backblast'll take your head off if their shooting don't." He crouched below the sill and the rim of the armor shielding him, peering through a periscope whose button of optical fibers was unnoticeable in the shadow. Faced inward toward the girl, Landschein hunched over the other launcher in the right corner of the protected area. His flechette gun rested beside him and one hand curved toward it momentarily, anticipating the instant he would raise it to spray the shattered convoy. Between them, Helmuth knelt as stiffly as a statue of gray-green jade. He drew a buzzbomb closer to his right knee where it clinked against the barrel of his own weapon. Cursing nervously, he slid the flechette gun back out of the way. Both his hands gripped reloads, waiting.

The cars' shrill whine trembled in the air.

Margritte stood up by the door, staring out through the windows across the hall. Dust plumed where the long, straight roadway cut the horizon into two blocks of forest. The women in the fields had paused, straightening to watch the oncoming vehicles. But that was normal, nothing to alarm the khaki men in the bellies of their war cars; and if any woman thought of falling to hug the earth, the fans' wailing too nearly approximated that of the imprisoned children.

"Three hundred meters," Counsel reported softly as the blunt bow of the lead car gleamed through the dust. "Two fifty." Landschein's teeth bared as he faced around, poised to spring.

Margritte swept up Helmuth's flechette gun and leveled it at waist height. The safety clicked off. Counsel had dropped his periscope and his mouth was open to cry an order. The deafening muzzle blast lifted him out of his crouch and pasted him briefly, voiceless, against the pocked inner face of the armor. Margritte swung her weapon like a flail into a triple splash of red. Helmuth died with only a reflexive jerk, but Landschein's speed came near to bringing his launcher to bear on Margritte. The stream of flechettes sawed across his throat. His torso dropped, headless but still clutching the weapon.

Margritte's gun silenced when the last needle slapped out of the muzzle. The aluminum barrel shroud had softened and warped during the long burst. Eddies in the fog of blood and propellant smoke danced away from it. Margritte turned as if in icy composure, but she bumped the door jamb and staggered as she stepped outside. The racket of the gun had drawn the sallow faces of every woman in the fields.

"It's over!" Margritte called. Her voice sounded thin in the fresh silence. Three of the nearer mothers ran toward the storage room.

Down the road, dust was spraying as the convoy skidded into a herringbone formation for defense. Gun muzzles searched: the running women; Margritte armed and motionless; the sudden eruption of children from the dugout. The men in the cars waited, their trigger fingers partly tensed.

Bergen, Della's six-year-old, pounded past Margritte to throw herself into her mother's arms. They clung together, each crooning to the other through their tears. "Oh, we were so afraid!" Bergen said, drawing away from her mother. "But now it's all right." She turned her head and her eyes widened as they took in Margritte's tattered figure. "Oh, Margi," she gasped, "whatever happened to you?"

Della gasped and snatched her daughter back against her bosom. Over the child's loose curls, Della glared at Margritte with eyes like a hedge of pikes. Margritte's hand stopped half-way to the child. She stood—gaunt, misted with blood as though sunburned. A woman who had blasted life away instead of suckling it. Della, a frightened mother, snarled at the killer who had been her friend.

Margritte began to laugh. She trailed the gun three steps before letting it drop unnoticed. The captain of the lead car watched her approach over his gunsights. His short, black beard fluffed out from under his helmet, twitching as he asked, "Would you like to tell us what's going on, honey, or do we got to comb it out ourselves?"

"I killed three soldiers," she answered simply. "Now there's nothing going on. Except that wherever you're headed, I'm going along. You can use my sort, soldier."

Her laughter was a crackling shadow in the sunlight.

●

Tall and stately Jayne Tannehill won her B.A. at Occidental College in Los Angeles and her Master's at San Diego State. She was born, she says, under a grand piano; her mother is a noted choral director. She was on stage when she was four, and is profoundly schooled in all phases of theater. She is a reading specialist with special expertise in dyslexia and hyperkineticism. After twelve years in the San Diego school system, she resigned to become an abridger for a major record company, and to write. When she isn't traveling, she divides her time between San Diego and Los Angeles.

"Eclipse" is the first story I have read which deals with the daily life and personal predicaments of an inhabitant of an "L-5"—the O'Neill space colony which the author feels is the most exciting idea in her lifetime. Good fiction isn't merely ideas; it is and must always be people, real people. I think you will agree that the people on Proxmire (*Proxmire?!*) are real—achingly, hurtingly real. This, by the way, is a first sale.

—Theodore Sturgeon
Los Angeles, 1978

ECLIPSE OF THE SON
by Jayne Tannehill

Dear Laura,

I don't know you very well, but Larry came by the house yesterday and happened to mention your dilemma. And Lord knows, child, you have to go through it alone. But I thought I might be able in some small way to help.

It was 1350 L5 when we overpopulated the first time. I was about your age, I guess, when it happened. We all knew the danger. There had been debates and commentaries and editorials for several years warning us of the problems of diminishing air and food supply and social pressures and all that. They even shipped up old literature from Earth, from back in the 1900s when they first faced the problem. And for a while we all worried and such, but after a while we sort of forgot.

Maybe forgot is the wrong word. We wanted to

stop thinking about it because it was too important, too significant, too loud in our minds. With loud concerns like that you forget to be happy on your first date, or even your wedding day. So I guess we just stopped thinking.

But anyway, that was a long time ago. Fred and I celebrated our 50th anniversary this year. And we have been happy even so. Oh, our health isn't all it should be. Fred tried to do too much and threw out his back last month. He spent so many years working in the laboratory he forgets how heavy things are on the rim. And my asthma kicks up now and again. But we really can't complain. We've made out OK and we've never wanted for anything.

Oh, Laura, who am I trying to fool? It's been hard to live with. Especially with what happened later. And it grieves me to see you struggling through it too.

I don't know whether an old lady's memories are much help though. Time dulls things somehow. But I came across something last week that maybe could help. It isn't much; only a diary I kept when I was a girl. But I noticed there were a few entries right around the time Fred and I were married and then a whole bunch when I found out.

Laura, you have to make up your own mind, girl. But I keep remembering wishing I could find out what somebody else would do, had done, so I didn't have to feel so alone and responsible. I guess that was silly. It's an alone thing to do. And Lord knows it's a responsibility.

But for what it's worth, I thought I'd send it on to you. Don't read it if you don't want to. I don't know you too well, so I don't know how you feel about such things. But it is sort of private, so please don't pass it on none. A lot of this I kept real quiet about. Didn't want to hurt no one. 'Specially Fred.

You can forget about the first pages. They were just about school and such. I marked the page I thought where it all started. Now looking back, I wish I'd written every day. But there was so much to do, to work through, so I guess I only wrote when I was troubled. There were happy days too.

But enough of this. I keep going on. Here's my diary. And best of luck to you, girl. Larry's a good man. I know he'll help all he can. He's been a good neighbor and his folks have been good friends for a long time.

Always,
Ruth

* * *

Shutter close. Standard date 5-12-1349
Dear Diary,
I went to the debates tonight. There was a scientist up from Earth and three specialists from the lab. I was really impressed with the debate and I'm glad I didn't have to judge it like the ones in school. I met one of the guys from the lab. His name is Fred and he likes my long hair. He called it cobwebs. He asked for my schedule and said he'd see me around. But I wonder. Why would he look for me? He's so handsome. Even Peggy says so. He's not much taller than I am, but that's OK. I'd sure like to visit the labs. I wonder if he would take me. Mom is worried about my exams. She says I

don't study enough.

Shutter close plus. Standard date 5-13-1349
Dear Diary,

I saw him again. I was afraid to say anything, but I know he saw me. I took my Sociology exam today and couldn't have done worse. I just couldn't concentrate. I hope my project will balance it out or Mom will be furious.

The debaters said last night that only 20 more children could be born on Proxmire at our current population. I wonder if it's really as much of a problem as they think. There's plenty of room on the rim to build. There are all those mountains they put over at 16 kilometers. They could put houses there. Or eliminate the mountains. After all, they put them there.

Shutter open. Standard date 5-20-1349
Dear Diary,

My cough is bad this morning and Mom says I have to stay home. Rats. Mom was talking last night about Earth traditions. Julie is getting married next month and Mom wants her to have a traditional wedding. I don't think there's been one on Proxmire since I was born. Mom says that brides wear white to symbolize purity. I wonder why Earth people put so much importance on that. Mom has a disadvantage, I guess, moving out here after growing up on Earth.

Shutter close. Standard date 5-25-1349
Dear Diary,

Finished an old Earth book called *The Population Bomb* today. They sure had big families. No wonder Earth was afraid it would overpopulate.

That could never happen here because nobody has more than two kids. Why would anyone want a bigger family? After all it only takes two of us to keep up the garden and do the chores. And where would they all sleep?

Julie had a long talk with Mom about her wedding and talked her into a simple ordinary wedding. So it looks like Tom will wear earth colors and Julie will wear sky colors, the way everyone else does. I'm glad. I wouldn't want everyone staring at us and talking about us as if we were from Earth.

Shutter open. Standard date 6-30-1349
Dear Diary,

I was just too tired to write last night. Julie and Tom had their wedding at shutter close and it was so beautiful. Everyone came to the glen strip at 7 kilometers and the trees were all strung with white lights—all the way around. It looked just like stars at eclipse. All the rest of the lights in the colony were turned out. So all you could see was the little lights. They said their vows and the whole colony sang them the welcome song. I stopped singing so I could hear the voices above us echoing. And then after the singing everyone lit his electric torch and you could see people all around the rim. And then there were parties all through the glen strip, and Julie and Tom and the families visited all of them. I drank so much champagne I got silly and Mom made me eat something.

And there was dancing. And Fred asked me to dance. And then he went with us to all the other parties. It was so fantastic. I wonder what it would be like to be married to Fred.

Shutter close. Standard date 10-20-1349
Dear Diary,

Julie lost her baby today and found out she can't have any kids. She is so very sick, she has to stay at the lab hospital. Tom is super upset and Mom has been crying all day. Funny, I didn't even know she was pregnant. Mom knew, I guess, but nobody told me. Right now I can't figure out whether Mom's more upset because Julie's so weak or because this means she won't be a grandmother. I wonder if I'm going to have kids. If Julie can't, I guess it's sort of up to me to carry on the family traditions and all.

Shutter close. Standard date 10-21-1349
Dear Diary,

Fred brought us news from the hospital about Julie. I was so shocked to see him. It never occurred to me that he would pay attention to Julie and her baby. But it was just outstairs from his office.

I was kind of mad at him though. He didn't tell Mom this. I guess he figured she was upset enough. But when we went out for a walk he told me it was a good thing Julie lost her baby because there were three other babies expected. Sometimes I think he takes his job a little too far. Just because he's an environmental studies technician doesn't mean he can decide whether people can have kids or not.

Shutter close. Standard date 10-25-1349
Dear Diary,

Julie went home today. She and Tom are exchanging quarters with a couple at 8 kilometers, over in the recreation area. It's an apartment instairs on level two. There aren't any little kids over there—just singles and couples who chose not to have children. Tom thinks it will be easier for her over there. I'll miss her. It was nice to look out my window and see up to her house. It made it seem like she was still part of the family more. But I guess I'll see her a lot. Tom suggested I come over and meet some of the guys at the club.

Shutter close. Standard date 12-1-1349
Dear Diary,
I just realized I haven't written anything for months. After Tom and Julie moved I went over to the club and the first person Tom "introduced" me to was Fred. Imagine that. My own brother-in-law sets me up with the one guy I've been dying to date. And it's been so great. He's so thoughtful. He sends me flowers and fruit. He even sent me some things called pomegranates. The seeds were sent up from Earth. And he writes such beautiful poetry and songs. Last week he took me to his neighborhood to meet his parents. He knows mine, of course. I'm so lucky.

Shutter close. Standard date Holiday 1-1349
Dear Diary,
There was a big celebration at the labs today and Fred took me on a grand tour. It was incredible moving through the pressure lifts. Everyone wanted to try flying in the core and Fred got us permission so we got to spend a few minutes in weightlessness. It was so strange. I sort of had to work up to it. It was so disorienting. I can't imagine working there. But Fred says the most important research goes on in the very core we visited. The walls are lined with magnetic clips and tools. We could only stay a little bit and I was sort of glad when it was over. Fred showed me where he works. Even there everything is so light. His experiments

now don't need the environment, but they didn't have anywhere else outstairs to move him so he just works there anyway. But sometimes he works on projects like getting people used to less gravity. He explained it all and why they do it, but it didn't make sense. Something about space conversion. Who knows. It was a super day. We spent the whole day together.

Shutter close plus. Standard date Holiday 2-1349
Dear Diary,

After shutter close today Fred and I took a long walk into the glen strip. It was so romantic. I kept remembering the night of Julie's wedding and how Fred danced with me and how happy I was, and then, when we reached the very spot Julie and Tom said their vows, he asked me to marry him. This is the most beautiful day of my whole life. We came back through the glen across the other side so we could see the house while we were walking. I didn't know what we were going to tell Mom and Dad. But Fred handled the whole thing and told them how he felt about me and taking care of me, and his job at the lab and all that. And Mom cried. And Dad got out a bottle of champagne to celebrate. It was so fantastic. I never dreamed I could be so happy.

Shutter open. Standard date Holiday 4-1349
Dear Diary,

I have to dash. Fred is picking me up and we are walking over to the club to meet Julie and Tom. We spent all yesterday together making plans and seeing friends to tell them. Julie and Tom don't know yet. I can't wait to tell them.

Shutter close. Standard date Holiday 5-1349

Dear Diary,

Now that holiday is over, I won't get to see Fred every day for a long time. I asked Fred today why we have 5 day holidays every 13 months and he said to try to keep our years like Earth. Since Earth has a year of 365 days, we do too. But we don't have seasons so we just divide up the year into 13 equal parts, with a few days left over. I asked him why 13, but he didn't know. Oh, well, I guess that's as good a reason for a holiday as any. At least I got to see Fred for five days.

Shutter close. Standard date 1-1-1350
Dear Diary,

This is the first day of the year in which I'm getting married. That calls for a celebration. Mom's been talking about New Year's resolutions all day. She really tries hard to keep all the Earth traditions. I feel kind of sorry for her sometimes.

Today Fred and I decided to get married on 3-1-1350. It happens to be a total eclipse so we can have the shutters open for our vows and have real stars as well as the tree top stars. I'm so excited. I picked out the material for my dress today and Mom is going to start it tomorrow. It's so pretty. It matches my eyes.

Fred said he doesn't think we'll be able to have children so we'll probably move near Julie and Tom. He's going to check the population studies tomorrow. I hope we can. I love kids. And I don't want to disappoint Mom.

Shutter close. Standard date 1-5-1350
Dear Diary,

Fred found out today that only 5 more children can be planned for this population. He thinks we should pass it up and let someone else have the kids. I guess there are some advantages, but I can't help thinking about Mom. Julie can't have kids and Mom's been waiting to be a grandmother ever since we were born. I guess it's mainly because she has no family here on Proxmire. Me, I've got more cousins and second cousins and aunts and uncles than I could ever need. But Mom just has us, and Dad, of course. Dad's family just never took her in, bein' as how she was from Earth.

Shutter close. Standard date 2-30-1350
Dear Diary,

I had to stop tonight and write. It's been so busy with parties and sewing and fixing food and making arrangements. But today is all mine. I'm sentimental about things like holidays and celebrations. I really enjoyed my graduation, and today is the next most important celebration of all. Tomorrow, of course, will be the most important. But today is my last day before I get married. Fred wanted to come with me today, but I wouldn't let him. Today I just wanted to be alone and go to all the special spots where all the special things have happened to me. So this is my last entry. Starting tomorrow, I'll be busy at shutter close. I wonder if Fred likes to talk afterwards before he goes to sleep.

This morning I walked around the rim to where Mr. Kramer has his farm. Bob Kramer was my first boyfriend ever. And it was fun to walk all over the farm where we used to walk. From there I walked up to the shutter ramp. That was always my favorite place to sit alone and look at the stars and at Earth. Funny how it feels to look at Earth and know I've got all kinds of kin-folk there. Doubt I'll ever see them. From there I went to town strip and walked the whole row of stores. I don't think I'd walked the whole row that way for 5 or 6 years. Stopped for lunch at the cafeteria, just for a special treat. They painted little houses and grass on the ceiling since I'd been there last. To make it look like you were looking through to the other side. Somebody must have taken a picture from the roof 'cause it looks just like it would if there weren't a ceiling. I wonder why all the stores have solid ceilings. It makes sense on the houses—privacy and all. But why don't the stores have mesh ceilings like the schools do? It would make it a lot more open inside.

Anyway, this afternoon I walked through my school and then I came home and just sat in the living room. Mom kept asking why I was just sitting there so I came into my room so I wouldn't upset her. She looks like she's been crying a lot. Sure can't figure out why. But she cried when Julie got married so I guess it's just another Earth tradition.

I wonder if I'll cry at my kid's wedding?

Shutter open. Standard date 6-4-1350
Dear Diary,

I'm not sure yet, but I just have to tell someone. I think it worked. I think I'm pregnant. For the last couple days I've had sharp cramps that sometimes make me sit down for a while. And my breasts are bigger and heavier and sort of ache. And this morning I just threw up. I'm so excited. Fred doesn't know yet. It's so hard to keep secrets, but I don't want to tell anyone until I know for sure. After all, I wouldn't want everyone to get their hopes up. It's been three months and nobody's asked when we're going to have a baby. They probably figure we decided not to. They'll be so surprised. I'm so excited. Now I've got to find out who we can trade quarters with so we can move to a section for children. I'm going to miss Julie and Tom.

Shutter close. Standard date 6-14-1350
Dear Diary,
It's for sure. I went to the labs for a test and it's sure. I'm going to have a baby! I told Mom this afternoon and she is delighted. We went into town strip and bought all kinds of little clothes. It's like playing with dolls again. I don't know who is more excited, Mom or me. And I can't wait to tell Fred. Why, oh why did this have to be the first night of his big conference? Why did he have to be gone this one night out of the whole year? I hope we have a boy and he looks like Fred. That would be so perfect. Mom says "Be happy either way." But I really do hope it's a boy.

Shutter close. Standard date 6-15-1350
Dear Diary,
Tomorrow Fred will be home at last. I'm going out of my mind, I'm so excited. I found us a new place to trade into. It's just perfect and right near the school. And I'll be closer to Mom. She'll like that. And the baby's room is so lovely with a view of the glen.

Oh, Fred, please hurry home!

Shutter open. Standard date 6-17-1350
Dear Diary,
I can't. I just can't. I'd rather not live. How can he expect me to? I didn't even get to tell him myself. He already knew. Damn that lab technician. Why did he have to tell him? Why couldn't I at least

have had that much? It's not fair. He was so cool. So logical. Doesn't he feel anything? After all, it's his baby too. All he could do is tell me to be grateful. Why should I be grateful? How can I be grateful? What have I got to be grateful about? Be grateful we can project environmental impact? I don't give a damn about environmental impact! I want my baby! Why did I have to be the one? Nobody else has to build up hopes. They all know they can't conceive. They all got to know ahead of time. It's just not fair. I can already feel my body changing. I'm already becoming a mother. Why oh why did I have to be number 6? Why couldn't I have been number 5 or 4? It can't be true. He just stared at me. He looked almost, no, it can't be, almost angry. He didn't even stay this morning. Back to the lab. Damn the lab. Oh, Fred, I'm so scared.

Shutter close. Standard date 6-18-1350
Dear Diary,

I've been wandering out by the shutter ramp today. I didn't want to see people. I thought a lot about transferring down to Earth. I could have my baby there. And Mom's family is there. They'd take care of me, I'm sure. I wonder what it would be like to live on Earth. I think I'd get lonesome not seeing neighbors all around me. Mom says you can see stars most any night just by looking up. And sometimes it gets cold. I wonder what it's like to be cold. And not to see Mom and Dad and Julie and Tom, or the Kramers or the Jordays. I wonder if Fred would go with me.

Shutter close. Standard date 6-20-1350
Dear Diary,

I had to go to the lab today. They want to take my

baby now, but I wouldn't let them. He can't be hurting anything right now. I went past the nursery in the hospital. I want my baby to be in that nursery.

Fred met me for lunch. He asked me to go up to his office to look at the charts. But I don't want to see them. I believe him. He wouldn't lie to me. He doesn't have to prove anything to me. I just wish he'd hear my side. I wish he'd take off work and just stay home and talk to me. I can't make the decision all by myself.

Shutter open. Standard date 6-21-1350
Dear Diary,

I just threw up again. It's been like that all morning. How can I want so much to feel so horrible? Mom says she knows women who got sick so much they didn't want to be pregnant. Right now I'm afraid to feel that way because that hurts even more.

Shutter close. Standard date 6-22-1350
Dear Diary,

Fred spent today with me. We walked through the glen strip just like we did on holiday. I guess he does understand. I want this baby so much. What scares me now is I know he doesn't want the baby. It's not just a matter of his job and knowing there can't be another baby now on Proxmire for maybe another fifteen years. He really doesn't want a baby. I asked him if we could go to Earth. He said it's no better there. They just don't have the controls we have. People can't see the problem. Not like we can. But I don't think he would want to go anyway. And I don't really want to go without Fred.

Shutter close. Standard date 6-23-1350
Dear Diary,

Mom and I talked about Earth today. She said they might have other ways to solve overpopulation now. But I'm sure Fred would have heard at the conference. I thought about it, though. Like what if there were another colony? What if we could go there and have our baby? But we'd have to go alone. Mom and Dad are too settled. It wouldn't be fair to make them start over. I think they would though. At least Mom would. She wants to be a grandmother in the worst way.

Shutter close. Standard date 6-24-1350
Dear Diary,

I walked today. I went into town strip. I saw people I hadn't seen in months. They all remembered my wedding. They were all excited and happy. I smiled on the outside. I couldn't tell anyone. I wonder if anyone knows. We've debated and talked so long about overpopulation. I wonder if anyone knows what it feels like to carry the one extra person that cannot be.

I walked passed the playground and found myself wishing just one of those children would die so my baby could live. I don't like feeling that way.

Shutter close. Standard date 7-12-1350
Dear Diary,

I stopped writing. It seemed pointless to say it over and over. Every day I've waited hoping there would be some alternative. Fred has even stopped pressuring me to get it over with. I guess I've been waiting for someone to die. And what I'm afraid of is that I'm the one who is dying. It's been a month since I've had any time with Fred that we didn't talk about it. He's almost a stranger to me. At first he was so busy with the conference and catching up work. But recently I just haven't been around. I walk a lot. I even walked to the other end of the colony. I was a zombie when they found me and brought me back. I really didn't care any more.

I've been thinking today that I can't wait any more. I'll forget that I can't have the child. I'll forget that it's a nightmare waiting for someone else's child to die.

I saw Julie today. Funny, when she found out she couldn't have kids I sort of felt I'd have them for her. But now I can't do that. But I guess I only really saw Julie today. It had never occurred to me before. She's happy. She can't have kids and she's happy. Maybe I can be happy too.

Shutter close. Standard date 7-20-1350
Dear Diary,

I laughed today. I met Fred at the lab after my check up so we could go the folk's for dinner. And one of the guys was fooling around, making jokes with statistics. Suddenly he looked absolutely serious and asked Fred, "How come they call this godforsaken place Proxmire anyway?" And Fred got that strange look on his face and said, "God only knows." And we all laughed. I'd forgotten how humorous he is. And how he lights up when I laugh.

* * *

Dear Laura,

If you've gotten this far you'll see I stopped writing there. Not living though. I went to the lab on the 13th. Fred was very proud of me. We spent a lot of time together after that. And he sure has been the very best husband. He let me cry a lot the next year when a whole flood of children were born. The technicians figured it was sort of a protest. I could sure understand it. As I remember it your mother was born about then. Could be mistaken. Anyway, we had some good times.

Mom got a job at the nursery school the next year. She always loved babies, and she sure found a good spot to put all that love down. We stayed in the recreation complex until Mom died; then we moved out here to take care of Dad. He missed her. We all did. Funny thing, the older I get the more I sound like her. Seems like farm folk just talk like farm folk even out here in space.

It wasn't easy to do, Laura. But we made a good life for ourselves. And things settled down in a few years. I never thought it would happen again. Not so soon at any rate. I thought we'd learned our lesson back then. Fred says things are worse on Earth these days too.

Laura, don't be afraid to be angry. That's where I went wrong. I was afraid to let anyone know it hurt and that I was mad. Found out later people really knew all along.

I found myself wishing for your sake that somewhere on Proxmire a child would die so you could keep your baby. But that's no good. I went through that craziness once. I don't wish it for me or for you.

It's all about life, Laura. No matter what you decide, don't forget to go on living.

Always,
Ruth

A lot of people come from Peoria, like it that way, and never go back. Philip Jose Farmer, who is unlike anyone else on this planet or any of its associated universes, does come from Peoria and did go back. This extraordinary man, with a cut-rock face like those you'll find on Mount Rushmore and a surprising component of gentle shyness, this prolific and often outrageous giant is owed a profound debt by all of science fiction. In 1951 he wrote a story in which he revealed that spacemen after a long voyage are horny and need relief; further, the exquisite creature who supplied it, caught him by the glands and then by the heart, turned out to be of another species—indeed, another genus. This short novel, *The Lovers*, was pivotal, shackle-breaking. Whether or not you find the sexual content in science fiction enjoyable or deplorable, I don't think you'll argue with me that freedom is good and slavery—censorship—is bad, and the appearance of that one courageous story (through the insistence of an equally courageous editor, Samuel Mines) gave sf a quantum leap into its current status as the only field of literature which, in its breadth and scope and freedom of thought, can rival poetry. The victory lies not in that sex must be in sf, but that it may. Farmer told me wistfully not long ago that everyone had forgotten *The Lovers* and its effects. This is to tell you, Phil, that we haven't.

All of which is a fairly heavy preface to one of his lighter effusions, typically outrageous and full of inside jokes. Have fun.

—Theodore Sturgeon
Los Angeles, 1978

THE LAST RISE OF NICK ADAMS
by Philip Jose Farmer

Nick Adams, Jr., science-fiction author, and his wife were having the same old argument.

"If you really loved me, you wouldn't be having so much trouble with *it*."

"There are many words for *it*," Nick said. "If you didn't have a dirty mind, you'd use them. Anyway, there are plenty of times when you can't complain about *it*."

"Yeah! About once every other month I can't!"

Ashlar was a tall scrawny ex-blonde who had been beautiful until the age of thirty-seven-and-a-half. Now she was fifty. A hard fifty, Nick thought. And here am I, a soft fifty.

"It does have a sort of sine-wave action," he said. "I mean, if you drew a graph ..."

"So now *it's* dependent on weather conditions. What're we supposed to do, consult the barometer when we make love? Why *don't* you make a graph of *its* rises and falls? Of course, you'd have to have some rises first..."

"I got to go to work," he said. "I'm months behind..."

"I'll say you are, though I don't mean in your writing! All right, hide behind the typewriter! Bang your keys; don't bang me!"

He rose from the chair and dutifully kissed her on her forehead. It was as cold and hard as a tombstone, incised with wrinkles that read *Here Lies Love. R.I.P.* She snarled silently. Shrugging, he walked up the steps toward his office. By the time he reached the third floor, he was sweating as if he were a rape suspect in a police lineup. His panting filled the house.

Fifty, out of breath, and low on virility. Still, it wasn't really his fault. She was such a cold bitch. Take last night, for instance. Ashlar's eyes had started rolling, and her face was falling apart underneath the makeup. He had said, "Did you feel something move, little rabbit?" (He was crazy about Hemingway.) And she had said, "Something's *going* to give. Get off. I got to go to the toilet."

Once it had all been good and true, and he had felt the universe move all the way to the Pole Star. Now he felt as if the hair had fallen off his chest.

He sat down before the typewriter and stroked the keys, the smooth and cool keys, and he pressed a few to tune up his fingers and warm up the writing spirit. He could feel the inspiration deep down within, shadow-boxing, rope-skipping, jogging, sweating, pores open, heart beating hard and true, ready to climb into the ring.

The only trouble was, the bell rang, and he couldn't even get out of his corner. He was stuck on the first word. *The. The* ... what?

If only he could see some pattern in his sexual behavior. Maybe the silly bitch's sarcastic remark about making a graph wasn't so stupid. Maybe ...

A bell rang, and he sprang up, shuffling, his left shoulder up, arm extended ... what was he doing? That was the front doorbell, and it was probably announcing the delivery of the mail. Nick gave the mailman ten dollars a month to ring the doorbell. This was illegal, but who was going to know? Nick could not endure the idea that a hot check was cooling off in the mailbox.

He hurried downstairs, passing Ashlar, who wasn't going to get off her ass and bring the mail to him. Not her.

Since this was the first of the month, there were ten bills. But there was also a pile of fan mail and a letter from his agent.

Ah! His agent had sent a check, the initial advance on a new contract. Two thousand dollars. Minus his agent's ten percent commission. Minus fifty dollars for overseas market mailings. Minus twenty-five for the long-distance call his agent had made to him last month. Minus a thousand for the loan from his agent. Minus fifty for the interest on the loan. Minus ten dollars accounting charge.

Only six hundred and sixty-five dollars remained, but it was a feast after last month's famine. By the time he'd finished reading the fan letters, all raving about the goodness and truth of his works, he felt as if he was connected to a gas station air pump.

Suddenly, he knew that there was a pattern to the decline and fall of the Roman Empire he carried between his legs. In no way, however, was he going to take the edge off his horniness by explaining the revelation to Ashlar just now. He dropped his mail and his pants, and he hurried to the kitchen. Ashlar was bent over, putting dishes in the washer.

He flipped up her skirt, yanked down her panties, and said, "The dishes can wait, but *it* can't."

It would all have been good and true and the earth might have moved if Ashlar hadn't gotten her head caught between the wire racks of the washer.

"You're getting fat again, aren't you?" Ashlar said. "That's *some* spare tire you got. And you missed a patch on your cheek when you shaved. Listen, I know this isn't time to talk about it, but my mother . . . what's the matter? Why are you stopping?"

Nick snarled and he said, "If you need an explanation, you're an imbecile. I'm pulling out like a train that stopped at the wrong station. I'm going back to my typewriter. A woman will always screw you up, but a typewriter's a typewriter, true and trustworthy, and it doesn't talk to you when you're making love to it."

Two minutes later, while Ashlar beat on the door with her fists and yelled at him, the typewriter keys jammed and he couldn't get them unstuck.

You couldn't even put faith in a simple machine. You could not trust anything. Everything that was supposed to be clean and good and true went to hell in this universe. Still, you had to stick with it, be a man with *conejos*. Or was it *cojones*? Never mind. Just tell yourself, "Tough shit," and "My head is bloody but unbowed. You have to die but you don't have to say Uncle."

That was fine, but the keys were still stuck, and Ashlar wouldn't quit beating on the door and screaming.

He got up, cursing and yanked the door open.

Ashlar fell sobbing into his arms.

"I'm sorry, sorry, sorry! What a bitch I am! Here's the whole earth about ready to move all the way down to its core, and I pick on you!"

"Yes, you're truly a bitch," he said. "But I forgive you because I love you and you love me and no matter what happens we have something that is good. However..."

He wasn't going to say anything about his discovery of the pattern. Not now. He'd test his theory later.

An hour afterward, he said, panting, "Listen, Ashlar, let's take a vacation. We'll go to the World Science-Fiction Convention in Las Vegas. We'll have fun, and in between parties and shooting craps, we'll make love. The good true feeling will come back while we're there."

Or should he have said the true good feeling? What the hell was the correct order of adjectives in a phrase like that?

It didn't matter. What did was that Ashlar decided to go to the convention and didn't even complain that she had nothing to wear. Moreover, his theory had worked out. Up to a point, anyway, and that wasn't really his fault. The fans crowded around him, begging for his autograph, and he heard never an unkind word. As if this wasn't heady enough, not to mention the stimulation of his male hormones, three of the greatest science-fiction authors in the world invited him to dinner and paid him many compliments over the bourbons and steaks.

The first, Zeke Vermouth, Ph.D., the wealthiest writer in the field, didn't mention that they were going Dutch until after the meal was eaten. Even this didn't lessen Nick's pleasures. And then, glory of glories, Robin Hindbind, the dean of science-fiction authors, had him in for a private supper. Nick was as happy as a man with a free lifetime pass to a massage parlor. It was fabulous to sit in the suite, which was as spacious as Nick's house, and eat with the creator of such classics as *Water Brother Among the Bathless, I Will Boll No Weevil* and the autobiographical *Time Enough For F°°°ing*, subtitled *Why Everybody Worships Me*.

Then, wonder of wonders, the grand old man, Preston de Tove himself, asked Nick to a very select party. De Tove was probably Nick's greatest hero, the man who had rocked the science-fiction world in the 40s with his smashing *Spam!* and *The World of Zilch A*.

De Tove, however, hadn't done much writing for thirty years. He'd been too busy practicing a science of mental health originated by another classic author, old B.M. Kachall himself. This was M.P. (Mnemonic Peristalsis) Therapy, a psychic discipline which claimed to enable a person to attain through its techniques an I.Q. of 500, perfect recall, Superman's or Wonder Woman's body, and immortality.

In essence, these techniques consisted in keeping your bowels one hundred percent open. To do this, though, you had to work back along your memory track until you encountered in all details, visual, tactile, auditory, olfactory, especially olfactory, your first bowel movement. This was called the P.U. or Primal Urge.

Kachall had promised his disciples that all goals could be reached within a year through M.P. Therapy. However, de Tove, like the majority of Kachall's followers, was, three decades later, still taking laxatives as a physical aid to the mental techniques. He had not lost faith, even if he did spend most of his time during the party in the bathroom.

De Tove had refused to go along with Kachall's S.P.L. Religion, a metaphysical extension of M.P. Therapy. Perhaps this was because de Tove had to wear a diaper at all times, and attendees at the S.P.L. services were forbidden to wear anything. In any event, the religion required that the worshipper send his C.E. (Colonic Ego) back to the first movement of the universe, the Big Bang. If the worshipper survived that, he was certified to be an E.E. (End End), one who'd attained the Supreme Purgative Level. This meant that the E.E. radiated such a powerful aura that nobody would dare to mess around with him. Or even get near him for that matter.

Aside from having had to sit by an open window throughout the party, Nick was ecstatic. Nothing better could happen now. But he was wrong. The next day, two Englishmen, G.C. Alldrab and William Rubboys, invited him to a party for avantgarde writers. This twain had been lucky enough to be highly esteemed by some important mainstream critics and so now refused to be classified as mere s-f authors. Nevertheless, when the convention committee offered to pay their airfare, hotel expenses, and booze if they'd be guests, they consented to associate, for three days at least, with the debased category.

Alldrab was chiefly famous for stories in which depressed, impotent, passive, and incompetent antiheroes passed through catastrophic landscapes over which floated various parts, usually sexual, of famous people. He was also hung up on traffic accidents, a symbol to him of the rottenness of

Western civilization, especially the United States. He sneered at plots and storylines.

And so did his colleague. Rubboys was famous for both the unique content and technique of his fiction. It drew mostly on his experiences as a drug addict and peregrinating homosexual. Otherwise, he was a nice guy and not nearly as snobbish as Alldrab, though some were unkind enough to say that his camaraderie with young male fans wasn't entirely due to his democratic leanings.

Lately, he'd been getting a lot of flack from feminist critics, who loathed his vicious attitude towards all women, though he claimed it was purely literary. They couldn't be blamed. Try though they might to ignore his bias because of his high reputation as a writer, they'd gotten fed up with his numerous references to females as cunts, gashes, twats, slits, and hairy holes.

Rubboys' technique consisted of putting a manuscript through a shredder, then pasting the strips at random for the finished product.

Nick didn't care for either man's works, though he did admit that Alldrab's fiction made more sense than Rubboys'. But then whose didn't? However, to be their guest was an honor in some circles, and these were the critics with clout. Maybe they'd take some notice of him now—glory through association.

Nick was told that, even though he was middle-aged and wrote mostly square commercial stuff, he had been invited because of his experimental time-travel story, *The Man Who Buggered Himself.* This was great stuff, obscure and unintelligible and quasipoetic enough to satisfy the artiest of the arty.

Nick just grinned. Why should he tell them he had written the story while drinking muscatel and smoking opium?

The party was a success until midnight. Alldrab pissy-assed drunk by then, tried to get his mistress to take Rubboys' rented car out and drive it at 100 mph into a lamppost. Thus he could witness a real crash and transpose it into sanguinary poetry in his next novel, *Smash!*, get to the root of the evilness in Occidental culture.

His mistress didn't care for this. In fact, she became hysterical. Rubboys wasn't too keen about it either.

Result: a stampede of pale tight-faced guests out of the door, Nick in the lead, while the girl-friend was dialing the police.

Ashlar was curious about why Nick had been so horny during the convention and for some weeks after that, then had quickly reverted to steerhood.

"What's the matter with you?" Ashlar said after one particularly distressing attempt. "Again?"

She dropped her cigarette ashes on his pubic hairs, causing him to delay his reply until he put out the fire.

"I'll tell you!" he roared. "You're always putting me down, literally and figuratively. Criticising me. You deflate my ego and hence my potency.

"The same thing happens when I get bad reviews or fan mail that knocks me or a rejection slip. But when fans and critics and authors praise me, which doesn't happen often, I'm inflated. There's no doubt about it. I've determined scientifically that my virility waxes and wanes in direct proportion to the quantity-cum (no pun intended) -quality of the praise or bumraps I receive."

"You can't be serious?"

"I drew a graph. It isn't exactly a bell-shaped curve. More like a limp cactus."

"You mean I got to say only nice things about you, keep my mouth shut when you bug me? Treat you like an idol of gold? You're not, you know. You have feet of clay—all the way up to your big bald spot."

"See, that's what I mean."

They quarreled violently for three hours. In the end, Ashlar wept and promised she's quit pointing out his faults. Not only that, she'd praise him a lot.

But that wasn't honest, and so it didn't work out. He knew she was lying when she told him how handsome he was and what a great writer he was and how he was the most fantastic stud in the world.

To make things worse, his latest book was panned by one hundred percent of the reviewers.

"Thumbs down; everything's down," Nick said.

A week later, things got good again. Better than good. He was as happy as Aladdin when he first rubbed the bride given him by the magic lamp.

Dubbeldeel Publications came through with some unexpected royalties on a three-year-old book. The publisher offered to buy another on the basis of a two-page outline. Nick got word that a Ph.D. candidate at UCLA was writing a thesis on his works. The fan mail that week was unusually heavy and not one of its writers suggested that he wrote on toilet paper.

It did not matter now that he doubted Ashlar's sincerity. People with no ulterior motives were comparing him with the great Kilgore Trout.

He was so happy that he suggested to Ashlar that they take another vacation, attend a convention in Pekin, Illinois, which was only ten miles from their hometown, Peoria. Ashlar said that she'd go, even if she didn't like the creeps that crowded around him at the cons. She'd spend her time in the bar with the wives of the writers. She could relax with them, get away from shoptalk that wearied her so when the writers got together. The wives didn't care for science-fiction and seldom read even their husband's stuff. Especially their husband's stuff.

Nick wasn't superstitious. Even so he regarded it as a favorable omen when he saw the program book of the convention. In big bold letters on the cover was the name of the convention. It should have been Pekcon, fan slang for Pek(in) Con(vention). But it had come out Pekcor.

Later, Nick admitted that he'd interpreted the signs and portents wrongly. Had he ever!

At first, things went as well as anyone could ask for. The fans practically kissed his feet, and the regard of his peers was very evident. Some even paid for the drinks, instead of leaving him, as usual, to sweat while he settled a staggering bill.

Ashlar should have been happy. Instead, she complained that she couldn't spend the rest of her life attending conventions just to have a good sex life.

Nick got to talking with an eighteen-year-old fan with long blonde hair, a pixie face, huge adoring eyes, boobs that floated ahead of her like hot-air balloons, and legs like Marlene Dietrich's. Her last name was Barkis, she was willing, and he was overcome by temptation. They went to her room, and the sexual-Richter scale hit 8.6 and was on its way to a record 9.6 when Ashlar began beating at the door and screaming at him to open it.

Later, he found out that a writer's wife had seen him and Barkis entering her room. She had raced around the hotel until she found Ashlar, who hadn't wasted any time getting the hotel dick and three wives as witnesses.

All the way to Peoria, Ashlar didn't stop yelling or crying. Once there, she swiftly packed and took a taxi to her mother's house. She didn't stay there long, since she had been so angry that she'd forgotten her mother had recently gone to a nursing home. Unfazed, she moved into an expensive hotel and sent her bills through her lawyer to Nick.

Each day he got a long letter from her—each deflating. Throwing them unread into the wastepaper basket didn't work. He was too curious, he had to open them and see what new invectives and unsavory descriptions she had come up with. So, after long thought, he sold the house and moved from Illinois to New Jersey. Only his agent had his forwarding address, and Nick told him to return all letters from his wife to her.

"Mark them: *Uninterested*."

But he knew that she would find him some day.

Three months passed without a letter from her. Things went as well as could be expected in this world where hardly anybody really gave a damn how you were doing. He did find a young fan, "Moomah" Smith, who was eager to spend a night with him when he got good mail, good notices, and good royalties.

And then, one morning as he was drinking coffee just before tackling the typewriter, the phone rang. His agent's new secretary, one he didn't know, was calling. Her employer was in Europe, (cavorting around on his ten percent, Nick thought), but she had good news for him. Sharper & Rake, really big hardcover publishers, had just bought an outline for a novel, *A Sanitary Brightly Illuminated Planet*, and they were going to give him a huge advance. Furthermore, Sharper & Rake intended to go all out in an advertising and publicity campaign.

The first letter was from a member of the committee which handled the Pulsar Award. This was given once a year by SWOT, the Science-Fiction Writers of Terra. Nick belonged to this, although its chief benefit was that he could deduct the membership dues from his income tax. However, one of his stories, *Hot Nights on Venus*, had been nominated for the Pulsar. And now, and now—the monster felt as if it were the *Queen Mary* heading for port with a stiff wind behind it—he had won it!

"Under no circumstances must you tell anyone about this," the committee member had written. "The awards won't be given until two months from now. We're informing you of this to make sure that you'll be at the annual SWOT banquet in New York."

Nick read the second letter. It was from Lex Fiddler, the foremost American mainstream critic. Fiddler informed him that he had nominated Nick's novel, *A Farewell to Mars*, for the highest honor for writing in the country. This was the MOOLA, the Michael Oberst Literary Award, established fifty years before by a St. Louis brewer. If Nick won it, he would get $50,000, he would be famous, his book would be a best seller, and an offer from Hollywood was a sure thing even if it didn't get the award.

Nick was so happy he put off opening the third letter.

Whooping with joy, he whirled around and around, the end of his mighty walloper knocking over vases and flipping ash trays from tables. He stopped dancing then because he was so dizzy. Leaning on a table for support, gazing at the ever-expanding thing, he groaned, "I've got to get Moomah here. Only ... I hope she doesn't faint when she sees it."

It was Nick who fainted, not Moomah. The blood spurted from his head, driving downward as his heart constricted in a final massive endeavor to supply what the ego demanded. His blood abandoned the upper part of his body as if the gargantuan paw of King Kong had squeezed it.

Had Nick been conscious, his terror would have halted the process, reversed it, and put the brobdingnagian in its normal state, limp as an unbaked pizza. But his brain was emptied of blood, and he was aware of nothing as he toppled forward, was held for a moment from going over by the giant member, the end of which was rammed into the carpet, and then he polevaulted forward, his grayish slack face striking the floor.

He lay on his side while the pythonish member, driven by the unconscious, expanded. It swelled as a balloon swells while ascending into the ever-thinner atmosphere. But balloons have a pressure height, a point at which the force within the envelope is greater than its strength and the envelope ruptures violently.

The mailwoman was just climbing into her Jeep when she heard the blast. She whirled, and she screamed as she saw the flying glass and the smoke pouring out from the shattered windows.

The police found it easy to pinpoint the source of the explosion. The cause was beyond them. They shook their heads and said that this was just one of those mysteries of life.

The police did find out that the third letter, the one from the Swedish Embassy in Washington, D.C., was a fake. Whoever had sent it was unknown and likely to remain so. Why would anybody write Nick Adams, Jr., a science-fiction author, to inform him that he had won the Nobel Prize for Literature?

More investigation disclosed that the letters from the Pulsar Award committee and Lex Fiddler were also fakes. So was the call from his agent's secretary telling him that Sharper & Rake was giving him a huge advance. This was eventually traced to Mrs. Adams, but by then she was in Europe and there to stay. Besides, the police could not charge her with anything except a practical joke.

Ashlar is living in Spain today. Sometimes, for no reason that her friends can determine, she smiles in a strange way. Is it a smile of regret or triumph?

Did she write those letters and make that phone call because she knew what they'd do to her husband? Of course, she couldn't have known how much they would do to him; she underestimated the power of ego and the limits of flesh.

Or did she try to bolster his pride, make him feel good, because she still loved him and so was doing her best to make him inflated with happiness for at least a day?

It would be nice to think so.

●

Karen Jollie, as I am sure you erudite people out there are aware, is the author of *Two New Genera (Thoracothrix Gen. Nov. and Polydiniopsis Gen. Nov.) and Five New Species of Spirodiniid Ciliates from the Caecum of the African Elephant: and a Revision of the Subfamily Polydiniellinae Nom. Nov.)* Honest. And it earned her a Master's in biological sciences. She lives in L.A., which is Cleveland, Ohio's loss, and teaches science in a girls' high school. She is one of the very best students I have ever had—a beautiful person who has more separate talents than she has toes. She is a meticulous bio-illustrator and a fine artist and calligrapher. And a writer. Oh, a writer. This is her first sale. By the way—I am far too genteel to have inquired who held the elephant while she captured the ciliates. So don't ask.

"The Works of His Hand, Made Manifest" is one of the finest short stories I have ever read anywhere. It stands every test for structure, for pacing, for suspense, and for that indefinable "something to say" quality. First sale indeed ... where do you go when you start at the top?

—Theodore Sturgeon
Los Angeles, 1978

THE WORKS OF HIS HAND, MADE MANIFEST

by Karen G. Jollie

I

I just want to know what Edmund is. He won't tell me and he knows I won't record the question in my personal log, nor the events that led to the question. Of course he knows. Maybe that's why he chose me. Oh yes, I know now that he chose me. Why did he choose me, what for? What *is* he?

Exceptional. Brilliant, yes, a savant, or whatever they call such phenomena. Only he's a savant on everything, I mean *everything*. Command knows that, everybody knows that. Or assumes it. He's only a lieutenant, but even the Captain treats him with reserved respect. His reputation has preceded him. It's never come to a matter of authority yet, and I hope it never does. I doubt it, though. He has a kind of built-in aura of authority that no one questions, not even Harvester. It is more than authority. He inspires an unflinching sense of trust that begs no alternatives, requires no proofs. He could have chosen to remain apart, share himself with no one, but he chose me.

Why?

I am an ensign, a lowly ensign in my second year of service. I am a science officer—well, an aspiring science officer. Nine long sweaty years and several scary decisions have given me my own small reputation. I'm not going to be humble about anything... I'm good at what I do. I've got a lot to learn yet, I'll be the first to admit it. But I know a lot too, and I'm good at correlating what I know. I've had command officers in engineering or life science, and even one in diplomatics, ask my opinion and follow it. Don't ask me where it comes from. I was born to it, I guess. And worked to it, worked hard. But I see each new problem as a unique challenge, and this is no career to follow while resting on laurels. I still anticipate with horror my first massive flub. Flubs cost lives on starcruisers. I kept wishing they wouldn't keep asking my opinion, until Edmund came along. Now, I actually look forward to an occasional inquiry. I miss them.

Edmund exploded nova-like in the very center of Academy Science Research. I was out on my first starcruiser assignment (where I reaped my first commendation medal) during his phenomenal arrival, so I didn't learn about it until we docked. Already the news was wild, though vague.

This guy had come out of nowhere and sidled into Professor Mayeda's office with a suggestion. The suggestion was the complete plans for a gravity conversion generator that would make warp drive obsolete when it became fully operational... give it seven years, tops. They immediately wrapped him and it under thick covers marked "Top-Secret" in red and green stripes. Nobody knew the physics of the thing except the privileged few in the top-flight Astroengineering Research core. Mayeda tried to recruit this fellow, Edmund Something-or-other (odd name: Finnder, Finnagle, something) into the earth-based research team, but no dice. He just wanted to go home. He'd made his suggestion, now let them work with it. Well, how about Starfleet duty? Join the service, see the Universe. No thanks, says this guy. Too rigid. Mayeda is pulling out his hair. Then Mayeda—my professor Mayeda, my mentor, my second father, my demigod of Astrophysics, Cultural Sapiology, and Engineering—Mayeda figures out the way. He askes questions about unsolved problems. Digs at Edmund's curiosity, at his expertise (where in hell or earth had he picked up his expertise?). Got him into a book, then a lecture series, then a library then a lab, kept him busy with asking and asking Edmund—the walking demeanor of blond country boy, reticent, self-contained, courteous, slightly shy—began to unfold the lotus of his potential. The man with the quiet suggestion that would completely revolutionize galactic travel began to want to learn it all.

(Just like me. Is that why he chose me?)

Mayeda played his fish well, knew the touch of the hook must be light, inviting; the bait must be infinite diversity, that most tempting of draws. And it worked until he tried to make his entry into the Academy official. The coaxed victim broke the surface, lashing sprays of violated privacy. The Federation asked too many questions, buttonholed their people down with ranks and titles, positions and duties; the Federation demanded mind-pattern readings and proficiency tests, physical and mental exams. No, said Edmund nononono.

Mayeda nearly lost him, but Mayeda is nothing but resourceful and influential. He nudged the brass, used his full armory of colleagues in an intimidating chorus of protest, beguiled, threatened, begged. Edmund was an exception. Edmund must be accepted on an exceptional basis. The Federation would be mad to lose him. The whole teetering juggernaut of bureaucracy shuddered under the onslaught, whimpered in anxiety, and melted into powerlessness. Mayeda rose above the steaming rubble, victorious, and Edmund was slipped into Academy Level One without as much as a security clearance.

They never tried to find out what Edmund is. They don't ask.

Edmund started taking course final exams. He was jumped to Level Three in two weeks. He studied on his own, got his own lab for independent research. He could have graduated Level Six within six months, but Mayeda put him in for Postwork, Exam-Proficiency, and enrolled him for Ensign Training, Level Two, simultaneously. So he trained on Star Ship Engineering—Manual, mornings; and Telemetry—Accelerated, afternoons; and passed one advanced course a week. In another four months he came out of Postwork at Level Ten, the highest possible attainment, with the same seven degrees it took me years to get (at level eight)—Engineering and Computer Tech, Life Science, Geology, Sapiology, Astrophysics, Chemistry, and Navigation. Ten *months*, I'm saying, and at level Ten! That made him an operating Lieutenant, Science, and eligible for prime assignment. Man, you just don't pick up seven doctorate-level degrees in ten months! *You* don't.

259

That's when I got back. I went to see Mayeda almost as soon as debriefing was completed, but I was aware of the flying talk already, so when I got into the Academy grounds, I didn't expect Mayeda to even remember his number-one son of a year ago. I had been the first Science Officer candidate he had gotten completely through the program in more than four years.

Now I was the second. And I felt like an idiot. I decided I wasn't going to like this Edmund What's-his-name.

Mayeda wasn't there. Mayeda wouldn't be due there until Friday. He was off at the Sprague Research Center doing theoretical run-throughs on a new project (read: gravity converter generator—this is supposed to be unofficial rumor). Sorry.

I meandered across campus miserable, feeling rejected, the runt of a two-pup litter. I stopped in the Union for lunch, but somebody at the next table started talking about this Edmund fellow who was, I gathered, killing time until his starcruiser assignment was cleared by writing a couple of books of poetry and doing some silicon-lead sculpture that was blowing everybody's mind. I lost my appetite and wandered out again. I decided to check into my assigned quarters.

I'm only an ensign and would normally rate a six-man bunker while on interassignment standby, but for some reason I had been given two-man accommodations in the junior officers' residence. I puzzled gleefully on that one, wondering whether my earned Medal of Commendation had anything to do with it. I almost forgot my disappointment over Mayeda's defection. I called to have my kit transferred from Docking Central: Personnel and went up to check into the mysterious depths of an officer's *sanctum sanctorum*. The lounge came complete with mystical indirect light and personalized Muzak per chair. I settled a moment, sighing, toying with the periodicals like I belonged there. I ignored the sideways scrutiny of two junior lieutenants who didn't question my presence with more than their eyes. An Engineering newsletter seemed to cling at my fingertips, so I glanced at it, noted a name—Findell—a piece on an electronics mastermind. Yes, Findell. Edmund Findell. Would I never stop being reminded? I cast it down in disgust and sought out my personal quarters. M-31.

The corridor was beige, buzzing with the low murmur of offical voices and air conditioners. I glanced at the paired name-plaques beside each door, all looking very permanent, though most were there less than a month and some for maybe two days, tops. Harrison, Giardo, Turner, Hasselblad, Arthur, Chellopsa, Tlitgli. Aliens, probably. I'd met few alien enlisteds, even fewer officers. I'd worked under one on my first assignment, a Morkadian. Like every human, I had had to go through those wrenching steps of adjustment, learning to raise humanoid to human, then non-humanoid vertebrate to human, then carapasoids, then inverts, then non-carbons. You've got to be flexible and open-minded in this service, or they'll cash you in, no refund, in a minute. They select for it, looking for that unique paradox in the human perception that combines the ability to discriminate to the finest degree, with the resistance to discrimination by prejudgment. Aliens can be fascinating, but you've got to keep a tight rein on your initial human inclinations.

There it was. The gleaming black plaque with the white embossed letters: Steward, Jeremy A., Ensign. The door had its white symbols too, M-31. Under mine was my roommate's plaque: Findell, Edmund G., Lieutenant.

I stopped. About eighty different impulses collided with my voluntary motor functions simultaneously. I was angry, flabbergasted, red, green and purple. I was confused. I wouldn't go in there. I would go to Housing Central, blow my top, get it changed. No. That would be too obvious. Why the hell was I letting rumor buffalo me? He probably wasn't in there right now anyway. I wanted to fight, I wanted to run. Hold it now, just hold it.

I went back to the lounge and sat for maybe a half-hour, letting my glands and my rationality battle it out. Face it, Jeremy, old kid, you're jealous. The guy's got a brain, Mayeda starts drooling for another good Federation Science Officer candidate, and ol' Jer gets jealous, just because he's used to being Mayeda's pride-and-joy. This Edmund is a brother-technician, remember, interested in the same things you are. He won't look at you like a stunned toad if you make some offhand remark about magmic convection currents or hyperspace flutter or correctional molecular manipulation on hydrocarbon synthesizers. Face it, Jer—with the exception of Mayeda, there are few others you *can* make diverse offhand references to, without being stared at. Whole-Field Scientists aren't just hanging around in every department, you know. Give the guy a chance. Who knows, you might even like him!

Well, tolerate him.

When I finally decided to enter my assigned quarters, no one else was there.

He was tall and well-muscled, yet so proportioned that there was no impression of massiveness. He stood easily; the slant of his hip and the bend of the knee showed no nervousness. The most startling feature about him from a distance was his hair. Worn long and full, it was neither the washed-out anemia of platinum, nor the hedonistic fullness of honey; but gold rather, metallic in distant gleam. No wonder he intimidated people. I watched from the Union steps after making inquiries at the Physics Department. He stood under a tree talking with two navigation students, explaining some concept with broad sweeps of his long-fingered hands. The group erupted into laughter and broke apart in fragments, the students drifting away toward engineering, Edmund turning to continue on his way to the Union. After two steps, his eye caught me standing there regarding him. Waiting. He paused a fraction of a second, as if he knew who I was and what my intent. He never took his eyes from my face as he approached, and he stopped at the bottom of the steps and waited too.

His eyes stole the lights from his hair. They were grey. Not a flat, nor a colorless, lifeless pure grey as the name of the color implies, but a shifting and subtle hue full of complexities, acting as if grey were actually made up of infinitesimal droplets of all of the spectrum as intermixed evenly, constantly moving. The eyes were a flat, depthless surface at first, as if seeing were inward or through other portals than merely his eyelids. They opened out suddenly, drawing all in like the mouth of a whirlpool, inward to some unknown bottomless distance. Yes, one could get lost in those eyes and forget one's own thoughts and intents. So I blinked and looked down, while a prickly sensation began racing up through my spine.

"Did you want something?" he asked quietly.

I expected the voice before I heard it. It was low and carried well, but there was a slight accent I couldn't interpret that softened the consonants and made the vowels broader.

"Yes," I said and tried to project an open smile. "You're Findell, aren't you?"

He sighed and nodded. Perhaps he thought I was another curious student, who'd heard of The Genius and needed some outward manifestation of his mental prowess to convince myself of his reality. I saw it all suddenly, felt myself slipping into his place, becoming a Phenomenon, gaining an astounding reputation in an astoundingly short time.

A Freak.

A man on display like a two-headed calf that people felt justified in holding at arm's-length, examining and exclaiming their wary and delighted surprise. He was used to it, though. He had armed himself long ago, and his expression of weary patience was edged with a touch of sardonic humor, as he examined me and waited for my first probe into his unlikely existence. I knew that feeling of apartness from my own descent into the crushing demands of Federation Academia, that terrible isolation that comes from being exceptional even among many exceptional people.

I didn't want to hate him any more.

"We're assigned to room together," I said. "I'm Jeremy Steward. I just wanted to meet you, maybe have a talk over coffee or something."

He relaxed visibly. He came up the steps and held out his hand. "I'd be delighted to," he said. His grip was dry and sure. "So you are the intrepid Mr. Steward, late of the *Liberty*. You must explain to me that unpleasant interlude on Penelgir IV. We share the same advisor, did you know?"

"Yes," I said, and locked my jealousy in the right rear drawer of my mental bureau. But I didn't throw away the key. Not yet.

He wanted to know all about the Penelgir Expedition, so I told him about Penelgir. He wanted to know about starcruiser service in general, so I told him about that. He wanted to know about my training, my childhood, my interests, my hopes. We spent three hours in the Union, finally had dinner, left and went back to the junior officers' lounge and spent another three hours. I talked, he listened, I stopped, he asked, I talked some more.

It was a fascinating evening.

It was only after I bedded down that I realized I knew nothing more about Edmund G. Findell than I did this morning. Tomorrow, I decided, I would have to remedy that.

I have since found that there is no remedy. Edmund was a lot of things, but one thing he was not was garrulous. He was very private, never rude, always punctual. By the time Mayeda got back, I had been beating my head on Edmund's wall for a week and had finally decided to stop because it felt so good. Surprisingly, I felt no rancor or even annoyance, because at last I was beginning to figure him out, but not from what he said.

The reaction of people to Edmund is a wonderful thing to experience. Since I found him accompanying me more and more often, I had plenty of opportunity to observe it.

He awes people, just by being there. He causes some sort of distancing reaction that varies according to the perception of the one distanced. Sometimes it is unabridged hatred, but mostly it isn't that extreme. I have seen bombastic professors back off without the hint of a Parthian shot, ebullient coeds squeak to a mute halt, and even the crustiest of Starfleet admirals wilt and stammer. I haven't yet figured out what it is he *does* to elicit these reactions. He smiles pleasantly enough, is soft-spoken, and I have never heard a threatening remark pass his lips. There is often a shadow of regret passing over those grey eyes, however. I don't know whether or not he understands why he has that effect on people, but I do know how cut-off he feels, and I sometimes wonder how he stands it.

I have known only two people besides myself who can be close to him and still be completely at ease. One is Mayeda and the other didn't meet him until long after this episode occurred. Not that Mayeda or I remain unawed (Edmund can be positively scary sometimes), it's just that we don't allow our respect...no, call it wonder...to get between us and him. I'm almost at the point where I can take his more...well...unearthly aspects for granted. I'll admit there was a time there when I suspected he was an alien, but he's not alien—just unearthly. Sometimes.

I know he's psychic. I suspect he may also be telepathic to a degree. These things don't bother me much because I've met natural telepaths, and I'm slightly psychic myself—I get prickly feelings when something is going to happen. His impressions are more concrete. He was a little hesitant to tell me about them initially, until he understood that I wouldn't think he was crazy. (He told me about the crash of the *Dominant* two days before Starfleet found out.)

He uses those grey eyes like weapons. The day Mayeda got back, I watched him intimidate a nosy psychology professor who wanted to use him in knowledge-retention experiments. Me, I wanted to bust this jerk, just for making the suggestion. But Edmund didn't say a word, just raised his eyes from a coffee cup and leveled them at this guy. There was an aching moment of silence while the professor's face got paler and paler; he could only stare back transfixed. I began to get panicky, fully convinced that looks *could* kill, but just then Edmund released him by looking back down at his coffee. Freed, the shrink fled wordlessly out the side door of the Union. Mayeda was with us and he only glanced at Edmund with eyes that said, "you should have finished him off." Then Edmund began laughing, and I was relieved for him, because I'd seen the hint of pain that had drifted onto his features when he'd dropped his eyes.

Mayeda got busy pulling his usual batch of strings to get the pair of us assigned to the same ship. Meanwhile, Edmund and I began some researches of my own that I had wanted to follow up from the Penelgir Expedition. We used Edmund's own lab space. Mostly it was work on the molecular configuration of eye pigments from nightfliers, but a little was done on some improvements I had in mind for both neural depolarizer circuits and the antigravs that were already in general use. It wasn't the research that enlightened me so much as my "assistant."

By the time our assignments were finalized (I was to be back on the *Liberty* and Edmund was to be with me), I found that verbal communication with him while working on experiments became entirely unnecessary. He knew what I wanted without my asking, I knew what he would suggest without being told. I swear, we were becoming positively symbiotic!

It spilled over into moods, too, his and mine. Sometimes it was a connective thing, a kind of mental unity. I can remember when my mood of especial lunacy transferred itself to him.

We metamorphosed into a two-man disaster team,

spreading garish practical jokes through the Physics department computer read-outs. There were times, too, when he'd pull off to be by himself, spending all afternoon sitting in the middle of his bed with his arms about his knees and staring at nothing and thinking. I could feel that mood coming on, and I learned to respect it. I pursued my social life, or read, or descended into my own contemplative withdrawal, never trespassing, never wanting to.

And then the times of need. So rare, so vital. The first was near the end of our stay at the Academy, a time when the withdrawal became a tortured thing of isolation. I threw away the key to my mental right rear bureau drawer then. I found the strength to break through the wall and to soothe the hurt by being, just being, the friend with no questions asked.

I didn't ask him what he was then, nor will I ever. He will tell me when and if he chooses, but I will never ask. Maybe that's why he chose me.

II

Antibis looks beautiful from 20,000 kilometers, and even better at five. She was a multicolored jewel, a mirrored eye reflecting life in piebald. She was our first mission off the *Liberty*, a simple mission, relatively uncomplicated.

Antibis II was an M-class planet with no report of any sapient life forms. *Liberty* was to check her out for the possibility of colonization, sending down four separate teams to take her planetary pulse. Initial readings looked good. Although the planet was smaller than earth and the atmosphere thinner, it was 12% richer in oxygen and 4% in CO_2 with correspondingly less nitrogen, so acclimatization shouldn't be difficult for any carbon-based form.

A Life Science team was to land in the green belt and survey the ecosystem. The green belt measured great guns in photosynthetic rate, and it only remained to analyze the salient products produced.

A second team was to hit the poles and get a more accurate measure of ice volume, radiation, and cold air convection patterns, so we could start drawing up climate-cycle projections and water supply figures.

The third team was after the three small oceans. They were to take the aquashuttle and would spend a 6-day cruise, figuring out the salt content, currents, bottom configuration, and predominant life forms.

Edmund and I pulled the least desirable assignment, at least to my way of thinking. Mineral exploration. There was a vast grey-belt (it was yellowish actually, but they always refer to the desert expanses as "grey-belts") all around either side of the equator. Chances were good we might find platinum, iridium, or titanium deposits, but even a few base metals in large amounts would be extremely promising for colonization.

We were given Shuttle III and a Lt. Commander Shasudo to pilot. He was to act as our chauffeur to and from, help with the heavy hauling, if any, and generally keep an eye on us. Shasudo made it clear from the beginning that he had no intention of giving us any scientific advice, but we were under his orders and he'd pull rank if any emergency arose. I mentally dubbed him "Mother Henning" as Edmund and I strapped in and waited for the other shuttles to report a "go," so the launch area could decompress.

As we sat there, I began getting that horrible prickly sensation crawling down my back. I glanced at Edmund. He was looking at me, pale, with his lips compressed in a narrow line. "What?" I hissed at him.

He only rolled his eyes at Shasudo's back. I knew what he meant. Shasudo wouldn't abort a mission unless he had some concrete indication of malfunction or something—certainly not because of some funny feeling a raw lieutenant had. I hoped it was a malfunction, something that would show up on the boards. Something minor.

Edmund said nothing, just sat back in his seat, his face waxy, and closed his eyes. Please God, I said under my breath. Something minor. Please. I wondered what Edmund had seen.

We launched into flecked black enormity. The smooth white hull of the *Liberty* loomed above us only momentarily, then Antibis filled our view screen and our consciousness, blue and yellow, circling streaks of white. We glided in gradually, making a full orbit at 78° to the equator before we slipped down far enough to dip a toe into the atmosphere. Shasudo got down to subsonic and we arced over the green belt, watching ice become sea and sea become clouds—spinning streaks of gossamer bursting with the stuff of life—water. It was being spread with a generous hand here, the misty curling fingers encircling the midlatitudes' emerald sea of bluish-green autotrophs—plants waiting as plants have learned to wait over the eons, to nurse from the watery blue breast of the skies and draw their nourishment therefrom.

I longed to press the ship far down along the twisting silver cords of streams, for life drew me, but Shasudo turned then, angling toward the bulging yellow expanse at our left, aiming for the cloudless airs that proclaimed Nature's thoughtlessness. Clear and striking blue, the sky shone as we settled. We bellied into a vast current of speeding atmosphere and turbulence began to shake the craft. It bucked and skittered nervously on the strange fiery airs, and I watched the duned breadths below us skim and shift into golden swirls, a blur racing past fast, too fast. We ran with the blowing sand.

I peered uncertainly at Shasudo, pale and intent at the controls, battling the winds that strove to turn us. I was sure we had long since overshot our designated touch-down point. This was it. This had to be it.

Twice he tried to bring the shuttle around and twice the roaring airs shouldered us roughly. Nearly tipping, we were sucked deeper into the currents and they tightened their invisible grip. I glanced at Edmund, who was sitting forward, as if listening or peering, but at no focus I could locate. One hand gripped the arm of the seat, the other poised over his restraining belt.

"Don't unlatch," I warned. "It looks like a rough ride."

What happened happened in an instant. Edmund tore away his straps and flung himself at the control board over Shasudo's shoulder. Even as my mouth opened to shout and my eye followed his motion, I saw in our path that impossible wall of red-smeared stone, half-obscured by blowing sand. Rearing above it was a natural obelisk of black granite, the desert's finger of accusation or destruction. Shasudo cursed even as Edmund flung the levers far over and we arced to one side, tumbling. I knew Edmund was trying to impact us broadside, partially from below; there was no time, no alternative but impact. And impact bloomed around me and smothered me; the tearing, roaring noise of metal on stone, the spark and boom of instantaneous distortion. I spun and went oblivious.

There was a time, a silent time.

The hiss and crackle of sparks interrupted the time. The acrid stench of plastic burned and metal scorched lined my mouth. I was in some awkward, preposterous position and I had no legs. The electric crackle spat its warning at me, though, and I made myself open my eyes. They started watering immediately.

The stench was a black and white pall that hung over my head. The shuttle lay partially on its side. It hurt to turn my head, but I turned it. The compartment was bent into a broad curve and Shasudo had been flung against the instruments, then tossed under the far side of the panel. There was no face, only blood and brains and protruding sections of skull that stuck out in jagged pale curves like the pieces of a broken china teacup. I saw where my legs were now. My seat had broken free—with me in it—and had flown across the cabin toward the bulge of impact. It had flipped onto its back and had burrowed under the navigation panel, hiding from the carnage. A jagged tear in the hull plates had bloomed inward like a flower; its knife-like petals stretched out to meet my arrival, neatly burying themselves three inches into the side of my right thigh. As I dully watched, a black sheet of blood rose to caress the metal, then flowed down my leg and into my lap. I only vaguely wondered if my femoral artery were severed. It didn't really matter, because my torso was hanging back over the arm rest at a grotesque angle. I felt nothing below the waist. The acrid stench around my eyes swirled closer, reminding me forcefully that by some miracle the impulse engines hadn't blown yet, but they would at any moment. I wondered what had happened to Edmund.

I felt fingers in my hair. My eyes were watering so

bad, I had to blink and shake my head twice to clear them. I guess I was coughing too. The reek swirled and for an instant I saw his face over me. A gash, welling blood, ran from underneath his left eye and across his cheek, but he appeared to be moving freely. He didn't say anything, just reached toward my impaled leg, then paused in dumb puzzlement. The hand he'd used to wrench over the controls was gone, severed just below the wrist. Out of the mess of raw flesh, a sharp end of bone protruded, incongruously yellowish-white, unbloodied. We both stared at the stump a moment; then he drew the arm back, suddenly, almost apologetically. He squirmed around to use his left. I found a voice.

"Get out," I said hoarsely. "It's going to blow."

He only stared at me with a strange faraway confusion in those gray eyes, as if they had taken it all in, but would not accept what they saw. He reached stubbornly for the trapped leg again. Behind me, I heard the ignition unit spit astringent sparks. I got angry.

"Don't bother, dammit," I shouted at him. "I'm dead! My back's broken! Get the hell out of here before she blows!"

He turned slowly to look behind him, get his bearings, then sat back on his heels and closed his eyes. If I could have moved, I would have shoved him, hit him, done anything to get him moving. But I couldn't. I started to cry.

His left hand was over my eyes, touching my temples. For a moment, the stump of his hand stood out in my mind, raised up like that bloody black obelisk, defiant. Then I was out again, leaving him to his fate.

The hiss of sand is eternal. Clean dry airs, ever in

motion, suck and curve over, around, through the sand, turning it in reluctant eddies. It hisses and whispers back at its carrier, whining, truculent, content to lie, to be undisturbed. The brittle wind but booms and proclaims its mastery. Eternal.

Shade is good, even unseen. I lay and listened to the shade, heard beyond it the rattling of the sun-exposed; heard the omnipresence of the heat that hulked in a wavering mass, pressing close, aching to invade the shade, but intimidated by shadow. My shade hummed happily back at the heat, smug. I snuggled my shoulders, working the shade around me like covers on a cool night. Smug. I licked my lips again, tasted dust again, and promised myself not to again. I thought of water again, not wanting to.

The wet coolness was back. It began on my forehead with such shock that I moaned, so it went away. And my head was raised again and I drank again, drank of the dust and heat and brittle air; drank the flat water, so abundant, so unsatisfying, drank until I couldn't. But the drinking made the wet coolness less alien, and my body shuddered and laughed at the tickle of the water in my hair, the dripping from my earlobes, the cool sweet sheet of water on my chest and thighs and feet. But I had no feet.

The grit of sand pressed at the back of my heels, as I tried to thresh my legs, get out. I had no legs. No, I had them, they were impaled; if Edmund would... if...

Edmund, get out.

I raised my arms to push him away, stared into the grey sea of his eyes. How cool they were, not confused at all. He was a bronzed mass over me, tunicless, his grey eyes so cool, like water or wisdom, cool and easing. Don't die, Edmund, get out, she's going to blow. His fingers were in my hair. I swam in eyes, water like eyes, eyes like water, cool, how did one swim without legs? But I swam, then floated, then sank unfearing. So easy.

There was a time. It was not silent, for the eternal sand hissed, the hum of the shade crooned, and I floated or sank as I felt need. I knew the time, but little else.

Edmund came and went in the time; sometimes I fought to get him out, but he never yielded. He always had a mind of his own. Sometimes I'd just lie there. He bathed me, I think, with the musty-smelling water. He touched me where my head hurt and I slept. Or where my back hurt, but it was warm where he touched and that eased it. He massaged my legs once, I remember that. That felt good.

He'd be gone for a time too, a long time, not just away but far, and I would swim whimpering during that time, but he would always return, always a little darker, always a little thinner.

There was a time, a real time, when he had gone to his away-place and I was awake, and knew it for awakeness. I studied the sandy roof over me where roots extinct and living traced their patterns of thirsty search above my face, leaving behind the fibers to bind the soil. And the glare of the sun was over my left shoulder, locked out by the shade in this alcove of sand.

There wasn't much out there with the sun, just runneled flatness and a far bank, boulder-strewn. There was a boulder near my feet, too. River bed, I thought. Dry. Against the white floor, out near the center of the sand channel, were crumbling heaps of bleached ochre. He's dug there. For the musty water. There's lots of water here. Just know where to dig. I half-thought to turn over and better examine the well, but a warning engraved red on my brain said, no! don't move! So I didn't.

There would be time enough, little enough to be seen in time. So I swam awhile, and sank again, wanting to. There was time, and would be time enough.

Time enough to realize...

Edmund sat at the edge of the alcove with his back against the boulder. A small fire flickered on the other side. Beyond it, a twilight hovered in blues and purples, the sun unseen, reflected only in the boulders on the far bank. Edmund was watching the changing light, the distances, and his knees were drawn up to act as a pedestal for his thin tired arms, one bound at the end with a dirty bulge of layered gauze. I knew he was aware that I was awake, but he just watched the distances and let me stare. I was staring at his profile, his bronzed face, so terribly thin, unscarred.

Unscarred.

I sat up and he did nothing to restrain me. I was weak, shaking badly, and had to use my hands to keep me sitting upright. I made no attempt to move toward him or the fire, but set my back against the undercut gravel behind me.

"How long?" I asked.

The sky beyond him had gone violet. He didn't bother to turn his head to reply. "Four days."

I pondered that, wishing he'd lied to me, wishing he'd said it had been longer. I fingered my right thigh. He had helped me to eat earlier, helped me to dress—silently as always. The light had been good enough to see the ruddy purple line along my thigh. It had itched madly, but he had gently peeled my fingers away from it as he covered it with the cloth. There had been no thickening where the metal had dug. No scar.

Four days.

"Did it blow?" I asked.

"Yes," he said to the river bed. I looked around the alcove. Piled to the right was a jumble of food packets, blankets, wood. How much time had he had?

"Did you get Shasudo out?"

"Yes."

"Buried?"

"Yes."

"*And* the food?"

He sighed. "Yes. And the medikit. And the blankets. And the emergency water." He paused in irony. "And you, of course."

"Of course," I agreed numbly.

Edmund, I thought, just how the hell are you going to explain this to Starfleet Command? They must have found the wreck by this time, assumed all aboard her had been blown to tatters. How are you going to explain to them how you had stopped an imminent explosion long enough to pry a man's leg out of that tangled metal, stop the bleeding, somehow transport him—broken back and all—out and far enough away to be safe? How you stopped it long enough to go back in and get supplies out, then get a body out for burial? Then let it blow? *Make* it blow? How the hell can you explain that to them? How can you explain it to *me*?

I suddenly knew he had no intention of explaining anything to anybody. He would not even look at me. I made an effort and waited until my blazing disbelief settled into cold curiosity.

"Where are we?"

277

"About sixty kilometers northeast, more or less."
"Why so far?"
"Water."

Sixty kilometers. He must have made the trip twice. Once for carrying a man with a broken back and a ruptured artery. Once for supplies.

A broken back.

"Was it torn completely through?" I asked.

He knew what I meant. He finally turned his eyes on me, their light dulled; there was a spark of fear in their depths, fear of what I was asking, why I was asking.

"The spine? Or the cord?" His voice was weary.

"Either."

"Both." His thin smile belied his hollow eyes. He looked back at the distances, watching as their purple began melting to black.

My back prickled where the gravel dug into it, my back, my smashed, irreparable back—repaired. I rubbed my thigh. It itched achingly, healing.

"How's the hand?" I asked, casual.

He tensed, paused, then shrugged. "O.K."

"May I see it?"

This was it, the demand for a final incredible revelation. Show me what was in those bulky wrappings at the end of that thin right arm, show me the hand that had to be growing back. I knew it was there ... with all the rest, it *had* to be there. Show me.

He unwrapped it reluctantly, curl by curl of gauze. It was still smaller than the other one, and covered in a thin, ivory-smooth skin so translucent, like a baby's, that the network of blood vessels showed through. How, in that bad light, I saw it so clearly, I can't say. I ventured to move, then, crawling out of the back of the alcove, past the food, the wood gathered, the water bottles, the fire; crawled on hands and knees like the battered shard of humanity that I was; crawled to him, took the hand and all it meant, touched it, knew it, just held it, my eyes stinging.

You could have left me there, Edmund, I thought. I would have died and no one else need ever have known. No one.

After a time, I asked, "Did you get a communicator?" in a sticky voice. He still wouldn't look at me.

"Yes."

Time. He had to have time, and an excuse for time. "Badly damaged, of course," I remarked.

His glance flicked at my face. I watched as the fear behind it washed away. "Of course," he returned cautiously.

I gave him back his new hand. "How long before this is back to normal?"

"Morning, easily."

"O.K.," I said. "You repair the communicator. I'll bury the supplies." There had to be no trace of anything that might indicate we had had time to do more than run. Too many questions.

"No," he said firmly, back in command. The coolness of his eyes glinted back at the fire. "You haven't the strength yet. Work on the communicator yourself—you haven't forgotten your electronics already?"

"No," I smiled grimly. "Where is it?"

He indicated with a nod. I rummaged through the pile of food-concentrate packs, water containers, and medical supplies. I found the communicator, brushed off the sand, and noted that he'd neatly mashed the transceiver connectives. A simple soldering job. A few shards of metal rattled around inside the guts of the thing. I began shaking them out carefully, one by one. I would melt them down, use them for the solder. He arose silently behind me and went out into the night, his face averted, his hands empty, wanting to be alone with what he was feeling.

I called after him:

"All I can say is—that was a hell of an accident for two men to walk away from unscathed!"

He turned in the purple darkness and I barely saw the muted flash of his grin.

"Wasn't it, though?"

Shuttle I came to greet us out of the rising sun. I felt gritty and grateful, still wrapped in an unceasing sense of amazement. Edmund waited patiently, still stripped to the waist. I held his tunic, gathered and knotted. Somehow he'd found the time and strength to do our assigned job here—the tunic held an extensive collection of ore samples, each painstakingly labeled with scratched-in data.

I let Edmund make the report. I just nodded in the right places. How we'd gotten out, looked for water and wood, finally managed to jimmy the communicator into working order. Nothing else.

Once we were aboard the *Liberty*, they sped us directly to Sick Bay. In the corridor, I glanced worriedly at Edmund's hand, but it was full-size now, the skin the right texture. There wasn't even a line of demarcation. He looked so damned haggard—that must have been a hell of a strain on his metabolism. I realized that the skin of my own cheeks felt glued to the bone. Hell of a strain on both of us. Even with the food.

The scanners picked up nothing unusual, not even scar tissue in my vertebrae. They told us to eat, they told us to sleep even before we had to make our official report to Captain Harvester. We gratefully wolfed down the food, but now and then I caught

Edmund examining me over his plate, sometimes contentedly, sometimes worriedly. We said nothing to one another and there were no others around to bother us with questions; it was a meal of silence and gazes. They insisted we bunk in the sick bay section, with a nurse on call if we needed anything. There were always dim lights in the sick bay, and I found myself staring across at Edmund, who was staring at the ceiling.

"Jeremy," he finally said.

"What?"

He paused, trying to word it correctly.

"Before you, I was alone in the universe."

What do you say to something like that?

He knows I won't record the question in my personal log, nor will I record the events that led to the question. I didn't ask him what he was then, nor will I ever. He will tell me when, and if, he chooses, but I will never ask.

We went before Captain Harvester in the morning, and Edmund repeated the report with official glaciality. It was not questioned.

It has never been questioned. Edmund has a kind of built-in aura of authority that no one questions, not even Harvester. It is more than authority. He inspires an unflinching sense of trust that begs no alternatives, requires no proofs. He could have chosen to remain apart, share himself with no one.

But he chose me.

●

AFTERWORD

I don't write so good. That's why I asked my good friend Theodore Sturgeon to write the Introduction to CHRYSALIS II and the rubrics for the stories. By doing this, he saved me from the angst of writing and, more importantly, he saved *you* from my bumbling prose. Except for these few words, that is.

CHRYSALIS II was made possible by the authors whose stories appear in it. Many of the authors are my good friends, whom I see and speak with often. The others, I like to think, are also good friends whom I simply haven't met yet. All are fine writers and I thank them for allowing me to share in their creativity.

I love each and every story in CHRYSALIS II and could ramble on and on in praise of them. However, they speak for themselves and you have read them and formed your own opinions. That is as it should be. So, let me content myself by pointing with special pride to four stories which are either first or second sales: "One More Song Before I Go" by Craig Gardner, "Dragon Story" by Alan Ryan, "Eclipse of the Son" by Jayne Tannehill, and "The Works of His Hand, Made

Manifest" by Karen G. Jollie. When I see these four stories in print I'm going to feel like a proud new papa.

Enough from me. I've got to get back to CHRYSALIS III.

—Roy Torgeson
New York City, June, 1978

HAVE YOU READ THESE BEST-SELLING
SCIENCE FICTION/SCIENCE FANTASY ANTHOLOGIES?

CHRYSALIS (287, $1.95)
edited by Roy Torgeson
The greatest anthology of original stories from the pens of the most talented sci-fi writers of this generation: Harlan Ellison, Theodore Sturgeon, Nebula Award winner Charles L. Grant, and other top storytellers.

SCIENCE AND SORCERY (345, $1.95)
compiled by Garrett Ford
Zoom to Mars to learn how an Earthman can become a Martian or take a train ride with a man who steals people for a new kingdom. Anything and everything is possible in this unique collection by top authors Ray Bradbury, Isaac Asimov, Frederik Pohl and Cordwainer Smith, plus many others.

SWORDS AGAINST DARKNESS (239, $1.95)
edited by Andrew J. Offutt
All-original tales of menace, high adventure and derring do make up this anthology of heroic fantasy, featuring novelets and stories by the great Robert E. Howard, Manly Wade Wellman, Poul Anderson, Ramsey Campbell, and many more . . . with a cover by the unsurpassable fantasy artist, Frank Frazetta.

SWORDS AGAINST DARKNESS II (293, $1.95)
edited by Andrew J. Offutt
Continuing the same outstanding success of the first, Volume II includes never-before-published novelets and stories by best-selling authors Andre Norton, Andrew J. Offutt, Manly Wade Wellman, and many others.

SWORDS AGAINST DARKNESS III (339, $1.95)
edited by Andrew J. Offutt
Here is Volume III in the highly successful SWORDS AGAINST DARKNESS anthologies, including first-time published short stories and novellas by best-selling writers Ramsey Campbell, Manly Wade Wellman, Richard L. Tierney, Poul Anderson, plus 9 others!

Available wherever paperbacks are sold, or order direct from the Publisher. Send cover price plus 40¢ per copy for mailing and handling to Zebra Books, 21 East 40th Street, New York, N.Y. 10016. DO NOT SEND CASH!

SUPER SCIENCE FANTASY SELLERS FOR ALL *STAR WARS* FANS...

A PLAGUE OF NIGHTMARES (279, $1.50)
by Adrian Cole
Four titanic, masked horsemen charge through the dreams of Galad Sarian with a haunting message that he cannot ignore. Volume I of a fantasy trilogy in the tradition of Tolkien and Lovecraft.

LORD OF NIGHTMARES (288, $1.50)
by Adrian Cole
The evil of Daras Vorta permeates even the strongest mind shield. Not even the magic of Galad Sarian can thwart it! The exciting trilogy continues...

BANE OF NIGHTMARES (244, $1.50)
by Adrian Cole
The cosmic circle of power turns, and Galad Sarian must meet the destiny chosen for him by the Dream Lords. This is the third in a fabulous sword and sorcery series filled with great fantasy, adventure, and some of the most ravaging battles ever created.

ORON (358, $1.95)
by David C. Smith
Science fantasy at its best! Oron, the intrepid warrior, joins forces with Amrik, the Bull Man, to conquer and rule the world.

ERIC BRIGHTEYES (365, $2.25)
by H. Rider Haggard
With his magical sword Whitefire, and his wild Baresark companion Skallagrim, Eric Brighteyes meets adventure head on—battling man and beast in order to stay alive! This is the first in a new illustrated science fantasy series.

Available wherever paperbacks are sold, or order direct from the Publisher. Send cover price plus 40¢ per copy for mailing and handling to Zebra Books, 21 East 40th Street, New York, N.Y. 10016. DO NOT SEND CASH!

DON'T MISS THESE SUPER SCIENCE FICTION/ SCIENCE FANTASY BESTSELLERS!

THE BLAL (351, $1.75)
by A. E. Van Vogt
Space pioneers are met with unearthly resistance from blobs and sleep creatures when they disrupt the serenity and balance of new unexplored territories in the outer limits. Plus other short stories.

THE GRYB (331, $1.75)
by A. E. Van Vogt
Journey to Zand at the end of The Ridge where a desperate traveler is willing to sell a pair of very special glasses, or travel to the land of the blood-sucking thing known as The Gryb. It's a nonstop trip to the star worlds of tomorrow and beyond.

200 MILLION A.D. (357, $1.75)
by A. E. Van Vogt
Cross the barrier to a new unearthly dimension when a man of the present and a man of the future, inhabiting the same body, battle to rule the world. He is the great and mighty god they worship as Ptath.

CHRYSALIS (287, $1.95)
edited by Roy Torgeson
The greatest anthology of original stories from the pens of the most talented sci-fi writers of this generation: Harlan Ellison, Theodore Sturgeon, Nebula Award winner Charles L. Grant, and other top storytellers.

Available wherever paperbacks are sold, or order direct from the Publisher. Send cover price plus 40¢ per copy for mailing and handling to Zebra Books, 21 East 40th Street, New York, N.Y. 10016. DO NOT SEND CASH!

TALBOT MUNDY'S EPIC ADVENTURE
TROS OF SAMOTHRACE

Volume 1: LUD OF LUNDEN (372, $2.25)
A swashbuckling tale of adventure on the high seas, in which Tros comes to Britain, in 55 B.C., to do battle against Julius Caesar for the freedom of that barbarous isle.

Volume 2: AVENGING LIAFAIL (378, $2.25)
Tros of Samothrace, sea captain without equal, builds a ship called *Liafail* and sails the world, smiting strange fleets in his continuing quest to destroy Julius Caesar.

Volume 3: THE PRAETOR'S DUNGEON (218, $1.75)
Tros comes to the end of his journey — only to find himself ensnared by a deadly, monstrous enemy that defies description. Demons and druids abound in this exciting third volume.

Volume 4: THE PURPLE PIRATE (233, $1.75)
In which Tros sails to Egypt and meets Cleopatra, who could prove to be his greatest foe ever. Beneath the towering pyramids, amidst lusty battles with pirates, Tros matches wits with her and the wily Cassius.

Volume 5: QUEEN CLEOPATRA (342, $2.25)
Cleopatra fears Egypt's vanquishment by the mighty Caesar, and she must form an alliance with Tros. But Tros, who has the auguries of the Druids to live by, has premonitions of bloody battles and untimely deaths.

Available wherever paperbacks are sold, or order direct from the Publisher. Send cover price plus 40¢ per copy for mailing and handling to Zebra Books, 21 East 40th Street, New York, N.Y. 10016. DO NOT SEND CASH!